The Devil's Mixtape

The Devil's Mixtape

by

Mary Borsellino

The Devil's Mixtape
Copyright © 2014 Mary Borsellino
Cover Illustration Copyright © Michelle Duckworth

All rights reserved. No part of this book may be reproduced or transmitted in any form or by any electronic or mechanical means, including photocopying, recording or by any information storage and retrieval system, without the written permission of the author and publisher

This book is a work of fiction. Names, characters, places and incidents are either the products of the author's imagination or are used fictiously. Any resemblance to actual events or persons, living or dead, is coincidental.

Third Edition

For Audrey, Erinna, Beckah, Saoirse, Gwen, Kati, Lauren, and so many, many other people. You are the self-rais'd and the sharpest, and it is because of you that this book exists at all. Thank you.

ELLA

Dear Nattie,

There's a general perception that spree shooters are boys and men. I'm the anomaly, too famous to ignore but considered a glitch in the program. Fuck, if I didn't exist, I imagine that some dreamy fucked-up girlbrain would have had to invent me.

In a way, that's just what happened in the end. Ella Vrenna dreamed up *ellavrenna*, and the rest is history. Or the rest is silence, if you prefer to get your linguistic clichés from Shakespeare.

But I'm not an anomaly. Just like female scientists, female politicians, and female musicians get shafted by history, the violent women of the world only get remembered in snatches. (Pun not intended but apt enough that I'll leave it there.)

Jennifer San Marco killed seven people in 2006. Shot them all in a day in late January. One was black, one was Chinese-American, one was Filipino, one was Hispanic, and one was a white neighbor whom Jennifer personally disliked. According to co-workers, Jennifer had a history of being a racist dickbag.

When we were in the library, right after Stacey died, Chris started giving this kid Martin a bunch of shit. Calling him nigger and stuff like that. Then he shot him in the arm and in the chest and in the heart. Martin died, and Chris called him nigger again and kicked the body.

"Don't say that shit," Dean scolded him. "People will say

we were racist if you do."

I started laughing. I thought I was gonna pass out from lack of air, I was laughing so hard. I doubled over. My hair falling around my face smelled like my shampoo and the smoke from Darcy's cigarette and guns and fireworks.

"You're a mass murderer," I gasped out eventually. "But you're scared people will think you're an asshole if they find out you used racist language."

That made Chris laugh too. He aimed his gun under one of the other tables and shot the two white kids hiding there.

"There. Equal opportunity. Happy now?"

His broken nose muffled his consonants, and I thought of you, tucked up at home in bed with the babysitter checking your temperature and one of your cartoon tapes on the TV. I felt glad it was a tape because if it had been on broadcast, then the breaking news might've interrupted you.

xE

Dear Nattie,

You won't read these for a long time, I hope. If you ever read them at all. Sam thinks I'm using the idea of writing to you as a literary conceit, and the real intended audience is nobody but my own eyes. Sam's smart about things like that. He knows a lot about doing things for their own value — about integrity. So maybe Sam's right. Maybe I'm writing this for myself, and nobody else will ever read it. But maybe someday, someone will. Stranger things have happened, as the saying goes.

I fucking hate sayings. They're the suburbia of talking, the same beige stucco words that all the neighbors use, and so people copy them to fit in and never say anything that means anything.

Anyway.

One thing you obviously know as well as I do is that you gotta get the iconography right if you wanna be an icon. I took suggestions from everyone in Cobweb, but the final say was mine. If someone didn't like it... well, then, they could be a sad little story on the evening news with a single-digit body count and a footnote in the true crime section to be remembered by.

I made a scrapbook of ideas, stuff I tore out of magazines at the library or copied down from books. I think it's fucked to tear up books, but magazines don't count the same way. I had pictures of Carrie in her sleek pink gown from the prom scene in Carrie, her skinny body splattered slick with bright red blood. I had a picture photocopied from the back of this video that Chris had just gotten from Japan, this amazing horror movie about this ghost woman who could climb out of your TV and kill you just by glaring at you. She had long, long, black hair that covered her face and white robes, and she moved like a puppet on tangled strings.

Chris — do you remember him and Dean? Really remember them, from when you knew them, not just from the newspaper and documentary photos? Chris with his fair hair and summer freckles, thin face and slightly secretive smiles. Dean was taller than me, taller than Chris. His hair was brown and curly. He was goofy, but we liked him even if he was a dork. We were all dorks. Misfits.

Anyway, Chris said her look was based on ancient ghost stories in Japanese culture, which just goes to prove my point: the right iconography endures. Who knows how many other horror movies got made the same year Carrie, but that's the one you remember because she burned herself onto everyone's retinas.

Girls are better at it than guys, lots of the time. I bet you can't remember shit about the suit Kennedy wore when he got shot, but you sure as hell remember Jackie's pink Verdun with the pillbox hat, the nubby tweed splattered with the blood and brains of her husband. You remember Mia Farrow's little pixie hair in Rosemary's Baby, her wild terror as she carries Satan's child to term inside her bird-like frame.

But then again you probably also remember Charles Manson's staring eyes and the X he carved into his forehead, and the scrawl of helter skelter on the wall of the massacre he orchestrated. Sometimes guys do get the iconography down, with perfection.

After Cobweb, that was the one I got compared to. Manson. They thought what I wrote on the blackboard was my homage to the 'helter skelter'. They thought I had dreams of being a cult leader as notorious and destructive as him.

Which isn't true, by the way. Either part. Manson's Family only killed eleven, for one thing. I may have only murdered three by my own hand - four if you include Chris - but Cobweb's total count was forty-eight. If Manson gets the credit for the killings of his followers, then I demand the same treatment.

And it wasn't about anything to do with Manson, what I wrote. The words just came into my head. I didn't know they'd even work out that it had been me who wrote it. ONLY SKY, all in capitals like your band name years later. You were so tiny when it happened, sickly and worried about me on that last morning after I made you drink the mustard water.

You get the iconography thing. That's how you know what to look like and what to say, even what to change your name to, in order to make it as a rock star. We're so alike, you and me.

Like I was saying, girls do that iconography thing pretty well. Take Brenda Spencer, for example. You remember someone who stands at her bedroom window and opens fire on an elementary school playground. But what cements her place in history is that when she was asked why, she said "I don't like Mondays." Fuck! Fucking genius, right there. Action heroes on the big screen wish they had lines that fucking good.

She was only sixteen, too. I was already almost eighteen when Cobweb happened.

That's the name I picked in the end, as you already know. Cobweb. We made up an insignia, too, so that everyone would know that everything was on purpose, not just some awful random coincidence. Not that there was really much chance of that, not when we timed it so all six schools got hit at once. But we had an insignia anyway: a vertical line with a horizontal line through it, like a plus sign. Then two lines at angles through that, so it was all like a big asterisk. Then a spiral, starting from the middle point of the lines and coiling its way out to the edges.

A stylized version of a spider's web, waiting for the flies.

xE

Dear Nattie,

In Alabama in 2010, three people got wounded, and three people died when Amy Bishop stood up forty minutes into a university faculty meeting and pulled out a 9mm handgun. Before the meeting she'd taught her anatomy and neuroscience class. Students said she seemed perfectly normal.

In 2004, Holly Harvey and Sandra Ketchum, a pair of 16-year-old sweethearts, wrote out a detailed plan and broke it down into four simple steps. Holly wrote them on her arm: kill, keys, money, jewelry. They lit some pot in the basement to lure Holly's grandparents, who were raising her, down to where the girls waited with knives. They stabbed the grandmother more than twenty times, the grandfather around fifteen.

Why? Same old shit as always. The grandparents wanted Holly to attend church with them and had forbidden the girls to see one another. The two were basically Romeo and Juliet with better planning skills.

Schools teach kids the greatest love story in all of literature is the one where a 19-year-old guy and his 13-year-old girlfriend rack up a body count and then kill themselves together. Then when kids learn the lesson, everyone blames pop music.

In 1983, Cindy Collier (15) and Shirley Wolf (14) knocked on random doors in California. An elderly woman let them into her condo. Cindy found a butcher knife. Shirley stabbed the woman twenty-eight times. When arrested the girls said that the murder had been 'a kick.' It was fun. They wanted to do another one.

But in the end, ladies often pick poison. In 1988, Laurie Wasserman Dann drove to several homes and left packages of food laced with arsenic on the front porches. She made two more stops and started fires. She then drove to an elementary school and used a .357 Magnum to shoot six kids and kill an 8-year-old. After that, she drove to a house and knocked on the door. She shot the man inside, went up the stairs, locked herself in a room, put a .32 revolver in her mouth, and pulled the trigger.

xE

AMY

Her name wasn't Sally Oblivion to begin with. She stole the first part of it from Bonnie, better half of Bonnie and Clyde. Most people don't know Bonnie was a writer or that she named her heroine Suicide Sal.

The "Oblivion" was a jab at her father, a big old fuck-you at the bloke who'd spent the first fourteen years of Sally's life trying to beat the sin out of her and promising someday paradise would be her reward.

I don't want paradise, she'd told the old bastard. *Give me oblivion any day.*

This was 1952, and Bonnie was long dead. So little Suicide Sally Oblivion was a touch out of fashion with her name. Then again, I guess the classics never go out of style.

I first met Sally Oblivion in hot afternoon light on the side of a February highway. She was drinking something oily and amber-coloured, and her hair was the berry-red of too much cheap dye, well before cheap dye was a fashion of its own. Mine was pale and tended to coarseness. I wore it long in a plait. Some had charitably described my eyes as tawny, but they were closer to hazel.

But let me introduce myself later.

"The King is dead. Long live the Queen," Sally said to me and gestured for me to join her on the dusty ground.

I'd been walking since eleven that morning, and my fair skin was toasted to a darker, sorer shade on my bare arms and cheeks. My feet were fine, though. I always wore good shoes.

Sally passed me her bottle. Her skin was a warm,

cinnamon brown. Most would take it for a tan.

"To Elizabeth," I agreed, taking a swallow. It burned and stung my throat, and I coughed. "I don't know if the new queen would appreciate her coronation being toasted with something like this, though."

Sally laughed. Her laugh was a deep, belly-full sound, and it opened her mouth so big that I could see the dark gaps where some of her back teeth were gone. Not enough good food and too many parental lessons conducted with knuckle and palm. Her clothes were loose and charity-pale. They looked like they might've once belonged to a farm worker.

I was in one of my habitual cotton shifts, the yellow one I think, and my sturdy boots.

Her hair, which looked like it'd been dark blonde before the dye, had been bleached white at the root by the unrelenting sun of the summer.

"Caught any rides today?" I asked, even though I hadn't seen a single car go past in all the day's walk. Usually, I preferred to move at night. I was more comfortable that way.

"Not yet. Night'll bring 'em out. Blighters are too soft to brave the days in this weather."

"That makes them smarter than us, then," I said as I took another gulp from the bottle. My skin was beginning to ache a little less.

"I'm Sally."

"Amy," I told her for my part of the exchange. I've been so many other names, but with the sun beating down and the bourbon sharp in my throat, I went with what I knew best. Amy. It's not a bad name as these things go. "Are you a native?"

She choked on her own mouthful. "What?"

"You've got some in you, don't you? The only ones I've ever seen with hair that fair and skin that brown had native in their blood."

She'd always passed. Always. Nobody had ever thought to even wonder before me. Sally told me that later in the same conversation from which I learned the origins of her self-chosen name. The same conversation in which I told her a little of the truth about me.

"Yeah," she answered, there by the side of the road. "Great grandmother. Never knew her. Never knew the truth until I read the old diary of Mum's that I stole when I ran. Funny how diaries can do things like that, isn't it? Be letters from the dead, fulla stuff you never knew before."

ELLA

Dearest Nattie,

It's been a while since I wrote. Sorry. I didn't know what else to talk about and figured that just rambling about all the other girls who've done violent shit would get boring for you. This time I'm going to write about books and movies and television and rock music and how people say these things can make people like me do the things people like me do.

Chris and Dean and I all loved *Natural Born Killers*. My favorite part was always right near the beginning when they're in the diner, and Mallory starts snarling along with the L7 song playing on the jukebox while she and Mickey murder everyone. I wanted to be her so badly I could taste it, copper-sweet on my tongue like blood and sugar.

So, *Natural Born Killers*. You don't even want to know how many teenage murderers cite it as inspirational, but I'm going to tell you anyway. In addition to the various Cobweb participants, there's been Sarah Edmonston, Benjamin Darrus, Michael Carneal, Jeremy Steinke's unnamed 12-year-old girlfriend who helped him kill her parents and 8-year-old brother, a fourteen-year-old boy in Texas who decapitated a classmate, Nathan Martinez, Jason Lewis, an 18-year-old in Massachusetts who murdered an elderly handicapped man, and Eric Tavulares. And that's not even counting the just-turned-twenty killers or the properly adult ones. All because of one movie. And, I mean, I like the movie a lot, but it isn't like it's perfect or anything.

Kip Kinkel's one of the closest matches to me, crime-wise. He killed his parents before he went shooting at his school and only killed two of the twenty-four he wounded once he got there. He didn't have the guts to kill himself, though. I guess I'm lucky I had Dean there to pull the trigger. Sometimes you gotta ask a friend to rip the Band-Aid off for you, you know?

He looked as scared as I felt, face gone white and his hair dark and lank with sweat and blood maybe, I don't know. We were all a little gory by then. Weirdly, I felt better that he was afraid too. We were all in this together, to the end.

So, Kip Kinkel. When police got to his house, his stereo was still on repeat on the song he played all night after killing his parents, before heading off to school the next morning. The song was an aria from Tristan und Isolde by Richard Wagner; the CD in the player was the Romeo + Juliet soundtrack.

Kip Kinkel was only fifteen when he opened fire on his classmates. Those damn early achievers make me feel so old for having planned and waited for so long before Cobweb rolled out.

On his calendar, on Mother's Day the year before Cobweb, Chris wrote 'good wombs have born bad sons.' That's Shakespeare, same as Romeo and Juliet.

Everyone knows that Dean had a Marilyn Manson poster on his wall, but nobody cares that along with the KMFDM and Rammstein, Chris's favorite music was Loreena McKennitt, that new-agey floaty faux-Celtic stuff. Nobody cares that Dean's favorite Nine Inch Nails song was a slow song, a longing song.

When Dan White killed Harvey Milk and George Moscone, he said he had diminished capacity as a result of eating Twinkies.

Twenty-two people died in the San Ysidro McDonald's massacre in California. The gunman's widow said that the monosodium glutamate in the food should be held responsible.

Once the cycle starts, it sometimes keeps itself going. Sixteen-year-old school killer Jeffrey Weise's favorite movie was that one Gus Van Sant made about Cobweb. The movie changed our names, of course, but everyone knew it was about us, even if suddenly Chris was Alex and Dean was Eric and I was Izzy. Names get changed all the time. You don't even go by Nattie anymore.

Seung Hui Cho, who killed 32 people at Virginia Polytechnic Institute and State University, once wrote a paper about the Cobweb attack.

High school shooters Barry Loukaitis and Michael Carneal both read *Rage* by Stephen King, so King had the book pulled from circulation.

Thank fuck nobody told him how dog-eared my copy of *Carrie* was. Do you still have it?

Even while we were planning Cobweb, Chris and I kept getting excellent grades. Dean's were never as good, but they went up a little just before the end. All that strategic thinking, orchestrating a mass murder, made him smarter.

Dean wrote a report for class about *Natural Born Killers* a couple of months before he put his Intratec TEC-DC9 semi-automatic against my temple and fired. He wrote that Mickey and Mallory 'got lost in their own little world.'

We had names we only called each other. Dean was 'Cordovan,' Chris was 'Indigo,' I was 'Violet.'

Independently from one another, in a coincidence that would not be discovered until after we were dead, Chris and I had both written the same sentence in our diaries in the weeks before we set our plans in motion. Each of us wrote 'I want to burn the world.'

xE

SALLY

I've been on my own for two years now, though time's not a measure of much when you keep to your own patterns. I wear a coat in winter and sweat in summer, but for all I care the world might as well be one day over and over forever, overlapping itself like layers on a cake.

I went up first. Really I went North, but after looking at maps in school so often, I always think of North and up as one. I went up from Brisbane to Townsville, mostly in cars and walking for some of it. I've never minded walking, and since I read Mum's diary, I've started to wonder if that's important. I've started wondering that about everything. Nothing's just what it is anymore, now that I know The Secret. I like walking for days and days; does that mean something? I prefer the coast to the bush; does that mean something?

My mother was taken from her own mother when she was four years old. She had me at twenty-four and died at thirty-four. I don't know if my father ever knew she was quarter-caste; the family who adopted her wasn't too pale, and luck had given her unremarkable features. She passed for an especially sun-tanned Irish kid well enough. Annie Pegg. Sounds like just the kind of girl a young farmer like Duncan Fitzpatrick would take as a sweetheart, doesn't it?

They were happy enough, I think. Duncan ruined fast when she was gone, and I can only guess that this is a sign he loved her better than anything else the world had to offer him. He was smacking me around in earnest before she'd been dead a year. I left at fourteen, and I've never looked back. There's work enough out there for a girl who doesn't mind the sun and just wants food and shelter in return.

I went up to Townsville first. Townsville's where Mum came down from, and we went up once as a family when my grandfather died. Mum didn't cry for him. I don't know if that was just her way or if he was a rotten sort she didn't care to mourn for. I never asked.

After reading Mum's diary and finding out about what really happened when she was a kid, I wanted to see my grandmother again. Now that I knew we didn't share any blood between us, I wanted something else of hers to make a part of me. A habit, a gesture. Something I could inherit, now that I didn't know what anything meant.

She didn't seem surprised to see me when I banged my fist against her door one slow, thick afternoon. The heat in Townsville's enough to kill you even after growing up near Brisbane. Hotter than hell, Mum used to say when I was a kid. I'd end up wondering all the rest of the day if Mum had ever gone down to Hell to confirm the comparison.

My grandmother served us tea, despite the heat. I thought about taking that as the thing of hers I'd carry but couldn't see it ever sticking well. I'm not the sort to serve tea, summertime or not.

She put out the sugar bowl and a bowl of jubes, the soft little sweets I remembered Tom sometimes giving me during the War. The sight of a little bowl of them, there on my grandmother's lace tablecloth, made my eyes sting up a little. The War had been rough, but my Mum had been alive then, and we'd had Nell, and Tom visiting when he could.

"The blacks didn't get a sugar ration," my grandmother explained, seeing how I stared at the jubes. "They got jubes instead. So now we put out both with tea in case you're used to sweeting with one rather than the other." Her soft, old lips twisted up into something wry and ancient. "It'll stay like this for another few years, I reckon. Something like a war leaves the memory fresh for a while. Then we'll be back to the bad old ways. People will forget the reason they used to put out jubes and just do it out of habit. Then they won't do it at all."

I sat in silence for a few moments.

"Mum had a diary," I said finally. "I read it after she died."

My grandmother nodded, smoothing the already-smooth lace tablecloth between us. We didn't drink our tea.

"Annie was a good girl. She was going to leave off telling you until she thought you were ready. It's a crying shame she didn't last that long."

I felt my chin tilt up, incensed. "I'm ready. I'll never be readier."

My grandmother patted my knee. "Only because you've got no choice in it."

"It's still true."

She nodded. "You're like her, you know. I can see it better now than when you were here as a little one after Frank passed on. She was fiery when she wanted to be."

"Tell me about her?" I tried to keep the pleading from my voice, but it crept in anyway. "Tell me about everything. Her diary... I don't know anything anymore, not like I did. I've run off from Dad."

So my grandmother told me about my mother. About a childhood spent learning how to look and act as white as possible, about the ways to deflect hard questions. About a little girl who loved stories and reading and writing but who knew it was more important not to draw attention and to do the ordinary, expected thing and get married and have babies. She only had one of those, though: me.

I cried for her, for the mother I'd never known as anything but a parent, for all the things she'd never had. I cried because there was nothing to be done about it but to cry and then forget.

As the sun went down, darkening the room where my grandmother and I sat over our cups of tepid, untouched tea, I asked "What was her favourite story?"

My grandmother's smile was sad and fragile. "Little Red Riding Hood. I told it to her when she was small. It was almost the first thing I said to her, the day we got her. I told her the story. For almost a year, she wanted it every night before she slept. My tiny brown baby, curled in one of the box-beds we kept the smallest in. None of my own kids ever wanted stories as much as she wanted them. She'd make up her own ways of telling it, when she grew up bigger. I'd put her with the littler kids to keep them quiet, and she'd tell the strangest ways. Red Riding Hood marrying the wolf, killing the woodcutter. Weird stuff. She wrote some of them down, though I've no notion as to why she bothered. She liked stories better when they got spoken to a crowd than when they were on paper.

"I've got one of them here. You can have it to keep with her diary, if you want."

And I wanted. I wanted more than I knew how to say, so I just nodded my head. My grandmother went to fetch it, this precious treasure, and left me with our forgotten drinks.

I looked at the jube bowl and the sugar bowl.

After a long time, my grandmother came back. The papers in her hands were folded in the same careless, uneven way my mother's linens always ended up, and I had to swallow hard to keep from crying again.

"You can sleep in the spare room at the end of the hall. There's a candle by the bed if you can't wait for morning before reading," my grandmother told me. She sounded so tired.

I couldn't wait. Of course I couldn't. My mother had

been gone four years then, and I would have cut my own hands off to hear her voice again.

Once upon a time, little Annie Pegg began, speaking down the years to a daughter she didn't expect.

> A wolf lived in the forest with a girl, and they had many children. One day a hunter found them.
>
> The hunter said 'I will take these baby wolf-girls and I will tie ropes to their necks, and the ropes will wear welts into their beautiful fur, and they will learn to be obedient.'
>
> And the wolf snarled and bared his teeth and said 'You'll do no such thing.'
>
> And the girl snarled and raised her old, notched knife and said 'You'll do no such thing.'
>
> And the hunter said 'I can do as I please. How can you stop me?'
>
> And the wolf and the girl looked at each other, and their eyes were full of sadness because they knew this was the end of all that came before and the beginning of something else. And beginnings can be joyful things, but ends are often sad.
>
> And the wolf and the girl looked at each other, and in their eyes they shared a plan.
>
> The wolf pounced, the girl ran. She picked her wolf-girl babies up in her arms, and she ran and ran and ran and ran, out into the dark with her hair streaming golden in

the night and her feet bare and cut on the rocks. They kept away from the paths, even though the paths did not cut. The girl had sworn long ago that no child of hers would walk that path, down through the trees to the cleared land of the village and the lights of the houses. She had come from there; she would not go back.

The wolf and the hunter wrestled through a day and a night, and in the end the hunter won, as the wolf and the girl knew he would. The hunter wins; the wolf is defeated. That's how the ending always comes.

And the hunter tied a rope around the wolf's neck and wore a welt in the wolf's grey fur and made him a dog.

But the girl found a cave, safe and dark and far from the path, out near the cliff's edge where the waves crash and whisper all through the darkest hours before the sunlight starts again. And there she laid her wolf-girl babies to sleep and stood at the mouth on the rocky sand and watched the moon go down.

She didn't howl. She'd need her voice for stories.

There's more than one meaning in a tale like that. Maybe my mother wrote it about herself, about what she maybe wished had happened: a mother who ran, who wouldn't let her babies be stolen and taken to the village along the path. I wish I could ask her, but I never can. I've only got the words she left.

In the spare bedroom of my grandmother's house,

I dreamt I was that running girl, a notched knife at her hip, in love with a wolf and racing through the whipping branches of old, dry trees.

I think that's why I liked Amy the moment I saw her this afternoon, when we met there on that roadside. Me with too much henna in my hair (the blonde I cover with dyes is the only legacy my fair-skinned father left me that I can't outrun with distance), the Little Red lost in the wilds of a country she should feel a tie to but doesn't (does that mean something?).

And here was a girl not much older than me, with eyes like a wolf's, all tawny and intent. I'm sure that we're meant to stick together. It feels like fate, which I've never much believed in before but will give a try for once.

We're in the back of a car now, the two of us together, while a husband and a wife bicker in the front. The wife's belly's big and round under her dress, and I wonder if the baby can hear the snappy words between his mum and dad. I hope so. Better to get the disappointment done with early.

Amy's staring at me like she's got a question she wants to ask or a puzzle she plans to solve. I smile back, and she blinks her goldy-green eyes in surprise. Like she'd forgotten that I can see her, too.

CHARLOTTE

From *Reign in Hell: Two Weeks in the Life of HUSH*, by Charlotte Waterhouse, Amplify Press, Australia, 2011:

"Fuck that flight. That flight was fucking brutal."

Few people are at their best at five-thirty in the morning after a fourteen-hour flight, but Tash Vrenna may be among that few. Fresh from the customs crush, she stands beside the doors leading back into Melbourne Airport and smokes like a mountain climber taking hits of oxygen.

It's not that she isn't rumpled and grimy from the travel; it's simply that she wears it like she's woken from a good night's sleep on feather pillows. I get the sense she's slept in far less comfortable places and long ago learned the trick of emerging clean and new.

The rest of her band and their crew are inside, ordering coffee while we all wait for the van to the hotel.

"I'd tour Australia five times a year if it wasn't for that fucking flight," Tash says. Her voice is quieter than expected, soft beneath the smoker's gravel. She looks a little older than her years, a hard growing-up leaving its mark. She's beautiful, but it is a damaged beauty.

Tash isn't wearing any makeup, her hair is tangled and dull, and the tomato-red polish on her nails is chipped to slivers. In her oversized sunglasses and rumpled black clothes, every aspect of her screams 'rock star.'

"The seats in economy kill at least half the nerves in your ass, the flight attendants leave the lights off for about ten fucking hours so they don't need to cope with you, and you're breathing in other people's germs the whole time. I always get sick after that fucking ordeal. Give it two weeks, and I'll be dying of fucking swine flu or bird flu or whatever. *Plane* flu, that's what it really fucking is. A long-distance airlock full of coughs and sneezes. And I love Australia. It's fucking awesome here. But there's no country in the fucking world that's good enough to justify that flight multiple times in a year."

Her guitar tech, Gabriel, joins us and steals a long drag from Tash's cigarette. The knuckles of his hand read 'BURN.' Compact and dark, he has quite a bit of that rock-star aura himself.

"Tour manager says we should just get some cabs, and she'll have the label comp it," he tells Tash. "I think she's scared that Cherry's getting pissed."

He turns to me, explaining, "Last time Cherry lost her temper, she made a roadie cry and got thrown out of the venue. Two hours before the show. I practically had to promise all the kingdoms of the world to the bouncer to get him to let her back in."

Tash snorts. "If she's had her coffee, Cherry's practically a zen master," she explains to me. "She wouldn't care if we were stuck in the airport forever so long as there was espresso to be had."

I ride with Jacqui and Ben to the hotel, with them in the back and me in the front of the taxi, because I'm the only one of us who knows Melbourne and can help with directions. I point out that the cab is equipped with GPS, but they've spent the last two months in Los Angeles and refuse to trust the little computer.

"Fuckin' LA," Jacqui says derisively as we drive through

the early morning toward the city. "It's the most bullshit place in the world. Did you know almost four thousand people die there every year just from the pollution? Their life expectancy's cut by fourteen years from the exhaust fumes in the air. Wrap your head around that for a second. Next time you sort your cardboard from your plastic before you put your trash out, think to yourself: the air in LA is twice as deadly as getting hit by a car.

"Kind of makes you feel like you're trying to bail water on the Titanic with a thimble, doesn't it? What difference can any of us make, when LA exists? It's an evil fuckin' vortex of shit and superficiality and glossy plastic garbage in every color of the fuckin' rainbow."

Ben clears his throat as Jacqui's rant winds down to discontented grumbling. "Jacq and I are from Brooklyn. We're contractually obligated to hate the West Coast."

As well as similar accents and the rockstar-standard black wardrobe, Jacqui and Ben share a steely sort of melancholy in their mannerisms. I'm sure that most people who meet them assume that their sibling bond is by blood rather than adoption.

I tell Ben that Australia has a rivalry between Sydney and Melbourne that's very like the LA/NY divide, with Sydney as the Los Angeles and Melbourne as the New York.

"But Sydney's not as bad as you make LA sound, I guess," I grudgingly admit.

"You're from Melbourne?" he guesses with a smirk. I nod and say yes, I've lived here almost eight years.

"What do you love about it?"

I have to think for a moment, not because I'm unsure but because I want to phrase it properly. Putting words together is meant to be my job, after all.

"I love the way that people here will open a bar literally anywhere there are two square feet of space together. I love the art galleries with their abstract stained-glass ceilings and whitewash-clean hallways. I love the state library's panopticon reading room and the collage of eras in its architecture. I love the stencil art in alleyways and side streets, the riot of thought and message and design and brashness that spills over itself in a sublime tangle. I love the restored movie theatres that show blockbusters and sell cheap popcorn. I love its romantic buildings and facades."

"And where are you from before that?" Ben presses, quietly inquisitive. I laugh, a little defensively, and remind him that I'm supposed to be the one asking the questions.

As the cab draws closer to Melbourne, the skyline of the buildings greeting us in the pale blue dawn, I admit that I grew up in Brisbane. Brisbane's literacy rate is one of the lowest in Australia. It didn't have a proper sewerage system until the 1960s.

I have my own, personal reasons for having left Brisbane, but it doesn't take more than a general overview of the place to get people to understand why I don't live in the city where I grew up.

"I think that's where Jo's from," Jacqui says. "Sometimes, anyway."

Jo Domremy, the band's recalcitrant drummer, is known for giving inconsistent and contradictory life stories to different interviewers. She tends to choose small towns and places known for their dark histories when asked about where she was born. It's not hard to believe she'd count Brisbane among such places.

Jacqui goes on, speaking mostly to herself at this point. "And Cherry and Tash are from Colorado, of course. Colorado has the lowest rate of obesity in the USA, which sounds impressive as shit until you find out that it's also rated as the third best state for business out of the whole country. Anywhere populated by a whole bunch of rich corporate fucks is gonna be able to afford healthy food and lots of outdoorsy shit, isn't it?"

"It's too early for soapboxing," Ben replies in a mild voice. Jacqui snorts. "I'm jetlagged as fuck, so I don't feel like it's early at all."

    Much of the band's earliest publicity focused on Cherry and Tash, to the point where it seemed for a while that their 'celebrity' might overwhelm any chance the band had at a real career. After a while, once it became clear that HUSH's songs contained neither evangelical messages of hope and faith nor dark whispers encouraging evil — except for the regular amounts of evil that some people are determined to hear in any and all rock music — the novelty of the band's Cobweb connection died down.

    Now it seems the band has accepted their dubious birthright of notoriety as best they can, confronting it head-on and getting it out of the way: 'And Cherry and Tash are from Colorado, of course.'

JO

Excerpt from the article "Boom! Crash! HUSH!: We talk to drumming sensation Jo Domremy," *Revolutions Per Minute* magazine, October 2009:

Jo Domremy is going to be one hell of a hard-assed middle-aged musician in a few more decades. You know the kind, the ones who look like they're half a beer away from breaking a chair over the bar and spending the night in lock-up while the rest of their band scrapes bail together. She's got the gutsy no-bull look that some ladies get when they've lived hard and fast for fifty good years of bad judgment. She's well on her way to that future self already: killer burn scars that she mostly keeps covered with long sleeves, a tendency to interrupt if she thinks you're bullshitting on too long, and a steely glare that'd suit a soldier's face better than a rock drummer's.

    Jo: "All four of them have essentially the same attitude to art and music. They willingly invite chaos. They use that raw energy as the fuel for what they create.

    "It doesn't always look that way. But the chaos is there. It's always there underneath. They thrive on it. I don't know if they'd cope with normal lives half as well as they do with the craziness.

    "Cherry's the example I use when I explain this to people. Cherry's perfect. It's vile. She spent her high school years doing volunteer work in a hospital. Her handsome, successful boyfriend adores her. And, she's in a rock band that gets good reviews *and* makes money. Even I hate her when I describe her out loud like that.

"However, the reality isn't anything like it sounds. Cherry opens herself up to pain and horror. She's always staring down the abyss. What 14-year-old kid decides to spend her free time sponging diarrhea off the terminally ill? Her boyfriend's a great guy, but he's Andrew fucking Davenport, you know? There's no white picket fence and babies and a dog at the end of that story. Not when the guy you're dating is a warzone photographer who gets halfway killed practically nonstop.

"Cherry is at her best when she's up against misery and chaos. And I'm one of the chaotic elements that they left their lives open to.

"HUSH had a practice space in Chicago. They were all living there. Summer break was on for schools and colleges. Jacqui was a junior, but she was the only one of them who actually made it to college, let alone graduated. Ben had just finished high school, and one of their grandfather's art friends offered this studio space they weren't using as a summer hang-out for the kids. Give them a summer in a new city, something wild and fun, you know? I'm sure that the art friend and the grandfather expected that Jacqui and Ben were going to just dick around and do stupid shit.

"And, I mean, they did. Of course they did. Jacqui was old enough to buy all the alcohol they wanted, and there's nowhere in the world like Chicago if you're a kid who loves music and culture. There just isn't.

"But it wasn't pointless, aimless dicking around.

"That's one of the things I found most interesting about them, right from the start. I..."

Jo stops for a minute, like she's choosing her next words. "I never had much of a childhood. I had to start making hard choices early. So I appreciate that quality in other people, that ability to get on with shit without too much fucking around. A *little* fucking around is okay

—fuck knows *I'm* no saint —" Jo pauses and smirks here, her eyes a little naughty and a lot hard. "But not too much.

"Jacqui and Ben had known Cherry and Tash on and off for two or three years by that stage, and the four of them had talked more than once about starting a rock band with the kind of dark, fucked-up blues they all loved — 'Hellhound on My Trail,' 'Shave 'Em Dry,' 'Mad Mama Blues,' all that crazy shit.

"So when they got to Chicago, Jacqui and Ben phoned Cherry and Tash to come, too, so they could, you know, get this band started. Cherry and Tash were only fifteen! It was nuts!

"But their dad is really permissive. He puts a lot of trust in the girls, even though I think he knows that they always dance as close to the edge of the apocalypse as they can, just out of habit. He said they could go live in Chicago with the others over the vacation.

"So they've got space, they've got time, they've got freedom... but they don't have a drummer. So instead of asking around or seeing if any of their friends want to learn to play — and Cherry and Tash were basically flying blind anyway, so it wasn't that the standard was too high to get in someone still learning — or any of the ways most people would go about it, what these four kids do is buy an old restaurant chalk board from a junk shop, the kind with a wood carving of a jolly old Italian chef on one side holding up the part you write on. They wrote 'Wanted: One Drummer' on it and dumped it in front of their studio. Inside they had mattresses on the floor and pizza boxes; the only thing they took any care with was their instruments.

"I happened to be the first passer-by who saw the sign and rang their doorbell. It's coincidental that I like to play drums. They would've taken anyone who applied, I think. They really were just inviting chaos in, and then they'd work with whatever answered the invitation."

ELLA

Dear Nattie,

Mary Flora Bell was eleven when she and a friend lured a toddler to an old air raid shelter. His resultant injuries were assumed to be the result of an accident.
When the corpse of a four-year-old boy was found two weeks later, people assumed that was an accident as well.
Then Mary went to the little boy's home and asked cheerfully if she could see the body.
Then two months later a three-year-old went missing, and Mary suggested where the searchers might find him. He'd been sliced with razors and scissors on his stomach and legs and strangled. The friend said Mary had done it all. A psychiatrist said Mary was manipulative and dangerous. Mary remained indifferent and seemingly bored throughout her trial.
Many, many, years later, when Mary had freedom and a new name and a little daughter of her own, the media tracked her down. They never let you get away — they want their ellavrenna, their marybell, forever; you don't get a life as a real person once you've been declared a monster. That's why I don't regret dying as I did.
Mary Bell's daughter forgave her, though. Their lives were ripped open, and they had to run away. But her daughter forgave her. I guess teenagers are occasionally capable of compassion, even if it's never been my strong suit.

"You were younger than I am now," Mary Bell's daughter said to her.

Sometimes, Nattie, I remember that I was younger than you are now. I don't know what to feel about that. Some would say that feelings weren't my strong suit either, but if there's anyone who knows better than that, it's you.

xE

Dear Nattie,

The one time the media really talks about girls like me — apart from Brenda Spencer because she got that song written about her — is when it's love that drives us.

Romantic love, I mean. Bonnie and Clyde, that's a myth that people understand. It's practically Romeo and Juliet. I guess that's why people get it when girls like me do what they do with a boyfriend beside them. That doesn't seem nearly so scary as a girl in a black trench coat, doing it for hate and being cool as ice about getting it done. Wild love is much less frightening than logical loathing.

But I was writing about Bonnie. Bonnie Elizabeth Parker. Died age 23. She was a writer from pretty early on, and once she was on the run beside Clyde, she started writing poems. Creating her own legend in a lot of ways. *The Story of Suicide Sal*. She had a diary when she was a teenager where she scribbled down her loneliness and kept record of her impatience with life.

Seems to me like the fact that she fucked a guy was hardly the most important reason she became who she became. Clyde was just the catalyst, the spark that lit the keg. And when you're a girl like Bonnie, you seek out the spark, desperate for an excuse to explode sky-high.

History points to the Depression, to the sadness and poverty all around, as a way of explaining why Bonnie and Clyde were so important. They were a mouthpiece for the rage. Like rock stars, I guess. I think there might be a bit of truth to that. But what history forgets is that there's always someone — a LOT of someones — hurting. Someone whose rage needs a mouthpiece. That's why there's always music. But you'd know about that better than I would.

Another girl, a lot like Bonnie, was Caril Ann Fugate. I think Caril's a pretty name. Sounds kind of light and musical, like it should belong to a little yellow bird in a cage.

Caril did like me and offed her parents. She killed her baby sister, too, though, which is shitty as fuck. You don't fucking do shit like that. Or maybe what I really mean is that *I* don't do shit like that. As far as I can see, if you kill your baby sister, then what's the fucking point of doing any of it? Who're you doing it for, if it's not for her?

Wow, way to put your own issues on someone else's plate, Ella. Caril killed her sister. That's her thing. You don't have to make it yours. Sorry I got so riled up there. I just love you, kid, that's all. You were what made any of it worth doing — without you, without knowing you'd have to grow up in the ugly fucked up world that was all around us, I wouldn't have bothered with any of it. I'd just have offed myself, strung a noose up in the garage or some shit. But going out quiet like that, just giving up without a bang, that's not an option when there's a little kid looking up to you. It's a big fucking responsibility, being a big sister. Maybe that's why Caril did what she did. Maybe she didn't want to carry the future of some other little girl in her heart and head while she whipped down highways with her lover and her gun, killing whoever got in her path.

She was younger than me. I was so fucking ancient it's fucking pathetic. Caril was only fourteen when she and her boyfriend Charles Starkweather got rid of her family and hid them in her shed.

Charles was obsessed with James Dean — felt like this was a guy who got what it was to be lost and angry. He killed a gas station attendant so that he could get a stuffed toy dog for Caril once. I think that's sweet. He cared about the little things.

Lots of people fell in love with the legend of Charles and Caril Ann. They're probably the most well-known of the spree killers who did it side by side as lovers, along with Bonnie and Clyde. There is this boring as fuck movie that lasts a million fucking years that we had to watch in school this one time that is based on them. It's got the chick who played Carrie in it as the Caril Ann character.

Speaking of Carrie, Stephen King was obsessed with the legend of Charles and Caril when he was a kid. Kept a scrapbook on the spree.

True Romance and *Natural Born Killers* are both based on it, too. We've been over that stuff already, though, so we'll move on.

And now it's twenty minutes later, and I'm still looking down at my paper, trying to know what to write next. Because that's just it, isn't it? I'm never going to move on. I'm stuck right where I am, forever and ever. Turning these thoughts of murderers and love over and over in my head until the end of the world. It's not the worst Hell I could've ended up with. But it sure as fuck isn't as good as I'd like.

xxElla

Dear Nattie,

The day before, I got sick. It wasn't cold feet or anything. My friend Nicolas says he felt the same, before they went ashore at Guadalcanal. It suddenly hits you like a physical smack: this is probably the last full day you will spend alive. This time tomorrow, your muscles will be cooling, stiffening with rigor. Your brain will be clammy and silent meat inside a skull, a skull that's only different from the billions of other skulls in the history of the dead in that it has your teeth, the molar that hurt as it came in crooked, the incisor with the tiny rough bump at the back of it that you can touch with your tongue. Your tongue, which has begun to swell and rot in your mouth, another slab of useless purple flesh.

I didn't want Dean or Chris to know, though. In retrospect, they would have understood better than anyone else at the school that day. They were feeling it, too.

I felt nauseous and horny and bitter and giddy and sad. I went to the girls' bathroom, not sure if I was going to jill off or throw up. I ended up doing both, one after the other. I was vomiting into the bowl of the toilet when there were footsteps outside the stall, quiet steps that stopped behind me.

"Are you okay? Do you need help?" a voice asked. A kind voice. I rarely have time for kind people — I think they're mostly hypocritical and weak, but I was shaky and felt strange. Not like myself at all. So in reply, I gave a wry little laugh as I wiped my mouth with the back of my hand. I stood and flushed and opened the stall, stepping past the girl to reach the sinks.

In the mirror, we were side by side, our reflections decorated with the spots and Sharpie scribbles of any public restroom. Her hair was a dark honey-gold, thick and wavy around the small dainty features of her heart-shaped face. Her eyes were brown and looked at me with concern. Your friend Cherry is paler and has a larger frame, wider shoulders and more flesh on her. You'd be able to tell that the two were related if you saw photos side by side. But sisters might not be your first guess.

"It's too late for help," I told her. My voice sounded as

shaky as I felt as I rinsed and spat into the sink. The water gurgled as it went down the drain, bouncing down through empty pipes into the dark. "Stacey, right?"

She nodded. "You're Ella."

I nodded back.

We were in English class together. Our current topic was Kurt Vonnegut's *Slaughterhouse 5*. Some other kid in the class had been whining about how he didn't think the book was appropriate for us to read because it treated something serious like war with all this dumb fantasy stuff and narration that was sort of funny in a horrible way.

"I don't think you're looking at it right," Stacey had replied, her voice soft and reasonable. Her copy of the paperback was dog-eared, scribbled with pencil margin-notes. "Sometimes the only way you can talk about serious things is with dumb fantasy stuff and things that are horrible and funny. Just being serious about it isn't serious enough."

I didn't participate in the argument — speaking up in class was never my style—but I'd appreciated what she'd had to say. She seemed pretty smart even if she was in those bullshit Evangelical groups who made life so miserable for me and Dean and Chris so much of the time. So, as far as people to run into in the bathroom on that last full day, Stacey wasn't the worst it could have been.

I finished washing my hands and face, grabbed a paper towel to dry them off, and said to her "Don't worry, I'm fine. It's just the monster that's inside me using my stomach as a trampoline."

Her eyebrows arched up like surprised punctuation for a moment, but after a second of silence all she said was, "Oh. Look, if you ever need information about —"

Realizing what she thought I'd meant, I barked a laugh, turning to face the real her instead of the reflection. "I'm not pregnant if that's what you think. And if I was, the last thing I'd need would be your fucked-up pro-life propaganda."

Her eyes narrowed as she scowled, but she didn't turn away. One of her small tanned hands curled and then uncurled, like she wanted to slap me. "You don't know me as well as you think you do, Ella Vrenna."

It was just a name, then. Just my name. It wasn't like now. She left me alone in the bathroom, and I threw up again in the sink, thin bile, because there was nothing but acid left in me.

On the 911 tape from the library, just after the exchange between her and Chris — you know the one I mean, everyone fucking knows the one I mean — the moment when she stopped being Stacey Reardon and became Saint Stacey, just like I stopped being Ella Vrenna and became *ellavrenna*, all one word, a name that was more than just a name. People can become symbols so easily once they aren't around to contradict the iconography anymore. Their names can become shorthand for entire concepts.

On the tape, a few seconds after the gunshot, while Dean is laughing at Chris because the recoil of the shot has knocked the butt of the gun back into his face, broken his nose, and left him with blood streaming over his chin, you can hear me say something quietly. I say, "So it goes."

That's from Vonnegut, from *Slaughterhouse 5*. I felt a twinge of regret that Stacey died because she'd been right. I hadn't known her. I've always been good at knowing how people will act, how to manipulate them. But I've never been good at knowing them, knowing why they do the things they do. How and why are such distinct things, though, I think one matters more than the other. I don't really give a shit about intentions. I'm already in Hell, so I don't need to pave a road with good intentions in order to get here. *How* is more important than *why*. Like, who cares if Joan of Arc really saw visions of the Virgin Mary or not? Either way, she was a fantastic general who led armies to victory. Shouldn't *that* matter more?

Vonnegut wouldn't have liked me. There's lots of stuff in *Slaughterhouse 5* about how shitty massacres are. But years after the day me and Stacey died, he said he thought suicide bombers were brave. So who knows? Maybe we would've got along. I think he and Stacey would've. He's dead now, same as us. But I don't think they're in the same place, and neither of them is here with me. So, I guess none of us will get to have a conversation about all of it. Shame.

You're too young to read it yet, but when you get older, you should look at *Slaughterhouse Five*. It's a fucking awesome book.

Love,
E.V

AMY

Aesop was the first thing I thought of when Sally told me her mother's version of Little Red Riding Hood. Her mother had heard the fable of the wolf and the dog.

    Sally told me about her mother on the first night, after we'd been dropped off in front of a creaking, lopsided boarding house with a room ready to let so long as we were nice Christian girls of good character. Sally seemed to think it a wonderful joke once we were upstairs and safe behind a squeak-hinged door. She kicked her shoes off and flopped on the bed, crossing her ankles and drinking another gulp of bourbon. Whatever else she was, Sally was the child of a mean drunk, yet she never hesitated to swallow down more than a fair share of alcohol. I think that for her, drinking was just another sort of running away.

    She told me the story of her mother. The rest of the tale of her family would come later. We were still getting to know each other at that point, and so she dealt out the details of herself with as much care as she ever gave to any secret.

    When she was done, the two of us, side to side on the narrow bed now, passed a bottle back and forth between us. I said the first thing I thought. "Aesop."

    So then, it was my turn to tell a story. I chose one I'd first heard as a tiny child on my father's lap. It was one of his favourites, and I liked hearing it as much for the relish in his telling as for the words themselves.

    A wolf was walking down the road, coat

thin over bone and skin and not much else. The wolf was starving. Then he met a dog, sitting by the side of the road. The dog was fat and sleek and happy.

"Wolf," the dog said. "You look miserable."

"I am miserable," the wolf answered. "I haven't eaten for days."

"Come home with me. There's plenty to eat there," the dog said, "You won't be miserable then, will you?'"

"I'm tired, as well as hungry," the wolf answered. "I haven't slept for days."

"Come home with me. There are soft carpets at the fire," the dog said. "You can rest after you've eaten."

"All right," the wolf answered. "But tell me, dog, why is the fur at your neck worn away? You've heard my troubles, please tell me yours."

"Oh, that," the dog said. "That's nothing. My fur is worn where my collar rubs, that's all. You'll have one just the same, when my master's met and fed you."

And with that, the wolf walked away. For it's better to be hungry and tired and free than to be fat and sleek and at a master's mercy.

By the time I finished telling it, Sally was asleep. She snored a bit, softly, and her fingers stayed curled around the smooth glass of her little bottle. I blew out the candle, and settled down to dream beside her. I dreamt of wolves and missed my father.

HUSH

Excerpt from "Track-by-Track with HUSH: Ben, Cherry and Tash take us through their debut album," *Revolutions Per Minute* magazine, September 2009:

> 10) 'Limp'
>
> Sample Lyrics:
>
> *I pump and shudder, beat and stutter, bleed and seize, convulse*
>
> *I won't lie cold and blue, I don't care if this is hard for you,*
>
> *Or if it's easier to love me when my limp wrist has no pulse.*

Ben: 'Limp' is one of the most straight up dirty punk songs the band's done. We recorded it live on our first take. We wanted it to be as raw and unpolished as we could get.

Tash: We didn't want to overthink it. If you think too much, the primal power gets lost.

Cherry: I don't especially agree with this approach to recording as a general principle — I think all art, no matter how spontaneous it seems, has to have a strong element of consideration beforehand in order to contain precisely what you set out to capture — but in this particular case I think this was the best way to make the song what it needed to be.

Ben: 'Limp' is my favorite to play live, without a doubt.

CHARLOTTE

From *Reign in Hell: Two Weeks in the Life of HUSH*, by Charlotte Waterhouse, Amplify Press, Australia, 2011:

When I ask what song Cherry finds most powerful to play live, the answer comes without hesitation.

"'Limp.' It's the closest thing I have to a mission statement among the songs," she says, pushing her blonde hair behind her ears. Apart from her eyes, Cherry has a very young-looking face, a baby doll sweetness that's at odds with her no-nonsense tones.

"What I'm saying is that the truth is always better than the lie, even if it's harder. Part of that lyric is actually a quote from a movie, the movie *Heathers*. 'I love my dead gay son!' That's what this guy says at his son's funeral.

"Christian Slater, whose character was responsible for the death of the boy, wonders aloud if the father would still be saying that if the boy was limp-wristed with a pulse. We all loved that line; the song was built around the line. Tash and I had that movie on VHS when we were thirteen, and we wore the tape on that scene until it was almost completely static over the picture."

I remark that *Heathers* is a surprising choice of viewing for the girls, considering the film's plot is concerned with the exploits of a pair of teens who decide to murder their classmates. Cherry shakes her head.

"My dad decided early on that he wanted me and Tash

to live in the world. We were never sheltered. We could watch whatever we wanted, movies or documentary, so long as we watched it with an understanding of the context around why it was made that way, what it's saying about the world. It makes him the perfect parent for someone in a rock band, really.

"So on one hand there's me, coming from that background of support. And the other person in the band who writes the lyrics is Jacqui, who is the most earnest person in the world and whose grandfather is a completely amazing, no-bullshit guy through and through. Jacq and I kind of spur each other on to greater and greater heights of activism and righteous proselytizing!"

She laughs self-deprecatingly, her full mouth pulled into a crooked smile.

SALLY

I wake up to the weight of an arm across my belly, the puff of sour-sweet breath against the crook of my neck. I feel comfortable and safe. I've never liked waking up alone. Funny, considering the life I've picked out for myself.

Then I get the panic, the sinking dread that I've gone and mucked things up again. This won't be the first time I've crawled out a boarding house window and left some poor blighter alone in my bed. Someday it's all going to come back to bite me; an army of irate landladies brandishing dusters and skillets and chasing me down some windy main street on a Saturday morning.

'She looked like such a nice girl when I rented her the room,' they'll say. As if I've ever looked anything like a nice girl.

Amy. I remember now. Amy, with the wolf-eyes and the odd way of looking at me, who listened to me retell my mother's version of a fairy tale. She'd started to tell me one in return, I think, before the day caught up with me and sent me under.

She's moved up against me while we slept. She looks younger with her eyes closed, maybe no older than me. Something brittle's missing from her face right now, and she's just as soft and clear as anyone. Her hair's rough, the plait gone to tangles on the pellet-hard little pillow, and the cotton of her light dress is soft from a hundred washings. I wish I didn't have to wake her. There are tiny freckles below her eyes.

Bumps and thumps come through the thin walls from the room next to ours. A creak of bed springs and a blue streak of swearing is followed by the tinkle of piss into the pot. The noise wakes Amy, and her eyes meet mine, a smile on her wide mouth.

"How... symphonic," she says and yawns, wide and fast, like a cat. She doesn't move her hand to cover it or apologise when she's done.

Amy sits up, the sunbeams catching stray strands of her hair and giving her a halo. The angelic look is spoiled a little by the deep purple-black shadows at her eyes. There's a faint twist of cruelty in her easy grin, and that spoils the composition. She's a poorly-painted angel, maybe. A cut-rate spirit.

Her look turns quizzical, and I'm trying to think of something to say when my belly says something for me. Amy snorts at the gurgle of hunger from my gut, apparently as entertained by it as she was by the piss orchestra a moment ago.

"Hungry?" she asks, as if there's any question about that.

I nod and move to get my bag from the floor. It's made of old canvas, worn to threads at the corners. Nell used to wear it, strap stretching across her shirt from shoulder to hip like a holster belt, when she did her Land Army world of picking the early fruits from trees in our tiny orchard. Even now, I think of it as my apple-bag.

"I've got some bread and cheese," I say, scrabbling around for the wax paper square. My fingers brush my notebook, and I wonder if Amy will let me draw her later. I could make her a dragon tamer or a sea siren.

"I'll find us something better," Amy says and shoves her feet into her boots. Her boots are clunky, hobnailed things, and I don't know how she can bear to have her feet bound up in them in weather like this. Even with the blush fading from morning's first light, I can feel how hot the day will get.

"Where are we, anyway?" I ask. Amy's smile curls up in amusement for a third time.

"You don't know where we are?"

I rub my face with my palms, forcing the last of my sleepiness away. "Hmm. New South Wales. Near the middle, on the edge. I can smell the sea."

Amy nods. "We're in South West Rocks. Trial Bay. I saw the sign as we drove in last night."

Trial Bay. I've heard the story a few times before from some of the wanderers I've crossed ways with. There're more of us than the rest of the country likes to know about, I think. Most of them are soldiers who never got the hang of being back home or kids like me who didn't fit in at home to start with. We wanderers keep the fruit picked and the paddocks fenced and the sheep sheared, but nobody really wants to see that we're about.

The *Trial* was a boat that a bunch of convicts stole back about 140 years ago. In 1816, I think. It'd be shit to be a convict, sent off a world away from everything you had just for breaking some idiot law. None of them was the worst of the lot, either. If you were a real devil, they just hanged you. The convicts who got sent over here from England were just kids who stole food and pocket watches, for the most of it.

The *Trial* got wrecked around here somewhere, which is how the bay got its name. Nobody ever found any of the convicts. The story goes that they all died, but there's no more proof of that than of any other outcome. A bit of me hopes they didn't. After all that, they deserved some luck.

"I want to go to the jail today."

Amy doesn't say it like an invitation, and my spirits sink a little. It was nice to have a friend, this girl who repaid a story with one of her own. I should have made more effort to listen to hers.

"After that I should get back on track," she goes on. "I'm on my way to Brisbane, but I'd rather move at night. What about you?"

I shrug.

I've been wandering my way down to Sydney these past few weeks. There's a family I've stayed with before down there, and their eldest died over in Korea just before Christmas. I thought they could use the company and an extra pair of hands. I never got the knack of peace, but I remember how to cope with war. There're always bombs and blood and mourning mothers somewhere in the world, it seems.

"I was going South."

Amy seems to consider me for a minute at that, like I've said something she didn't plan on. Then she shrugs too. "There's no hurry for Brisbane. I'll go South, too. Tonight?"

My heart flops over behind my ribs. "Sounds all right with me."

She nods, pleased with my answer, and smoothes her hair back and heads for the door.

"I'll find us breakfast. Wait here, "she says.

I've been on my own long enough to know better than to pass up an extra minute of sleep on a soft bed, so I settle back down and watch the light play on the ceiling. There must be a water trough for the horses in the back yard because reflected ripples and waves dance gold on the old whitewash over my head.

My fingers twitch for want of a line and shading, and I haul myself back up to sitting. I drag my battered drawing book and a couple of dark chalks out of the corners of my bag. I try not to put down faces without a subject I can copy from, so I settle for a landscape instead. I draw gum trees, thin and ghostly as a girl in a cotton dress, their branches spidering out and up from willowy trunks. I add some magpies in the branches. Nell told me once that the magpies in America aren't like the magpies here. American magpies don't sing, only caw. I almost wanted to cry when she said it. I was still a dumb, dreamy kid then, and the thought of a place without that lilting magpie cry in the mornings broke my heart.

I don't go inland much. It's too big at night. I feel like I'll fall off the flat of the earth, up into the endless stretching stars. I think I'm like a beach vine, the sort that grips onto the sand so tight that even the winds and tides don't drag it free. Mad from drinking seawater.

I haven't been inland in a long time, not by more than a few hours' drive. I think the country would guess that I'm an impostor if I go any deeper than that. It'll swallow me up.

From out the window I hear the cracka-thunk of a blade splitting a log of wood. It comes a second time, shorter and sharper. I've chopped my fair share in the past, so I know the sound of someone taking out a hefty dose of fury on a blameless block. I go to the window and look down, wincing at the brightness of the sun-dots glinting on the trough. Bourbon is not my friend come morning.

Amy. Her slim hands on the broad handle of the axe look about as strong as pale moths, but she brings it down again with a crack to wake the world. Then, as if she can feel the weight of my gaze, she turns and waves up at me.

I wave back.

AMY

The boardinghouse owners gave us breakfast in return for my chopping, and I stole a handful of shillings from the small box hidden atop their bookshelf before joining Sally out on the front step. They'd get us dinner, bed, and food for the next day or two, at least.

We reached Trial Bay Jail shortly before midday. The weight of misery trapped in the walls hit us before we could even see the building. It was a roiling, burning day, but Sally shivered.

"Can't we go down to the water? See where the *Wooloomooloo* sank?" she asked hopefully.

I shook my head.

" Who cares about a bay where ships wrecked a hundred years ago?" I called back to her over the wind, walking ahead towards the old prison. Forces of nature don't leave anything behind. They just are, and then, once they're finished, they aren't. If I wanted to see that, I could stare at the moon or the lines on my palm. I didn't want that; what I wanted was ghosts.

Judged by sight alone, the prison is beautiful. The ruins look romantic against the green of the hills and the blue of the water when the weather is good, and when the weather is bad; the grey and the wind give it an even more romantic cast. It looks haunting rather than haunted.

Sally, as if deciding that company was better than solitude in surroundings like this, caught up with me by the time I reached the jail itself.

"This place is awful," she muttered accusingly, like it was my fault that sorrow pressed us down like damp cloths on our skin.

"It closed just after the turn of the century," I told her. "But they opened it again to put the local Germans in during the first of the wars. Just in case."

I walked down the long, claustrophobic corridor, keeping my steps as light as they could be with the heavy boots on my feet. The plaster was falling to ruin slowly, like it knew it would have forever to get the job done and wasn't in a rush. Even after several empty decades, the jail felt like a squatting, watching predator. The nape of my neck prickled beneath my braid. Even a place as powerful as this jail should have known better than to challenge the likes of me.

"Some of them died here."

The wind wailed and whistled through the cracks and windows.

"The prisoners did what they could with it. They made a tennis court down that way." I pointed.

"But it was still a prison."

"They were Germans." Sally sniffed unsympathetically, a child bruised by war. As if the State-sanctioned theft of her mother hadn't been a hatred based on race, too. Then her face went softer, apologetic, as if noticing for the first time the paleness of my hair and skin.

"Sorry. Was your family from Germany?"

My mother. Elsa was German. I could remember her face a little if I thought about it. I inherited her milk-pale skin and long limbs.

I shrugged. "The nationality doesn't make a difference. Atrocities are the birthright of everyone. It can happen anywhere and often does. Humans are fundamentally horrible."

That made Sally snort. "You reckon you're special and

different, then?"

I grinned. What I was fell far beyond Sally's wildest imaginings of 'special and different,' I was sure.

"Come on, let's find the cells."

As we walked together, I pulled a little block of wood from my pocket. I'd picked it up while chopping and liked the weight of it. There was a knot hidden under the grain. With my pocketknife, I started to shape the edges. The light was low this far into the corridor, but I've always been able to see well in the dark. Carving always calms me. Making something beautiful and new out of worthless discards.

"You like carving?" Sally asked, clearly glad for something normal to discuss, her posture relaxing and her voice losing some of its sharpness. She still held her forearms crossed before her like she was holding herself against a gale.

"I like scrimshaw better," I said. "I used to carve faces down at the docks in Melbourne for the English visitors on holiday. People like seeing themselves reflected in a bone. I don't know why."

"I like to draw. Never done it for money, though." Something small and furred skittered in a nearby shadow, and Sally jumped. "Damn it! This place is stuffed. I'm going to wait out the front, all right?"

I shrugged, putting the knife and wood in my pocket again. Mutinous, she turned and left me there.

I walked until the floor began to creak threateningly under me. Then I chose a cell, the iron of its barred door cold like winter in my palm as I stepped past the threshold. The pain and despair in that tiny square of a room was almost enough to send me backwards, but I braced my feet and moved carefully to the far corner. It was like temperature's effect on arthritic bones or loud noises buffeting a headache. An intangible force, capable of inflicting a battery of sensation against those sensitive to it.

The remains of a hammock-ring, long ago torn from the wall by looters, jutted out of the water-warped wall beside my head. This is where the most hopeless of dreams were dreamt, once. I closed my eyes.

CHARLOTTE

From *Reign in Hell: Two Weeks in the Life of HUSH*, by Charlotte Waterhouse, Amplify Press, Australia, 2011:

For a long time, HUSH was the band all your cool friends claimed to have liked from the start. The truth is that even your cool friends probably hadn't heard a note.

First came a four-track EP, *HUSH Presents Skyline Splinters*, with the six song *Jazz Funeral* soon after. These releases were vinyl-only, and the band's already cult-like followers did their best to keep the songs off the internet.

"Music's so easy to dismiss now," Jacqui says. We're in the hotel dining room, collecting fruit and coffees from the breakfast buffet to take upstairs to the others. A pair of teenage girls, still in their pajamas, have abandoned their cereal bowls to whisper frantically to each other while staring at Jacqui. She's wearing a shapeless T-shirt that might have been black a thousand washings ago and a pair of jeans held together with silver duct tape at one knee. Like Tash, she seems to wear red lipstick as a permanent fixture no matter what the time of day or location.

"You download an mp3, you listen to it, and then you forget it ten seconds later," she says, oblivious to the adolescent excitement she's causing. "You go see a live show, and by the time you get home, all you retain of it is the smell on your T-shirt.

"We wanted to bring the adventure back into rock. Make it something exciting when you finally found the B-side you were looking for in a used record store. Or when you heard about your favourite band playing a show in your town.

"Jo was the one who always pushed for proper representation. Without her we'd probably still be playing dives. Jo's a really fuckin' driven person. Really fuckin' driven."

We go back to the band's rooms, where every suitcase and satchel seems to have spontaneously exploded with crumpled black T-shirts and makeup cases already covering every visible surface. Jacqui sighs happily at the sight of the mess.

"I fuckin' love the tour life. Only place I feel like I'm normal is when I'm travelling, you know?"

The band's tour manager orders them all to get some sleep before their show that night, advice which is promptly ignored by everyone. The tour schedule is pretty standard for an overseas act: Melbourne, Sydney, Adelaide, Perth, Brisbane, and then back to Melbourne for a hastily-added second show tacked onto the end of the tour due to popular demand. No longer the best band you've never heard, HUSH is now the fastest-rising star of the alternative world.

The band's first full-length album, *Harlequin Razors*, was described by *RPM* magazine as 'the closest genuine successor to David Bowie's *Diamond Dogs* the world has seen, crossed with the prickly, visceral resistance of Nirvana's late work.' No reviewer gave it less than three and a half out of five on any rating system.

The band members state time and time again, however, that they don't care about approval, sales, or popularity. For them, the point is and always has been to create a place that feels like home and live there as long as they can get away with it.

They put up with the 'fucking brutal' flights to Australia and the publicity bullshit of having a would-be book writer tag along with them in order to play to as many crowds as they can. They suffer through all this to reach as many kids as possible with the idea that there are kindred spirits out there, just as restless and malcontented and hungry for something different as they are.

"Basically," Jacqui says, "We decided to go mainstream, to actually listen to Jo, because… I read this Kurt Cobain interview this one time, right. And in the article he's saying how the Walmart guys wanted to change the title of a song or the album artwork or something before they'd sell it. All these people around Kurt were going 'No, man, you can't compromise your integrity, you can't sell out to the man.' But Cobain was all for it because he knew there was no place in the world more fuckin' important for his music to be than Walmart.

"The kids who find shit in indie record stores are, like, they're already saved, y'know? Or anti-saved, I guess. They know it's okay to be weird and different and damned already. It's great to appeal to that group because they're already trained in how to try new things, open themselves to new ideas. I'm super-glad we went that way first with the vinyls.

"But once we were thinking about going maybe to a label and real distribution and shit, I thought okay, yeah. Yeah, we gotta fuckin' be in Walmart, we gotta get to those kids who don't know yet about the little record stores. Like my grandpa always says, 'there's no point in preaching to the fuckin' choir.'"

In the afternoon Jacqui and I sit on the floor of the paved courtyard behind the hotel bar. Jacqui is drinking a vanilla sorbet and Red Bull smoothie and plucking at loose threads on the frayed cuffs of her jeans.

Jacqui is stunning and surprisingly delicate up close. Surprising because the reckless, infectious joy she exudes onstage seems too exuberant and wild to permit anything close to fragility. Put simply, when Jacqui's got a microphone in her hands, she looks like she could fight the whole world and win, and you don't expect someone like that to also have small, even white teeth just crooked enough to make her smiles lopsided.

Her wide green-grey eyes have black spiky lashes, and her skin is death-pale, traced with delicate blue veins beneath the surface. Jacqui seems much too… *pretty* to be a rock star.

She seems that way until she snaps her gum and says "If I keep texting while we're talking, that's okay, right? Gabe's shitty at following directions, and I'm trying to explain to him how to get to that great comics shop here, the one up the elevator? I've got a craving for some action figures."

After that, her prettiness is less distracting because her personality fills the air like lightning crackles.

"So now that we've got an album out there, we've done the touring all over, and it's… I never know what to say to describe it. Success is kind of heavy, a heavy responsibility. How can you not feel good when kids come up to you after a show and say that your music kept them going when everything else made them wanna die? That's a good kind of heavy, I think. It means we're doing something important.

"We just finished recording the second album in LA just before we came out here. I think that… I don't know. It's weird to talk about it. Right now I'm super-stoked about the new album because it's all fresh, so it's hard to get perspective. I was excited about the last one at first, and now I've got nothing but dislike for it.

"From a personal perspective, I mean. I know a lot of people out there love it, and I love that they love it. But for myself? After a while the songs get to feeling like used tissues almost. You know when you're sick, and you need to sneeze and you grab a tissue, and that first second when you sneeze, the tissue is the best thing that's ever been invented, ever? And then, you can't get it into the trash fast enough because it's disgusting and full of your snot?

"Songs get to be like snot for me. They're a part of me that I've expelled out of my body, that I've purged. They're puke. You're glad you got the puke out of you, but you don't wanna have to keep dealing with it for eighteen months on the road, you know? You don't wanna replay your snot and puke every night on a stage."

While she may wish for greater distance from her metaphorical excretions, it's clear that Jacqui has no fear of her literal tears, saliva, or blood. She regularly cries onstage. Screams and sobs intermingle in the furious, unbound sections of the band's shows. She'll spit mouthfuls of water over the crowd, sometimes hurling herself down onto their waiting hands afterward.

Her blood has only made one deliberate appearance, though. Jacqui is regularly scraped and scratched by her uninhibited performances, but there is a wide divide between that type of injury and what happened at last year's Anarchy in the Park festival in England.

The day of the festival, the Daily Mail carried the headline STRANGE SINGER SEX-CHANGE SHOCK with the accompanying article declaring with salacious faux-horror that Jacqueline Caramano's 'shameful secret' was that she had been born as Jacob Caramano, transitioning in preadolescence.

Onstage that day, in front of 40,000 music fans, Jacqui stepped up to the microphone with a glass of water in her hand. She drank the liquid down calmly, then crouched down and smashed the empty glass against the stage. She stood up and brought a shard, pointed sharp as a switchblade, to the veins on her forearm. A swift slice and the blood welled up and began to drip.

"It's fuckin' red, same as yours," Jacqui said into the shocked quiet that followed her self-inflicted violence.

Arm held aloft, to avoid bleeding so much that she fainted, her hand a raised fist, Jacqui began to sing. She prefaced the first song with the dedication "This is for all the lamia girls and nephilim boys."

In the photos and footage of the set HUSH performed that day, Jacqui looks like a steel-spined war general, battered but unbroken, leading her army of misfits forward to victory.

"The record company went into damage control," Jacqui says, her voice soft as she talks about the hours leading up to her powerful, gory moment on the stage. "Publicists argued about whether to address it or not. What the best thing to do was, to avoid alienating the fan base, you know?

"Cherry's the one who called a meeting of everybody who worked with the band. I was fuckin' terrified because I'd never talked about being trans with them. I assumed they all knew — Ben knew, obviously. I'd never talked about it one way or the other with the others, but I assumed they all knew. But now, I was like, what if they didn't? What if they're freaked out, or angry, or both? Was this the end of HUSH?

"I thought for sure I'd destroyed my damn band. I was a wreck.

"Cherry stands there at the end of the table, in one of the meeting rooms at the record company's HQ in London, and she's got her arms crossed and looks like she's some motherfuckin' dictator about to lead an army.

"And she says, 'I don't give a shit about alienating the fan base. Anyone who feels alienated by something like this isn't someone I want as a fan of my band. The only person who gets to have an opinion about this is Gabe, or whoever else Jacqi wants to sleep with.

"'The only media statement I intend to make is this, and I will make it on every music blog and website on the entire fucking internet if you try to 'damage control' anything:

HUSH supports every person's right to be who they are and do what they want, and that is *the whole of the fucking law*.'"

"And then we went out and played the show. After, I got stitches in the First Aid area while Jo screamed at me and threatened to quit if I ever did anything so dangerous and stupid again. We all went back to the hotel and had pizza with extra mushrooms — I fuckin' love mushrooms on pizza, and usually I gotta fight Jo and Ben because they hate them — but not that night. That night Gabe and I watched *Blade Runner* on the TV until I fell asleep. That's how I spent my day, the day the world found out that I'm transgender."

Jacqui swallows the last of her Red Bull smoothie and offers me a crooked, weary smile.

"I avoid people's discussions about my gender where I can. That's a hard thing to do because I try to monitor the media we get, y'know? So I can help out with publicity stuff a bit. But I set up the email alerts to be like, show 'HUSH' except when 'Lady Gaga' is also present. Because Lady Gaga always gets mentioned when they talk about my body, and never otherwise, because of that bullshit that was around for a while about her being intersex. I don't know what the fuck that has to do with my band, but who the fuck knows what goes through the fucking media's heads, you know? No offense.

"Doing the Gaga alert-filter thing is a good way for me to avoid having to read people's bullshit. I don't care what anyone else thinks about me. The only people who matter are the people I love, who love me."

Jacqui pauses, chewing her lip for a moment. Her presence is magnetic even here in the courtyard of a hotel bar, though it's a very different kind of magnetism to the wild energy she exudes onstage.

"I try to be like my granddad," she says. "He's the most

badass person I've ever known, so when I start to feel sorry for myself or like the world's too hard, I pretend I'm him. I try to react to shit in the way I know he would. One of his favorite phrases, one he says all the time, is 'drink a cup of concrete and harden the fuck up.'

"He jokes that Ben and I are in this band because we fuckin' owe him. We got to be David Caramano's grandkids; now he gets to be known for being Jacqui and Ben's grandfather."

David Caramano has been taking remarkable photographs since he first picked up a camera in 1942. As of last year, he has two Pulitzer Prizes, a World Press Photo of the Year, and countless other accolades and awards.

Of all those photographs, however, there are two for which he will be best remembered: *Rosie Remembers*, taken in 1945, and *Death and her Sister, Love* in 1994.

ELLA

Dear Natasha,

I apologize for saying you're too young to read Vonnegut. When I stopped to think about it, when I remembered how you're older than I ever was, I realized how dumb I sounded in warning you away from it as being too grown-up.

You don't even go by Nattie anymore — the fact I haven't been able to bring myself to say 'Dear Tash' can tell you at least a little about how hard it is for me to reconcile my perception of you with the truth. In my heart you're still little Nattie, fat and laughing-eyed, with your dolls and plastic trucks. I can't think of you as an adult.

I'm not the first to write from this place. C.S Lewis wrote the *Screwtape Letters* — which is fiction, but still — and Jack the Ripper said that the messages he sent the police were 'from Hell.' So there must be some kind of postal service here, even if that postal service is unreliable and partly made from fiction. Maybe you'll read these words one day after all.

I could tell you about the people I know, I guess. 'People' is a kind of relative term; a lot of those I love the best are monsters, metaphorical and otherwise. Chris and Dean are still around of course — I couldn't get rid of those two even if I wanted to. The three of us, when we aren't in human form, sometimes fuse into a kind of three-headed hydra, a many-limbed spider with a trio of grinning, bloodied mouths. We scuttle down school hallways in the nightmares of parents, leaving gleaming leech-trails of gore across linoleum.

Jo's rarely anything but person-shaped, even when she's here. People get weird about their scars like that, as if the very fact that they're hard-won and painful in the gaining makes them valuable somehow. The scars become a badge, a mark of what the wearer has gone through. She doesn't want to give them up in favor of a prettier shape.

I feel like I should write about Jo since she's the one you're closest with, the one who matters most in your life. But I don't know her very well. She doesn't like me. She thinks my death was stupid.

To tell the truth, most of the time I feel the very same way. These days being dead is tedious, even for famous wicked souls. I envy all the kids who've grown up beyond the age where I stopped. But it gets my hackles up when Jo insults me. She's so self-righteous. That's why she's always so clipped when she talks — it's like nobody is properly worthy of her attention for more than the minimum amount of time.

The friends I do have are Nicolas and Sam, Chris and Dean. I always got along better with boys than girls. I like it when I hang out with Vivi, but I don't think either of us would ever say that we were friends. We both hate people far too much to open up like that.

The winds are too hot and the view too variable for me to have a window in my quarters. I live alone. I've always liked my space. A poet once said that no man is an island, but I've come pretty close in my time in the world and out of it.

No windows, and strong locks on the door. Hell is other people (a poet said that, too — more pretty words I want to defy). Nobody sleeps here, and I get bored a lot, but there are books to read and always music. It isn't so bad.

Love,
E.V.

Dear Natasha,

Richard Loeb was eighteen, rich and clever. Raised by a controlling governess and finding solace and rebellion in obsession with crime. He thought of crime as a game to play and win.

Nathan Leopold was nineteen, smart, and the son of a millionaire. His obsessions were songbirds and Nietzsche.

When I first read about Leopold and Loeb in a book of true crime at the library, I was fourteen, which meant I was basically cross-eyed with horniness all the time, no matter what I was doing. The story of those two made my heart thump and my cheeks flush.

They reminded me of Dean and Chris. That was the first day I realized I was in love with Dean and Chris. It's funny, the way we learn things about ourselves.

Dean was a lot like Nathan Leopold. They'd both have done anything if they got to be the accomplice in their best friend's folie au deux.

Like Caril Ann, Dean and Leopold may very well never have murdered at all if not for the whims of their lovers. The world will never know.

Chris, like Richard Loeb, was cold and logical with a strange kind of brain. They carefully planned out their wicked deeds as meticulously as a traveller setting out on a complex adventure.

I've always been a natural tactician — at this point that really goes without saying — but even I was impressed by some of Chris's strategies and systems.

They were caught and went to jail. They became teachers at the prison school. Nathan Leopold was at Richard Loeb's bedside when he died. Another prisoner claimed that Loeb tried to have sex with him in the shower and that slashing his throat and cutting him fifty times was self-defense.

This was a lie, but nobody except Leopold really cared. The other prisoner wasn't punished. The newspapers wrote 'Richard Loeb, despite his erudition, today ended his sentence with a proposition.'

Photographs of black lynching victims used to get made into postcards for white people to buy. Fags murdered in jail make for hilarious puns in headlines for straight people.

Other people's deaths have always been the best joke, the great gag gift we give one another. If we laugh at those poor dead fuckers, then the grim reaper will know we're nothing like them. He won't come for us.

After Leopold left jail, he went to work in a hospital. He wrote a book about birds.

Love,
Ella

Dear Natasha,

Another saying I hate: 'Hell is empty, and all the devils are here.'

The first problem with this assertion is that it assumes the 'here' that the reader inhabits to be Earth, when actually an awful lot of reading goes on in Hell. There are no restricted titles lists, no burned books, no censorship.

For bookworms like me, Hell can get dangerously close to heavenly sometimes. We all make sure to pinch ourselves, hard, so that nobody starts to suspect how happy we are. We're cunning in order to keep our secret pleasures.

Hell is very far from empty. It's a lot of things, but empty isn't one of them. You may not be too young for

Vonnegut, Nattie, but I'm sure as fuck that you're too young for hearing about the things Hell is.

But it's not empty. The damned, the dead — there are a lot of us — would fill cities and countries and continents on Earth. But part of the saying's true enough: the devils are mostly on Earth these days.

The devils can get through the Dark, which the dead can't do. Except for Saints, of course. It's different for Saints. The ordinary dead only do it once. Once they're through, they never get a return ticket to come back out again unless it's to live another life from scratch, all that they used to be erased like a cracked hard drive.

On Earth, the devils have to be people-shaped these days. If they want to be able to get much done, anyway. Murmur's told me stories about times when that wasn't as true as it is now. They're good stories. Maybe I'll write some of them down for you.

But for the last few hundred years, demons are mostly people-shaped. I think humanity uses that as an excuse. We behave in such a way that there's no point in trying to tell one from the other at all.

Xe

Dear Natasha,

Because we were nerds, we were ahead of the curve, way ahead, when it came to computers. There was this one awesome punk zine that Murmur brought back to Hell in about 2001 or so, just as blogging and all that shit was starting up, years before MySpace or Facebook or anything was around. It was photocopied on colored paper and filled with a mess of thoughts and feelings. The cover listed the creator's name as Scarlet Slaughterhouse.

It had one collage-page made up of awkward stock photos of kids looking at computers, all smiles and learning and diversity and wholesomeness. Scrawled across the images in lumpy, uneven letters was:

THE FIRST SOCIAL NETWORK WAS A COBWEB.

The period at the end of the sentence was a biology textbook illustration of a fly. Buzz, buzz.

How's that for a test of genius? I was creating a social network when Mark Zuckerberg was still fucking around on Geocities. (I've also been on the cover of *TIME* magazine more times than he has, though his cover photo was more professional than the yearbook snaps and video stills that I got. Those pictures don't look like anything to me anymore. It's like when you stare at a word for long enough, and it becomes incomprehensible. Those photos of me have been used too many times. They've stopped being of a girl, of *me*. They're just a jumble of shadows and brights.)

So, Cobweb. It was an IRC chatroom first, a place where kids talked about gaming and books and music and how much we all hated school. I was the head moderator, with Chris and Dean as my lieutenants.

After a while, the chats about gaming and books and music all became less frequent, and conversations about school began to dominate. We were all of us miserable, most of us lonely, some of us cutting ourselves or drinking too much or fucking the wrong people. It was a clubhouse of fuckups, a place of solidarity.

After I had the idea, that night when I was babysitting, Cobweb became our recruiting ground.

We moved the location from a chatroom to an email list to make things more private and easier to keep track of. It was time to get serious about our discontent.

It was time to weaponize.

exx

P.S. I had a personal website, too. That got me into trouble. It could have ruined everything. But even super-smart murderer genius teenagers are still teenagers, and what teenager really thinks about potential unintended consequences?

I had sex with Chris and Dean, but we weren't dating. They weren't my boyfriends. They were my best friends. They were Chris and Dean — a part of myself.

So even though we regularly fucked each other, we dated other people outside our little world of three. Dean took Stephanie Ryan to the prom on the last Friday before the massacre. Chris sometimes hung out with this college girl who was pretty into him; she helped him get some of his guns.

And I had Darcy. He was pretty cool. He liked games and stupid jokes and messing around with AV equipment, same as I did. He made me laugh and was cute in that floppy-haired schoolboy kind of way, but after a couple of months he dumped me because he said I was kind of a psycho bitch.

Chris, ever chivalrous, came over and helped me write the most hateful and inventive screeds we could think of against Darcy to post on the website. We went all out, listing tortures and punishments and mutilations, swearing and cursing.

Then we fell asleep on beanbags in front of the TV and woke up with killer hangovers. I didn't think much more about it. The website had all kinds of stupid junk of it, *Doom* levels made by Chris and Dean's short stories and my pages of lame jokes. The stuff about Darcy was just another bit of junk in the jumble.

Then he found it and showed his parents.

SALLY

I should just leave Amy here. She doesn't even want to come down to Sydney anyway, so it's not like it'll be any real loss if she comes out and I'm gone. I throw another sharp-cornered rock into the troubled water below the headland and glare at the cloudy horizon.

I don't want to go. I don't want to be angry with her on our first full day in each other's company. She worked so I could have a better breakfast than old bread and dry cheese.

My chin's resting on my arms, arms resting on my knees. Curled in like this, my shivers are starting to go. It's not even a cold day, and here I am trembling and clacking my teeth like I'm frozen.

I've been places like that jail before. Felt that shiver. Back around Brisbane, there's a good dozen of them. Once, I went out to Gatton with Nell so that she could visit some of her Women's Land Army friends for the day, and there was a field out there that nerved me up so badly I had nightmares for a week. This jail's as bad as that was, but no worse.

Still, I've never known anyone who'd stay in a place like that by choice. Seek it out, that's what she did. Amy knew what we were in for when she said she'd planned to come here.

I should just leave. Even an idiot like me knows better than to mess with this stuff. The skin on my back is crawling. Everything in the air and in my skin wants me to get to my feet and run away from the ruin off in the distance.

Everything except her, and for her I wait.

It's more than an hour before I hear the crunch of her boots on the gravel behind me. There's a healthy, happy flush in her white cheeks, and the smile she gives me looks almost completely sincere.

"Do you still want to visit the beach?"

By the time we make it out to the main highways and flag a lift, it'll be late afternoon. "Nah. Let's get started if we've got both South and North to get to."

"You want to come to Brisbane."

I make a face, then nod. "Guess so. Gotta go home sometime, right? Might as well see how Dad's doing."

A little of the pretty blush fades, and she looks away from me, down at the water, below the headland.

"All right. If you want."

Damn it. I've said the wrong thing again. "What about you? Where're your kin?"

She shakes her head. "Not here."

"Overseas?" I don't know why I'm pushing it. She makes everything difficult and strange.

She looks up at me again, though, so that's something. The pall vanishes as quick as it came, and Amy nods like nothing was ever wrong in the first place.

"Yeah. Come on, let's go snag ourselves a ride."

CHARLOTTE

From *Reign in Hell: Two Weeks in the Life of HUSH*, by Charlotte Waterhouse, Amplify Press, Australia, 2011:

You've seen *Rosie Remembers* even if you didn't know the picture's name. Every montage of 20th Century images of despair and conflict include it, along with other mainstays such as Dorothea Lange's *Migrant Mother*, Kevin Carter's *Vulture and Child*, Nick Ut's *Napalm-burned Girl*, and Steve McCurry's *Afghan Teen*.

Rosie Remembers is the one of the young, dark-haired woman — David's wife, Lena Caramano, who died in 2007 — sitting at a kitchen table, her hands scratched and dirtied from a day of factory work. She's looking at a photograph. There are tears in her eyes, but she isn't crying. Her jaw is set, her lips blurred a little as the shutter of the camera attempted to catch the tremble of them, but she isn't crying. On the table in front of her is a tin cigarette box, an Army Medal of Honor, and a pair of wire-frame glasses with one broken lens visible inside. The image on the photograph she's holding can't be seen, but the handwriting on the back says simply 'Nicolas'.

If you've ever seen it, you know it. It's a difficult photograph to forget.

Later, *Rosie Remembers* became a much-duplicated symbol of the anti-Vietnam movement. David and Lena both vocally supported the picture's use by protest groups and peace activists.

For several decades, *Rosie Remembers* was unique

among Caramano's celebrated work not only because of its fame, but because it was the only one of his published photographs to feature a member of his family. Any number of his pictures from the intervening years can be held up as examples of excellent photojournalism, but not until David returned to the personal did his work, once again, reach the realms of exquisite.

Death and Her Sister, Love is a color photograph of two children giggling together atop a hospital bed. The gender of the pair is impossible to guess from the photo alone, as the two are dressed in matching Batman pajamas, and both are bald.

The smaller of the two girls is skinny, her limbs spindly in that way children who have been seriously ill for a long time begin to have. Her eyebrows and lashes are gone, along with the hair on her scalp, making clear the baldness has been brought on by chemotherapy.

The elder of the pair is sturdier, a child at the age where puppy fat starts to plump the face and arms. Her little sister kneels above her, wielding a large pair of stainless steel scissors that look better-suited to gardening or craft projects than for cutting children's hair. The two are laughing as the smaller girl snips away the last long lock of her sister's hair, leaving behind a patchy landscape of short, shorn clumps of dark brown.

The camera caught the blade of the scissors just as the light from the ward's window has struck them, making the sharp edge gleam in center-frame between the girls. The photo is haunting, heartbreaking, and yet it's almost impossible to look at it without wanting to smile.

The faces of the two girls contain so much joy and laughter along with the illness and sorrow that the picture is seen by many people as the iconic image of terminal childhood disease, as well as a depiction of impending sibling bereavement.

The children in the photo are Marie and Jacqueline Caramano. Less than a month after *Death and Her Sister, Love* was taken, Marie died of acute lymphoblastic leukemia.

"My little sister died when I was eight," Jacqui says. She is still visibly the little girl captured in the photograph, grown up and painted in harsher colors but the same underneath these trappings. "Our parents took off right after. Flaked out and hit the road. I hated them for a long time for that, but now I'm older I can be more Zen about it. Losing your kid in such a shitty way would make anyone wanna become a smack-head and run away from their life, wouldn't it? How the fuck do you cope with watching your own child get murdered painfully by her own body, you know? So I guess I don't hate them now. It isn't like they left me on the street or anything. My grandma and grandpa were the best parents anybody could fuckin' want in life. And Marie, she was the golden baby. She was their light. My actual mom and dad, I mean. They loved Marie so much. I was... well, I was, you know. They ordered a Jacob and they got a Jacqui. Who can blame them for splitting?"

"I can fucking blame them," Gabe cuts in as he enters the courtyard. His dark eyes flash with anger, wiry shoulders set back as if he's ready to launch into an attack. His tattoos are so extensive that there's no bare skin visible below his jawline, just a puzzle of color and shape. He hands her a paper shopping bag. "Here's your action figures. And what the fuck, baby? Did I hear you right? Did you just fucking excuse those dirtbags for what they did by suggesting that you *deserved it*?"

Jacqui shrugs, looking uncomfortable. "I just meant that it's, you know. It's complicated. Having one sick kid and one trans kid is —"

"Is the shit parents *sign up for*. There's no clause in the contract that says 'I'll only love and care for my baby if it fits in the traditional gender binary and is of good health.' *Fuck* ."

Gabriel's tattooed hands hold Jacqui's own hands tight, clasped between them as he speaks with a sincerity that's almost uncomfortable to witness. "You are so fucking beautiful, you fucking idiot. Any parent who can't see how deserving of love you are... well, they don't fucking deserve you. They don't even deserve *contempt*." There's a look of violence in his face that makes me think of predatory birds, creatures of talons and black darting eyes.

"Are you sure we're still just talking about my mom and dad here?" Jacqui asks with a cryptic, quirky smile.

The two of them look like the perfect punk rock prom king and queen, dirty and tattooed and makeup-stained, their sharp edges fitting together in the jagged, bright-bladed way of all beautiful machines.

I go into the bar proper, giving Jacqui and Gabe a few minutes alone together as I order us another round of smoothies.

Gabe's leaving as I come back out, taking the action figures he bought for Jacqui up to their room.

"You should totally show her the show from side stage tonight," Jacqui says to Gabe, nodding in my direction. Gabe raises his eyebrows in a wordless invitation, but I want to make sure that I won't get underfoot while the techs are working.

"I think we'll manage," Gabe promises, so I happily agree to meet up with him prior to the concert that night. With a final lingering kiss goodbye for Jacqui, he departs.

"Okay. What were we talking about before Gabe showed up? Oh, Grandpa's photos, wasn't it? Me and Marie. I decided to get my tattoo right after she died, you know. I had to wait years before I could get it — even sketchy fuckin' places aren't gonna put ink on an eight-year-old — but I knew exactly what I was getting and never changed my mind for a second."

Her left thumb rubs at her right wrist while she speaks, like she's seeking comfort from the words she brought back with her out of her pain. Tiny black print across the veins that trace under her honey-colored skin. *Fuck nobility*. Her scar from the Anarchy in the Park cut starts several centimeters further down.

"I guess you know that Marie died from cancer. That shit's a lot more painful and messy than it looks in made-for-TV movies, I'll fuckin' tell you that. So, anyway, when it wasn't completely hopeless yet, when there was still a chance she'd live, our local paper wanted to do a story on her. 'Brave little girl fights her brave fight bravely,' you know, that kinda feel-good bullshit.

"We wouldn't do it. We locked ourselves in her room, just her and me, until everyone went the hell away.

"Because *fuck bravery*. Why the fuck did they need her to be brave? She was six fucking years old, and she was in horrible pain, and she was gonna maybe fucking die, and here are some bullshit fucking journalists — no offence — demanding that she be some fucking poster child for a sweet and noble bravery. Fuck that. Fuck sweetness. Fuck *nobility*.

"After Marie died, for a few years there, it was just the three of us — me, my grandma, and my grandpa. Ben came to live with us when I was fifteen. He's two years younger than me. Things were really good for both of us at my grandparent's house. Ben only had his dad, and he was a quiet guy. Getting thrown out by his dad turned out to be a good thing for him. Having Grandma and Grandpa and me around to draw him out was really good for him, I think. Yeah, I don't think... I'm a big sister, I know, you know? Are you a big sister?"

I tell Jacqui that yes, I'm the eldest of four.

"Then you get it. You wouldn't know how to be *you* if

you weren't a big sister, would you? It's not just the context you're in, your place in the family. It's way deeper than that. Being a big sister is who I was, and then all of a sudden I *wasn't*. I wasn't *me* anymore. Having Ben there gave me a chance to be me again, to put myself back together into the person I wanted to be."

    This time, Jacqui's smile isn't weary or wry, just happy and a little surprised, as if her shock still hasn't worn off even after two albums and countless tours. She reminds me of Snow White from the old Disney cartoon, all whites and blacks and crimson lips.

    "I think I did a pretty okay job of it, don't you?"

ELLA

Dearest of dear, dear Natashas,

In the Middle Ages, people took long, difficult journeys to the shrines of holy people. The journeys were called pilgrimages; the people, pilgrims.

In the Bible, there's a part that talks about Paul's handkerchiefs having healing power and another part that says Elisha's bones could raise the dead. So people call the stuff a holy person owned or touched (or parts of the person themselves) *relics*. They believe relics have power. When a pilgrim went to a shrine, they'd purchase a relic and take it home with them as a way to be closer to God.

Relics became big business. John Calvin once remarked that there were so many pieces of the True Cross hanging around that a ship could be built out of them. There'd been enough finger bones attributed to some saints that the people in question must have been strange monsters indeed when they were intact and alive. Holy foreskins were popular, too. The Topkapi museum in Istanbul has a hair from Muhammad's beard.

The same's true on this side of the tracks, too. When Bonnie and Clyde were killed, their car was towed into town, and people came in droves to touch and look. School kids tore off pieces off Bonnie's dress and stole locks of her hair.

Fingerbones and foreskins by any other name.

Look on eBay sometime and see how much yearbooks with my photo in them are going for. It's a whole industry.

Everyone wants the magic object.

I guess I'm really just telling you things you already know. You've thrown guitar picks into grasping crowds. You've scrawled your name on album covers. This shit is all old hat to you.

XE

Dear Natasha,

Since we've established that you're old enough to read Vonnegut, I'm now thinking about other books that I should recommend to you. (If I were in a trite, smarmy mood, I'd make a crack here about how even just one trip to the library can be life-changing. But it's a bad day today. I can't find anything funny, not even myself or my own end. Usually those get a laugh out of me even when nothing else does.)

Books for you, part the first: *In Cold Blood* by Truman Capote. A predictable choice, but the classics are classics for a reason, you know? It's a novel about a true story, which if you ask me is cheating, but nobody's asking me so, whatever. This family got murdered in the 1950s, and Truman Capote and Harper Lee went to cover the story.

Harper Lee wrote *To Kill A Mockingbird*. Everyone says it's this amazing, perfect book, but I don't have a lot of time for a book that replaces the injustices of racism with the injustices of verbally badgering a woman and undermining her accusations of rape. I know what the point is; I just don't like the point. Why do we have to make another disenfranchised group the enemy in order to exonerate the first disenfranchised group?

You can always tell when I've been listening to Lucifer. My writing turns into an echo of hers. I think that's why

I'm so unhappy today. Lucifer always makes me feel the possibilities of the universe, the things we can do and the fights that need fighting, and I come away feeling useless and stupid and ineffectual. I wanted to burn the world once. Now sometimes I can barely muster a flicker inside my own heart.

Anyway, *In Cold Blood*. Capote started it before the killers were caught but didn't finish it until after they were dead. I think that's good. Well, obviously *I* do. I made sure that I'd die before my legend started growing. No living, ordinary, human can be as large as her mythology needs her to be. But I guess you know that, as a rock star. It's all airbrushing and PR after a certain point.

So it's better that Perry Smith and Richard Hickock were executed by hanging before Capote finished his book about them. (The gallows they died on is in a museum now, of course. Saint's fingerbones can't be left unworshipped.)

Perry dreamed of being a singer and wrote poems about birds. Richard, who went by Dick, was pragmatic and unromantic by contrast, but that's what Perry liked about him. When I read *In Cold Blood* over that last winter vacation before Cobweb, I kept thinking that Perry and Dick reminded me of Dean and Chris. There's a dynamic, a one-two dance. Art and machinery, maybe. Dreaming and building. One doesn't work without the other.

On the backseat of their car, Perry and Dick had a honey-colored Gibson guitar and a 12-gauge pump-action shotgun. If you ask me, that's practically as good as the thing about barrage balloons and theater curtains that your friend Ben loves so much in Nicolas's letters. The still lives of instruments.

The family of four that Perry and Dick murdered included a 16-year-old girl, Nancy. She kept a diary. I hate the way some diaries become profound in hindsight when the person writing them dies. As if we're not all, ultimately, writing foreshadowing of our own deaths while we're alive.

There are exceptions, of course — Anne Frank was a genuine writer, who revised and edited her diary in order to make it more like art and less like the same accidental narratives of any life. But since then, so many other dead voices have been printed and bound as if the banal crap they wrote about has become poignant simply because they didn't get any older after penning it.

I sound harsh, but I don't mean to be. Not really. I'm sure Saint Stacey would agree with me. I'm sure she'd rather not be remembered for the dumb scribbles she wrote down at night before going to bed. Even people who write in the form as a kind of literary conceit for telling more sophisticated stories are, in the end, just vomiting out what's stuck in their heads in that moment.

Christ, I guess in the future we'll start having profound bindings of Facebook status updates or something equally repulsive. Or, you will, anyway. I won't. I'm not on Earth at all anymore, except in a literal, my-ashes-are-in-an-urn-on-the-dresser way.

Nancy's diary has escaped becoming a saint's relic probably because Capote superseded it with the novel he built. But there are snatches of bittersweetness to be found in the words she put down sometimes: "Summer here. Forever, I hope."

Dick and Perry rode around in a black 1949 Chevrolet sedan. That's one part of the Bonnie-and-Clyde, Mickey-and-Mallory, *Badlands*, *True Romance* adventure I never got to have. The road trip on the run, helter skelter down the highway to the horizon with sirens on our heels and diner food in our bellies. I wish Dean and Chris and I could have had that. The wind and the open air and the three of us forever.

Xe

AMY

The first ride of our second night stopped in Port Macquarie as the sun went down. The sparse trees and narrow roads of the landscape were all tinted the same dim grey by the twilight, and the first few stars of the night sky were anemic glimmers against a sky not yet truly dark.

Our drivers were another pregnant wife and her husband — the whole country was about to give birth, it seemed. Stacked in two small piles on the floor of the car's back seat were old magazines, the dates on their covers stretching back a couple of decades.

"I remember this one," Sally held up a battered old copy of the *Women's Mirror*. "Nell, the Land Army worker who helped on our farm, used to get these from her friends in town. I learned to read on things like this."

"Keep it," the husband said without looking back at us. "They're just going to my cousin, anyway. He won't miss one or two."

Sally shoved her prize in her bag and smiled broadly at me.

I smiled back, heart still singing and jittering from its earlier nourishment.

They let us off outside their motel; I couldn't have made the situation more perfect if I'd planned it. "The Historic Well Motel" was shiny-new with paint and optimism, the perfect picturesque haven for young families or couples spending a night in a fishing town.

But I knew about the dark and seemingly endless pit

in the corner of its courtyard. There'd been a jail here, too, once upon a time. Not as devastatingly desolate as Trial Bay's prison, but terrible in its own way. That gaping wound leading down to nothing, now an historical landmark, had seen the executions of four prisoners in its time. The horror, left in after-image on the air like light on the eye when a room's plunged to darkness, was thick enough to swallow.

Sally took one look at the place and stepped back. "Let's find another ride. We can get a hell of a lot closer than this to Sydney tonight if we push on."

An hour by the well, on top of the afternoon's jaunt in solitary confinement, and I'd be set for weeks. But Sally looked determined to be anywhere else but there, and I quietly cursed the fact I'd picked someone so sensitive. Someone who names themselves Oblivion should, by rights, be more oblivious than she ever managed.

At some of those sites, in those days, I wondered at how natural the absorption of sorrow and pain seemed to be for the landscape. It was as if the yawning wounds of the landscape, scars of abandoned jails and holes that had been wells, gobbled misery with an appetite equal to my own.

I'd always considered myself among the most unnatural of the creatures scuttling on the surface of the world, but perhaps I wasn't so uncanny after all. Perhaps the world itself had an appetite for darkness.

"All right," I agreed. "Let's go get a drink or a bit of dinner before we set off, eh?"

Sally's footsteps lightened as we moved away from the motel and its history.

"That magazine I got, that really is how I learned to read, you know," she said, as if attempting to clear the air between us. "That's where I read my first comic, too.

"The *Mirror's* fella was the Phantom. I never loved him best of all of them, but I took what I could get. Mum was always yelling at me because I'd get my hands all covered in the newsprint, black all over the place." Sally went quiet for a few moments. "They mangled it up, but. Tried to make it all Australian; rubbed out 'New York' and put in 'Sydney.' Even with all the slang switched over, I still knew that it wasn't really about *here*.

"It's bloody stupid. We've spent the last hundred and fifty years bending over backward to be as much like England as we can get, and now that America's looking interesting, we're just trying to make ourselves into that instead. We're a country of kids waiting to be bossed around. I hate it."

She scuffed up some of the heavy dust lining the edge of the road. Her frustrated kicks sent the disturbed air swirling red around our shins.

"There," I said, pointing to a pub up ahead. "They'll have food."

SALLY

Amy slips away while we're waiting for our grilled sandwiches to arrive. Says she needs to go have a piddle in the outhouse, but I can tell she's gonna be tearing back to that damn motel. Maybe I'm just skittery from the jail at the bay, but it felt like there was something wrong with that motel, too.

The eagerness in Amy's eyes frightens me. I don't want to get mixed up in something mad. I don't want to get mixed up in anything.

I order myself a glass of drink, the strongest stuff they'll sell to a girl, and pull the battered *Mirror* out of my bag. Nell used to get these from Diana, her friend who worked at the Doctor Carver Club. The club was for the black American soldiers stuck in Brisbane, and the Aboriginal girls who got pushed hard to go along and dance with them. White soldiers, like my mate Tom, only got to visit if they were particularly asked.

Nell had come over from Brooklyn after her sweetheart got shipped out in the Marines. Now that she was so alone and worried, she said it was too hard to stay in the same street, the same city, the same *country* as where they'd been so happy together. Better to come across to the other side of the world and find work with an apple bag on her hip.

Diana, Nell's best friend, was lighter-skinned than I am, but she knew how to talk her way in anywhere. She pilfered newspapers and rations and nylons out of any bloke who came close enough to get dragged in. The war was one big business venture for her, and far as I could tell, she did a bang-up job at it. The spoils she passed along to me were mostly magazines and comics. I treasured them like gold. I musta read every page of them a thousand times.

    Revisiting those pages now, when I'm so far from home and from the past, is strange. The placement of a headline or a photograph drags me back to those endless afternoons hidden under the porch with my radio going and a stack of things to read beside me. I can almost hear the tinny songs, smell the dirt, see the spiders creep along the dead space of the margin-edges.

ELLA

Dear Natasha,

 Ever seen *The Doom Generation*? I keep thinking about it because of my last letter and because of how I wish I'd had that road-movie freedom in my own life. Not that anyone really gets a life like the movies. But you know what I mean.

 I didn't really like *The Doom Generation*. I should, probably, because it's about three kids and violence and love and open roads. It's got two boys and a girl and all the complicated things that means, and blood and death and shit like that. It's the middle film in Greg Araki's *Teenage Apocalypse Trilogy*. As one third of a teenage apocalypse trilogy myself, I should dig it. But it's just not my thing.

 Ditto for David Lynch — I know, I lose all my cool points admitting that. Chris and Dean couldn't get enough of his stuff. But I find him kind of pretentious. I'd rather watch Indiana Jones, which led to a fight one time, when both were on TV late at night — *Lost Highway* or *The Last Crusade*.

 I like Greg Araki's *Mysterious Skin*, made five years after I died. It's about kids who were abused when they were little and grow up into train wrecks. So it's a little ball of sunshine, obviously. But, you know, nice girls who like happy movies usually don't orchestrate massacres. I clearly got something cross-wired in the brainpan at some point.

Nicolas and I watch a lot of movies. He sometimes tells me about how when he was a kid in Brooklyn, he and his brother and Nell from down the street would go to the old-timey picture houses. (Later when she was older and wanted to be more sophisticated, Nell went by Lena instead, but in the stories he still always called her Nell. Lena was the grown-up who came later, but Nell was the girl who grew up beside them, the young woman who joined the Land Army so that she wouldn't be the only one of the three left behind by the war.) They couldn't go to the picture houses every week because it'd take them longer than that to save up the money, and the theatre owners were too sharp for them to sneak in.

When they'd miss some parts of the serial stories, they'd spend the intervening weeks making up their own things to happen next. Then they'd go back to see a later part of the real story, and the turns the narrative had taken were never as exciting as what they'd thought up between kickball games after school.

The movies back then all stuck strictly to this code that kept all the content squeaky-clean and morally righteous. I guess the people with the power wanted to make sure kids didn't get any ideas about picking up guns and going nuts. At least until all the plans for the next World War were drawn up. It was like the moment before a game starts, when everyone takes a roll of the dice to see who has the first turn.

The rules of the movie code were all shit like, "the sympathy of the audience should never be thrown to the side of crime, wrongdoing, evil, or 'sin' and 'the sanctity of the institution of marriage and the home shall be upheld' and 'dances which emphasize indecent movements are to be regarded as obscene' and 'no film or episode may throw ridicule on any religious faith.'

It's so ridiculous, it's funny now. Those rules were so

straight-laced and full of prudery, I laughed when Nicky first told me about them. But then we talked about it more, and I stopped laughing.

I'd been laughing at the fact that all these rules were basically trying to stop assholes like me from doing shit like I did. I think that I would have gone bugfuck crazy at an even younger age if I'd had to contend with all that.

Those rules also meant that Nicolas Caramano had never been able to look at a screen and see anybody like him while he was growing up. No gay heroes, no gay romances, no comedies with gay people being ordinary and stupid and funny like the straight people were. Old movies had subtexts and coded messages, but all that did was encourage the audience to see a villain as effeminate and mincing and not a real, manly man like the hero.

I'm glad your band holds up a mirror to kids who can't see themselves elsewhere.

xe

Dear Natasha,

There's no road to Hell, paved with good intentions or otherwise. It's reached by the Dark, and the Dark is made of nothing that can be put into human words. But there are roads inside Hell, and those roads are paved with broken things.

Everything else is made from scraps, too, but you notice the roads first. The surface is so uneven that progress is slow, every footstep forced to be deliberate.

The first time I walked the road, on the afternoon I died, I had guides. Caim and Murmur navigated with the ease that comes from practice. They got far ahead of Chris and Dean and me before we'd even gone a block. Under the scuffed rubber soles of my sneakers, I could see dozens of different textures: poorly fired clay, its gleaming glazes pock-marked with exploded bubbles; the rusted curves of old machine casings; cracked parts of red house bricks; moldy chipboard with clinging remnants of stained laminate; battered empty suitcases with rotted leather straps. A thousand stories pass underfoot on even the shortest of journeys.

It's always dark like night, but here there are no stars, and morning never comes. Lights dance between the bulbs of streetlights, though. Bulbs hang and flicker from a long cable strung between iron poles along the curbs on either side of the road. The poles lean at woozy angles. Some are needle-pointed like the spires of buildings, and some end in elaborate curlicue shapes. Some are just blunted off at the top, like a giant invisible hand reached down and snapped them off at roughly the right height. The bulbs are mismatched too. Most have a vague golden glow to the light inside, though some are made of stained-glass, and some are eye-searingly fluorescent-bright in their whiteness.

Thousands of tiny dark-winged moths flutter in the air above our heads, making the flicker effect of the streetlights even more crazed and uneven.

"They aren't drawn to the light, you know," Caim told me one time, nodding up at the swarm of soft insect wings against the dark. "People think moths want to get close to flames, to lights. But it's not true. The light just disorients them. They aren't drawn. They're just lost."

It's cold in Hell. Not cold enough to freeze it over, but a pervading chill makes the bones ache.

The thing I noticed most in that first walk behind the pair who'd collected us from the library when we died wasn't any of this. It wasn't any of the new and strange and captivating features of this afterlife we'd earned. The thing

I noticed was that Chris and Dean held hands.

Chris saw me looking and held out his other hand for me to take. I grasped it, trying not to tremble as we walked deeper into Hell to face whatever horrors came next.

Some say that Hell is other people. We knew that as well as anybody — otherwise we'd have just killed each other and nobody else — but what we also knew was that sometimes other people are the only consolation you can find when you're groping in the abyss.

In that spirit we walked together, the Dark at our backs and Hell before us, hands held tight to unite us in our fear.

Love
Ella

Dear Natasha,

Dean liked sex. Chris and I didn't really care, though Chris liked the idea of 'scoring.'

Conquest was the appeal, not the act itself.

People think we did it as a way to control Dean, a way of keeping him on our side and in our power. But we'd have been pretty mediocre murderous masterminds if we'd kept all of Cobweb in line by fucking it.

No, that wasn't why we had sex together, the three of us. It was because Dean liked it, and we had a familiarity, an intimacy, a world for just the three of us. Chris liked extra garlic on his pizza, so even if Dean and I didn't, we got it anyway because Chris liked it. Love is compromises, no matter how dominant one personality may be over another.

Sex, garlic pizza, killing sprees — you've got to respect the things that people you care about care about. Was it like that with you and Cherry?

Did one love music first and the other follow?

xE

CHARLOTTE

From *Reign in Hell: Two Weeks in the Life of HUSH*, by Charlotte Waterhouse, Amplify Press, Australia, 2011:

> Fuck nobility.
> Fuck music.
> Only love.
> Only sky.

> The four statements adorn the liner notes of HUSH's debut album and the top of their website like a short sharp list of commandments for a new kind of faith. The words can also be found on the inner wrists of four of the band's five members: *Fuck nobility* is Jacqui's, *Fuck music* is Ben's tattoo, *Only love* is Cherry's, and *Only sky* is Tash's.

> Jo, who wears long sleeves that loop over her thumb in order to cover more skin, tells me that she doesn't have any tattoos. "I have burns," she explains quietly.

> Each of the four tattoos contains a story of a loss devastating enough to make the world seem incomprehensible. That the four young musicians each found some kind of meaning in that horror and made those meanings into defiant declarations is one of the most remarkable things about the band.

> Like Jacqui's memorial to her little sister Marie, Ben's *Fuck music* is a testament to a lost sibling as well. All four of the band's tattoos share this motivation, but Ben's stands alone as the only one about a sibling lost to someone other than the owner of the tattoo.

"Nicolas was my foster father David's brother," Ben tells me. "He was killed in the Second World War. In David's photo, *Rosie Remembers,* Lena is looking at Nicky's stuff. I'm not sure she was even going by Lena yet when it was taken, actually. She might have still been Nell then. But I guess that's beside the point. The whole point is that her grief was common to a whole generation of women, like her identity as a Rosie the Riveter."

It's my third day with HUSH when I talk to Ben about his tattoo. He's still skittish, uncertain of me — for a group who has voluntarily put itself in the world spotlight, the entire band is extremely attention-shy — but after a few minutes, he seems to decide that I can hear the explanation.

"Lena told me about Nicky when I was fifteen. I got beaten up at school. I'd always been in fights, and they'd both yelled at me a thousand times for letting the bullies get a rise out of me like that. But this time, I hadn't fought back at all; I'd just taken it. I let some asshole from the football team break my nose and put a hairline fracture in my arm.

"I was so ashamed of myself. That's what scared them, more than the injuries. David's totally blasé about... I bet you that I could walk into his kitchen with one of my eyes hanging out the socket, and he'd say the same thing he always does, which is 'kids get hurt doing stupid shit. That's how kids learn not to do stupid shit anymore.' He used to let Jacq and me build tree houses much higher up than we should've, and swim in the lake, and all kinds of stuff that most parents wouldn't dream of letting their kids do.

"I guess he figured that Jacq deserved to feel immortal once in a while, y'know? Because of Marie. Jacq and I had both gone through genuinely awful shit in our childhoods. I guess David and Lena didn't want to add to that with dumb worries about broken legs from falling out of tree houses. What's a broken leg when you've seen your sister die slowly?

"What I'm saying is, I didn't expect David to give a shit about my arm and my nose. I knew Lena would fuss a little because she always wanted to take care of people. But they both looked pale as ghosts when they came to the emergency room. No, that's not right, not exactly. They looked as pale as if they'd *seen* ghosts.

"Like I said, it was the shame that did that. The shame on my face, I mean. They knew that look. They'd done every goddamn thing they could to stop me from ever having that look, but there it was anyway. I didn't know that, though. I thought they were mad at me.

"We were quiet in the car. David was clearly furious. His knuckles were white on the wheel. I was all clammy with cold sweat, partly because of all the painkillers I was on from when the doctor set my arm and nose, but mostly from fear. Even though I'd been with them for a while, I still had that kicked-puppy brain that kids in the system get, you know? I was always half-expecting them to throw me out at any moment, no matter how often they reassured me. It wasn't their fault. I was broken before they got me."

Ben pauses in his story and sips from his glass of water. Recounting the memories has made his voice slip into a quiet, flat affect, the matter-of-fact way that traumatized children often speak.

"I should tell you about Nicky and David and Lena first, I think. A lot of things will be easier to explain that way.

"Nicolas was David's younger brother. They grew up with Lena. Nicky wrote a lot of letters home to Lena, when the brothers both went off in the Second World War.

"A lot of times, he writes how sorry he is that he's not that good at writing. But he was a lot better at it than he thought; his letters are really evocative in this sparse, factual way. One of my favorite things in the letters is where he writes about how for this one USO band show he was in, they made the curtains out of a barrage balloon. I couldn't dream up a metaphor that perfect about war and art if I tried for hours, you know?

"The USO shows are where my tattoo comes from, sort of. David was a musician too, along with Nicky. Then Nicky died, and David completely renounced it. He wrote a letter home to Lena that just said "fuck music." Like, what was the point of music, if Nicky was dead? What was the point of anything?

"The tattoo is kind of my way of challenging that. Of honoring the fact that David had lost somebody, that Nicolas had died, but at the same time being determined to prove that there *was* something worthwhile in music. It's my challenge to myself: I have to make music that can't be dismissed."

ELLA

Dear Tash,

    Nicky survived Guadalcanal. That was where he felt the sick-feeling the first time. He was in the little boats they rode to the shore, soldiers standing together, waiting to die and fight.
    Nicky doesn't like what happened, by the way. Cobweb. But we're friends anyway.
    He says, "kids shouldn't have guns," but he's not just talking about me. He's talking about himself, too. I don't think he thinks what I did was evil, at least not compared to all the other things people do. It was just another thing, a terrible thing, but he's seen so many terrible things that what I did wasn't remarkable. I can't even imagine what would count as remarkable for him.
    His Hell is full of bombs and bullets and wire and knives and lush dense greenery and water and meat. I don't like it there. I try not to go there if I can help it.
    With all the strategy and planning and leadership and maps and radios and all the rest, it still doesn't feel like anyone is in charge. It doesn't feel like anyone is in control.
    "Anarchy, that's what it was. No matter what anybody tells you," Nicky said to me once. "That's all war is. Anarchy."
    So I guess we have a new saying we can add to the list of things that aren't true. War isn't Hell. You can only escape one of them by dying, after all.

    xe

Dear Tash,

Survivors tell different stories than the dead. The dead talk to the dead, who have no innocence left to lose. Survivors want to protect those who've never been forced to survive anything. Somebody has to stay innocent of all that was lost, to make the sacrifices worthwhile.

Survivors, well. Survivors tell stories to their grandchildren over Saturday lunch in a kitchen. In a house with ham and wholegrain bread and cordial to drink.

"We'd come back from a long run, and we were all stumbling on our feet, exhausted like we'd never been," David says to Jacqui and to Ben, and they listen because David is always a little sad, even when he is happy.

Maybe even that's when he's saddest, in a way their teenage worlds can only lightly comprehend, because being a teenager means such a different thing now to what it meant to him, meant to Nicky.

"We got back and there were these jugs on the tables. And I thought, oh, grape juice. Grape juice that was the best thing we'd ever seen. I took a huge swallow. *Beet* juice!" David laughs and punches a hole in the top of the can of beet slices and drains the juice into his glass. "Even now, I've got a taste for the stuff."

Ben eats sliced beets with cheese and ham on multigrain bread and listens to the stories. Jacqui eats the same but without the ham because at eighteen she has decided to become a vegetarian.

David thinks it's absurd to be a vegetarian, but he loves Jacqui and loves that she passionately believes in this absurd thing. He fought for that. His beloved baby brother gave his life so that a petulant stupid-ass kid can do stupid-ass things like refuse good ham at lunch, sneak cigarettes out of his pack when she thinks he isn't looking, and trade angry words with Lena when Lena won't let her stay out all night on a Sunday to see a band play at a club that Jacqui is too young to visit legally.

David thinks that Nicky would have liked Jacqui. They could have bonded over music, a love the two of them share. David doesn't love music anymore. It got stripped from him in the war, like a limb torn and cauterized by grenades and hot shrapnel.

David's right, by the way. Nicky does like Jacqui. He's glad that she's happy. So glad.

xe

Dear Tash,

Do you remember the first time you met Jacqui and Ben? I do, but I suspect that makes one of us. You were pretty wasted. So was Cherry, but she's always been better at hiding it than you. A better liar. Funny how that, and the blonde hair, make her the sweet one, when really the two of you aren't that different at all. More like sisters than you and me, in some ways. Guess nurture won out over nature in that battle. Not that you got a lot of nurture for a while in the middle there.

You were both twelve. Cherry and Stacey's dad — your dad, too, by then, really, in everything but blood, and blood's not anything special; it's just red and sticky and thinner than you think it'll be, faster moving over skin from any wound worth talking about — was one of the speakers at a gun control march. David was there, and Lena too, and so were Jacqui and Ben, and so were you and Cherry.

David is an excellent speaker, just as he was an excellent

singer when he used to sing. Jacqui may share her love of music with Nicky's ghost, but her skill of captivating an audience and holding them in thrall with her voice and gestures, that comes from David.

You'd stolen a bottle of whiskey from your dad. Watered it down with soda pop to make it drinkable. You thought you were so sneaky, you two. You thought he had no idea. But he knew. Of course he knew. You both giggled and stank, swaying on your feet in your best shoes and dresses. But he wasn't angry. Actually, he felt proud.

Proud because there you were, drunk children, fortifying yourselves in small and clumsy ways in order to be strong enough to stand at a lectern in front of thousands of people. You two, little Cherry and little Natasha — no longer Nattie, not yet Tash — were so determined to live, to fight. To be brave in ways Stacey and I had not been.

Nobody ever said I was brave (even if somebody thought it, who'd dare say it?), but in your new father's mind, Stacey never needed to be as brave as you and Cherry. Stacey had been very, very brave, of course. He was so proud of her.

But all Stacey had to do was die bravely. It's much easier to die bravely than it is to live bravely, and that's what you and Cherry were doing, in your patent-leather shoes and with your soda pop whiskey giggles. You were so fucking alive, and he was so proud of you.

xe

SALLY

The pub's door swings open, and I look up in case it's Amy come back from whatever daft game she's off playing. Two men, one a rangy old guy with short, greying hair the same colour as a caramel and scars on his cheeks and the other easy enough on the eyes in an unremarkable sorta way, walk in. I wonder if the scars are from some sickness he had when he was a kid, measles or chicken pox, or if they're from spots when he was my age. He looks like he's in his early forties, and one of his eyes is covered by a little black patch. He's tall and thin, like he's been stretched long by some machine.

    Back in the old days, before the war, I would've called a man like him a swaggie. They came by the farm every so often, and Mum would give them a bite to eat and let them sleep in the shed if it was bad weather. I remember hiding behind her skirts and giggling at how silly one man's hat looked, all rimmed with corks on string. I wore a hat like that myself, once. Down in Victoria, the first summer I spent on my own. The flies are murder there.

    Now nobody much calls them swaggies. I don't know why. Maybe because there're so many or because there're so many different sorts out and about on the roads now. People like me. Can't really call me a swaggie.

    Maybe he wouldn't have been called a swaggie even then. He doesn't look ragtag or lost like most swaggies I can remember. He just looks like he spends a lot of his time moving from place to place without settling. I've learned to spot the look of that in someone since I see it in myself in every mirror or reflection I catch sight of.

The other man's younger, maybe only a decade or so on me. Maybe not even that. His skin's a little weather-worn from too much sun and wind, and his clothes look like they're about as old and second-hand as mine. He's got the kind of colouring my mother might've had if she'd really been as Irish as she'd claimed: black hair, blue eyes.

On their own, either one of the men might not have been worth a second look, but the two of them together catch my eye. Something about the way the one with the patch claps the other on the shoulder once, a sturdy pat, and then heads off to where some other old blokes are playing cards in the corner. Whoever they are, they trust each other.

Lord knows I don't expect to see much of that anytime soon, not with Amy at my side. Girl's as trusting as a kicked cat.

He turns, the blue-eyed one, and catches my eye still caught on him. I look back down at the *Mirror*, but he decides not to take the hint and sits down in Amy's empty chair.

"I'm Pete," he says.

"Sally," I give him in return, torn between staying stuck in my paper and being polite.

Most times, I'd take a fella like him back somewhere quiet for a fumble and not think twice about it, but a day like the one I've had leaves a body too wound up for simple things like that. Still, looking doesn't take much effort. I close the *Mirror* and do my best to smile at him.

"Passing through?" I ask as if it's not plain as day that he is. He has a strange star-shaped pendant on a leather cord around his neck, a seven-pointed star.

"Yeah. Heading for Darwin, eventually. You passing through, too?"

I tap my fingers on the soft cover of my magazine, tracing the shape of the title. "Suppose. Heading for Sydney. Not sure after that."

"Can I buy you a drink?" Pete asks, gesturing to the glass of watery local beer beside my arm. "Something better?"

"If you like," I reply. "Bourbon."

AMY

I could smell them as soon as I stepped back through the pub's door. It's not actually a smell, of course, any more than it's a sound or sight. But of all the senses, it's most like a smell. The same cloying, lethal perfumes that flytrap flowers give off, luring prey in close.

One by the bar, getting a pair of drinks, the other in the corner with the card players. I walked to Sally as quickly as I could without drawing attention and grabbed her wrist to pull her up.

"We have to get out of here. Right now."

She glared at me, as cross as she'd been in the prison by the bay.

Oh, Sally, what you thought you knew about defiance couldn't fill a thimble.

"No. Pete's getting me a drink."

"Now," I repeated in a voice tight with panic, pulling her arm again. "Please. I'll explain it all, I promise. But we have to leave this instant."

The certainty in her face clouded when she saw how urgent I was, and then she stood. "All right."

At the door I felt the prickle of being looked at shiver the nape of my neck. I glanced around and sure enough, the card player had forgotten his cards and stared straight at me with his one sharp, gun-grey eye.

"Now!" I shoved Sally hard, out into the dark and relative quiet of the night. I shouldn't have gone to the well; I was overfull and sluggish. I grabbed Sally's arm and dragged her into the thin dark space between the wall of the pub and its water tank. It smelled like a cave gone to rotting damp, but I didn't care. Sally yelped. I clamped my hand over her mouth to keep her silent.

"Shut up," I hissed against her hair, squeezing my palm tighter to lock her jaw in place. "Please."

The door opened again, spilling momentary light and laughter out before swinging shut behind the two men.

"Christ, it gets dark out here," the younger one said. "I can't see a thing."

The other raised a hand to his eyepatch, and shifted it from one side of his face to the other. "I can."

That's an old trick. Keep one eye primed for bright, patch the other to keep it ready to see in the dark.

I kept as motionless as I could, my arms full of barely-stilled Sally. If I were the kind to pray, I might've sent up a small and heartfelt request to the heavens. As it was, I just hoped and hoped.

The old guy looked around, bending low to look under the few dusty cars parked around the place. Then, my luck holding true, he beckoned for the younger one to follow him around the corner of the pub towards the sheds out the back.

I waited until they were completely gone from sight — I don't need patches to see without light — and then dropped my hand from Sally's mouth. The sweep of headlights was coming closer down the road, and I crossed my fingers for one last piece of fortune.

The sleek little Holden pulled up beside my thumb, and the driver leaned out the window to take a look at us.

"Girls looking for a ride?"

There was no time for this, for the stupid flirting games lone drivers always want to play with hitch hikers. Those two from the pub could be back around at any moment.

"Get us to Newcastle by dawn, and I'll fuck you," I said

simply and pulled the door to the back seat open without waiting for a reply. I would do nothing of the sort; I find the whole production distasteful. But he didn't have to know that; he just needed to get us away.

   Sally looked a state, clutching her little shoulder-sack of clothes and diaries and magazines against her body. I put my hand on hers and squeezed, trying to make my smile into something comforting.

   "I'll explain everything," I vowed again, quietly, hoping that she'd accept it.

   "Yeah," she said, eyes wide with surprise and a fear she had no reason to feel for herself. "You're damn right you will."

CHARLOTTE

From *Reign in Hell: Two Weeks in the Life of HUSH*, by Charlotte Waterhouse, Amplify Press, Australia, 2011:

The venue for the Sydney show is the Roundhouse Theatre at the University of New South Wales. Fans are lining up outside the doors by early afternoon, teens and twenty-somethings who were strangers before today and are now chattering happily together, sharing bottles of soft drink and anecdotes related to their common love of the band. There's a warm, light breeze in the air, and everyone seems excited and happy.

"We played at the Roundhouse as the opener a couple of years ago," Ben says. "There's a beer garden out the back full of plastic picnic tables where we went after the show to meet people from the audience and hang out. That was our first time out here, in Australia I mean, but so many kids were excited to meet us. It was amazing. I recognize some of the same faces in the line there now — people don't think that bands can possibly notice individual faces in the crowd but it's not that tough.

"When they look up at the stage, they're so open and honest in their expressions. Most of the time, in ordinary life, people don't look like that. They never look so unguarded. But when they're at a show watching you, their faces are naked. I'd have to be a pretty horrible fucking guy if I didn't notice and cherish them giving me a reaction like that for my art. Of course I remember them."

We're walking toward the line, through the shaded grassy lawn area that divides the edge of campus from the suburb beyond. Ben says that hanging out with the fans is perfectly safe, that he's not one of the "high-profile, super-loved" members of the band like Jacqui and Cherry.

"And anyway," he says, trying to sound reassuring. "Our fans are crazy in the good way, not the steal-your-hair-out-of-your-head way."

In the ensuing scenes of delight among the crowd, the thing which especially strikes me is how considerate and kind Ben is with the younger fans. He goes out of his way to ask how they are, what their names are, what song they like best on the album. They seem overwhelmed by the attention. Their eyes take on the same wide, enchanted look that very young children get when faced with actors dressed as cartoon princesses or Santa.

"A review of our stuff back in the States a few months ago, that was trying to be complimentary, said that HUSH's music 'was better than should be expected from a band with legions of teenage girl fans who tattoo lyrics on their arms'," Ben says, "That got me so angry and sad. I was so insulted on their behalf.

"As soon as teenage girls start to profess love for something, everyone else becomes totally dismissive of it. Teenage girls are open season for the cruelest bullying that our society can dream up. Everyone's vicious to them. They're vicious to each other. Hell, they're even vicious to themselves. It's terrible.

"So if teenage girls have something that they love, isn't that a *good* thing? Isn't it *better* for them to find some words they believe in, words like the 'fire-proof and fearless' lyrics that Jacqui wrote? Isn't it better for them to put those words on their arm in a tattoo than for them to cut gashes in that same skin? Shouldn't we be *grateful* when teenage girls love our work? Shouldn't that be a fucking *honor*?

"It's used as the cheapest, easiest test of crap, isn't it? If teenage girls love a movie, a book, a band, then it's immediately classified as mediocre shit. Well, I'm not going to stand for that. Someone needs to treat them like they're precious, and if nobody else is ready to step up, I guess it's up to us to put them on the path to recognizing that about themselves. It was a band that did it for you, right? When you were younger?"

I blink in surprise. "I guess it was," I agree, with a wry smile. "I doubt anyone would become a music journalist without some extremely formative gratitude towards the medium."

That makes Ben laugh and nod. "I've met so many people who found those first little seeds of strength in the music they listened to. But it's only seeds, isn't it? You have to do the rest yourself."

"Or die trying," I agree, thinking of girls I knew in my own teen years, the ones who never made it out. Ben's smile turns sympathetic, the two of us sharing the silent truths carried with survival.

ELLA

Dear, Dear Tash,

The Devil Wears Prada — a book/movie title I know, not really a saying. Not factual, either: the Devil wears all kinds of stuff, but I doubt Prada makes many things that are interesting enough for inclusion in her wardrobe.

The Devil also doesn't hate God, except in the hot, wounded way that love gone bad always looks a bit like hate. Revenge is a fine and long-acknowledged motive, but it's not at all the same as hate. I'd know. And the Devil's not that interested in revenge anyway. Just in a regime change, the toppling of Heaven.

I don't think God's a tyrant, really. Tyrants are more vindictive. I think he's just one of those dads who's a little too old and staid to be a satisfactory parent for his younger kids. The world changed, and the old ways of doing things didn't work anymore. I think God's not a tyrant at all, just 50,000 years behind the times. All the Devil ever wanted was for Dad to stop being so old-fashioned and to get a grip, and she got grounded in the everlasting inferno for her impertinence.

When I think about people weeping over earthquakes and babies with cancer and how they ask 'Why God, why?' I keep getting the mental image of how our own father used to get sometimes. Remember?

"Why do I have to go to bed, Dad?"

"Because I said so, that's why."

As if any kid ever accepted that as the last word.

This all sounds pretty flip to someone alive, I'm sure. Here's the thing, though: being alive is like high school. You think it's everything, so fucking important, the end of the world... and then it's over, and you realize how small and unimportant it is in the scheme of the rest of everything. Sure, how you do there determines what happens right after, but even that changes after a while. It doesn't matter as much.

So, if the Devil doesn't wear Prada, what does the Devil do?

Lend books to people and then buy them again because she can't remember where they went (I say 'buy them,' but I mean 'get the demons on Earth to bring them when they visit Hell.' Lucifer doesn't leave her realm; this is the worst of her punishments.)

Get drunk on tequila and listen to Edith Piaf and cry.

Rule Hell with a ruthlessness that's only visible after you've been here for a while, unless you happen to overstep the wrong line.

Offer scathing critique of Hollywood blockbusters (obtained through illegal download, naturally).

All my love,
E.V. xxx

Dear Tash,

Kip Kinkel — he's the one I told you about whose murder-music of choice was the *Romeo + Juliet* soundtrack — he killed his parents because he'd gotten in trouble at school. Killing them was a way to avoid telling them. Disappointing them.

I remember when I was ten (you weren't even born yet), and Dean's dad died. My own parents were on the very brink of divorce, all drunken recriminations and screaming fights and broken glass after they thought I'd gone to sleep. Sometimes I wonder if you were an accident or an attempt to save the marriage. I can't imagine that they were fucking often enough for it to happen by mistake. For you to happen.

So Dean's dad, he died in the morning. A heart attack after his regular run. He was pretty old. Dean was the only child of his second marriage. Dean had older siblings somewhere overseas. He never really knew them, though. If you don't grow up with someone, they probably don't feel like a brother or a sister in the same way.

I probably don't, for you.

Dean's dad died in the morning, but Chris and I didn't find out until the afternoon. My mother was waiting at the school gate to pick us up, and that's when she told us. I felt annoyed because I'd wanted to go swimming after school, and now I wouldn't get a chance.

We went around to his house. My mother and father were upstairs with Chris's mother and father and Dean's mother. Chris and I were downstairs with Dean in his computer room.

Chris had brought this game he'd just gotten, *Police Quest 4*, and we installed it on the computer. I have to tell you, Tash, I was so grateful for that stupid game. Because near the start, you gotta go arrest this crazy guy who's jumping around and being nuts and shit, and it was so stupid and funny that Dean laughed. We'd found a way to make him laugh, even if it was just for a few minutes. Then he got quiet and sad again and ran out of the room, and things were awful again. Except...

"At least now he knows that they can never get divorced," I said to Chris. His parents were — and are to this day

— solidly and unshakably married. Chris knew exactly what I meant by my soft words and nodded in agreement.

I'm sure if an adult had been there, they'd have yelled at us, scolded us for saying something so untrue. How could divorce ever possibly be worse than death? But oh, it was, and Chris and I both knew it. Better to mourn and cry and have a happy memory, an idealized concept, than go through the wrenching pain of seeing the union of the two people you love most crumble and shatter and crack.

Better in every way. Better to see a parent dead than see a parent hurting, without question.

That's why Kip Kinkel did what he did, what a lot of spree killers do. What I did. Parents do it to their children, too. Kill them to protect them. To spare them the disappointments and betrayals and endings that come from being alive.

It's like how some people always stop *Moulin Rouge* before the end, so they can pretend it has a happy ending and not a sad one.

The secret to a happy ending is to know when to fade to black.

When to pull the trigger.

xe

Dear Tash,

'A match made in hell.' That's what people say about lovers who hurt one another or who are a bad match in some other way, or are both bad before they get together.

Here's one of Hell's love stories. It didn't begin here. It began on the way.

Sam Brightwater's name isn't as well-known as mine,

but it's not that far behind. *sambrightwater*. I don't think there's a word for Hell-Saints. But he's one as much as I am, or even as much as Bonnie and Clyde or Jo. A lot of people on Earth expect Jo to be in Heaven. A lot more expect Sam to be there.

Sam was pronounced dead at 12:53a.m. on the 12th of October, 1998. He was in Colorado, same as us. I wonder what we were doing that night. Maybe I was getting drunk with Chris and Dean, making wild ambitious plans for how our legacy would echo after Cobweb, unaware that a sinners' martyr was dying that very moment not so far away.

Maybe we were babysitting you. Those were good nights. Do you remember that time we let you shoot the cans?

Sam died of fractures to the back of his head and the front of his right ear. He had brain-stem damage, which stopped his body from regulating his temperature and heartbeat. He had a dozen small lacerations to his head, face, and neck. He was tied to a fence and left to die. The person who discovered him thought he was a scarecrow. He was beaten so badly that his face was covered in blood, except for the tracks made by his tears. Without regaining consciousness, he died in intensive care of intracerebral hemorrhage and hypothermia.

He was 21, and he was gay. The latter fact was also motive for his murder.

The Sam Brightwater Foundation was set up by Sam's parents in December of 1998. I gave you those pony toys for Christmas, remember? And you promised you were going to save up and buy me and Mom and Dad all presents for next Christmas because you were grown-up enough to do more than just draw pictures for us. But me and Mom and Dad were all dead by that next Christmas. You were already with Cherry's family by then, weren't you? I don't remember for sure. Maybe you were still in the foster system, or maybe you were already with them. Either way, I guess

Christmas wasn't all that merry for you.

Sam's parents set up their foundation in that December of 1998, before I died but after Sam did. The foundation still does educational, outreach and advocacy programs.

Those 'God Hates Fags' assholes got their first taste of some fame from picketing his funeral with signs about how Sam was burning in Hell for being gay. I fucking hate those vile shitbags, even if they are on the money. God really does hate fags, and Sam really was down here in Hell by then. But still. Truth isn't a good enough excuse to be a raging turd.

Friends of Sam, wearing white robes and wings, surrounded the protesters. Police had to stand as a barrier between the two groups. The wings blocked the protesters from the funeral. People called them the 'Angels of Peace' and 'Angel Action.' Oh the fucking irony.

Sam and Caim had already met by then. Caim's like Murmur; they both have a weakness for people who are skittish, a little damaged. The slightly dented baubles have more character.

Caim is a comforting collector. He genuinely likes Earth and likes people, and even if he can be kind of an asshole sometimes, I'm glad he came to the library for me and Chris and Dean. I'm glad he was the one who went to the field for Sam.

He took Sam's hand and pulled Sam up out of his body because even if Sam's heart was still striving and struggling, there wasn't much left to stay around for except more pain. So Caim pulled him out early. I think Oscar Wilde was the one who said that mercy was invented by the guilty.

Caim gave Sam the small mercy of leaving his body before the pain of his death was complete. Then they stood there together, two spirits in the dimness at the edge of the Dark.

"Stare at the back of me," Caim instructed. "Don't look

away. Keep your eyes fixed on my back."

He said the same thing to me later. When I died. Want to know something funny? The SWAT team said just the same words to the kids in the library. To the ones who were still alive at the end. Keep your eyes on me as we walk through. Don't look around you.

So Sam stared at the nape of Caim's neck, at the heavy dark fall of his hair, black as blackbird feathers. The Dark isn't just sights, of course. There are sounds as well. Nobody alive has ever heard sounds like the sounds of the Dark. Maybe some of the people in psychiatric hospitals, the ones who scream and scream in padded rooms, have heard the sounds. Like Oscar Wilde said, justice was invented by the innocent, mercy by the guilty. God's never felt guilty, and thus is merciless.

When you're in the Dark, the approaching lights of Hell are as welcome as a sunrise. A nimbus of Lights dances at the edges, like fireflies or lens flares. Instinctively, Sam narrowed his eyes against the brightness of them, before remembering that he was dead and that nothing hurt anymore.

Even so, he was afraid. Caim, who understands people (and, as I mentioned before, genuinely likes them, despite understanding them), reached out and took Sam's hand and squeezed. Comfort in the Dark.

That's what most love stories are when you scrape them down to the bone. Comfort in the dark or laughter in the light. A rare few are both.

Murmur and Jacqui are both, I think.

In 2009, Lady Gaga performed 'Imagine' at the HRC Dinner. She changed the lyrics from 'above us only sky' to 'Brightwater in the sky.' Sam still teases me about it sometimes, that he stole my famous lyric from me.

xxE

SALLY

Just before I wake up, I start to think about swaggies. I don't know why. I remember one in particular that came through in that first lonely summer after Nell left. He was a weird bloke, not all there in the head, and the stuff in his pipe never smelled like tobacco. Mum said it wasn't my place to be cheeky about him and that it was nobody's business but his own how he wanted to live.

The swag on his back was stained and worn, and the old billy-tin he kept tied to it was knocked around and blackened from fires and ash. When I touched it, I'd almost expected it to still be hot. He brewed me tea in it one afternoon, though I can't remember why he'd bother. Mum would have let him use the kettle and the stove if he'd asked.

He put his old, gnarled hand on mine, squeezing.

"You were born with two feet," he said. "So lift up them eyes and walk."

It seemed profound to me then because I was just a kid and didn't know nonsense when I heard it. It's always stuck in my head, though, as if one day it'll make sense.

I ease my eyes open and groan. My head feels like a plough ran over it. At least the curtains are drawn.

"What happened?" I croak. Amy, somewhere over to my left, makes a small, amused noise.

"Well, first your drinks happened. Then the table and your cheek happened. Then some snoring."

Sounds about right. I wrack my brains, trying to find

what little I can remember of the evening. "We get a ride?"

"Eventually."

My mind grudgingly offers up a flash of Amy talking to a driver, her face hard. "Did you..."

"No." Her voice is sharp. "I didn't."

"You don't like doing it?" Paying for a ride like that is bloody awful, but the disgust in her voice sounds a lot bigger than just one fella in a car.

"I don't like bargains of any kind."

Fair enough. I sit up carefully, easing my feet down to the floor beside the bed. This room's nicer than the boarding house back in Trial Bay. All decorated up with lace runners on the sills and patch-worked quilts on the narrow twin beds. There's a cross made of dark wood nailed to the wall beside the door.

Amy's sitting in a high-backed chair beside one of the curtained windows carving with that little knife of hers. The wood block's forming slowly into the shape of a cat with a tail held high in a looping question mark. Her boots are off, and she's changed her dress for another like it, this one a vivid blue. In the dim light, the hairs on her legs look like a fine, firey gold, barely visible.

"Where are we?"

"Inland a little. Not far from Newcastle. It's mid-afternoon; you must have needed the rest," she answers. I notice that the hand controlling her knife is bandaged tightly, across the palm and down halfway to her elbow.

"What happened?"

She drops her gaze, the new angle making it even more obvious how gaunt and tired she looks today. It might just be the shadows of the room, but I don't think so. She looks like she's been through a wringer. My head aches like judgment day, but I'll bet that even I don't look as bad as she does.

Her mouth twitches into what might be a smile, just for

a second. "Bar fight. After you passed out."

It's easy enough to imagine that. She might look small and frail, but I'd put down half a pound that she can hold her own against a room.

Yesterday's still hazy, but I remember the guilt I felt that I didn't stay awake to hear her story on our first night. "Hey, Amy?"

"Yeah?"

"Tell me a story. Since I missed the last one. It'll give me another minute to collect myself."

She slips the carved cat and the knife back into the sky-coloured pocket of her dress. "If you like. Do you know who Annie Oakley was?"

I nod, but she goes on anyway.

She was a sharpshooter in America. The Indians called her Little Sure Shot. When she was a child, her family was very poor, and she was sent to work at a neighbour's property. For the rest of her life, she'd never talk about the time she spent there. She wouldn't even say the family's name — she just called them the wolves.

Anyway, she was an amazing shot. Some said she was blessed, though what that means I don't know. She'd perform for royalty, for queens.

One day, the Prince of Prussia demanded that she shoot the ashes off a cigarette he held. She did it, of course; she could have done anything that needed a bullet and a trigger. That Prince grew up to be the Kaiser. Lots of people say that it's a damn shame that she didn't miss her shot and kill him there because she might've prevented the wars, but they speak without thinking. For time travel only works in one direction: we can look back, but never forward.

Are you hungry?

Her tone changes so fast it takes a moment for me to catch up with it. I blink. My head is aching, but I don't feel sick. My stomach is empty and sore with it.

"Yeah, I am."

"Pia said that we could have some of the lamb in the cold box. This is her house. She's not charging us; she says she likes having someone under the roof. I had a long talk with her this morning while you slept."

Old, cold lamb. Nothing has ever sounded more delicious to my empty belly.

We go downstairs. Amy's feet are back in her clomping boots, and my tender head feels every step of their noisy stride. I carry my drawing book in one hand but leave my bag. The rest of the place looks much like the room I woke up in, lots of hand-made lace, a few more crosses. There's a painted plaster statue of Our Lady on the mantle, so with a name like Pia, I'm fairly sure the landlady's Italian.

Nell's sweetheart was Italian. She'd tell me about him sometimes when she was in a chatty mood and not worried about him any more than the usual amount. She loved him. He loved her. They were good for one another.

And maybe the closest I'll ever get to a normal life was with an Italian, too. His name was Estachio, and we all called him Chio. I met him cherry-picking when I was still new to life on my own and didn't yet know better than to give my heart away.

He'd been a soldier with the Italian army, fighting in Libya. He got captured and, in true British style, got transported over here. Ended up deciding that Australia's version of what it meant to be a prisoner of war was better than the life he'd had when he was free, so when the war ended, he ran away before he could get deported.

He'd married a local girl. "Like you, dark on the skin with the golden hair, a beauty," he'd said, because he sure knew how to talk his charm to me, and they'd had a daughter. Chio's wife had died when the baby was still small and, without the help of the other fruit-picking families who worked the same circuit of farms through the year, both he and his daughter would have been left with no hope.

Little Theresa was four years old when I met her dad, and she took a shine to me almost as fast as he did. The first time she slipped up and called me 'Mama,' I thought my stupid heart would break. It seemed impossible that I could contain so much contentment without cracking apart and spilling it free all over the place.

The old women and the children stayed at the camp while everyone else picked in the daytime. In the evenings, our hands stained with cherry juice halfway up the wrist, I'd go collect Theresa from the women who cared for her. They were so generous to me even though they had almost nothing themselves. They loved me because Chio loved me and because Theresa loved me and because I loved them. That was all that mattered.

All in a row down the road, the men would cycle to town to get us fresh food for dinner. The women, our bones weary from the work of the day, would sit together and play with our babies and talk and laugh together. I was not quite fifteen, and to be treated the same as all the rest felt like a wonderful prize.

When the men came back, we'd cook the vegetables and the pasta and the spices and the meat and make a feast. The whole camp would eat together around one great big fire in the centre of the tents, and we'd tell stories and sing songs and make up the rudest jokes I've ever heard. Then, when it got late and the fire began to die, we'd carry Theresa back to our tent and lay her down carefully on the plump rag-bed she slept on.

Then, after a long time, I'd fall asleep, too, with Chio's breath on my cheek and my skin glowing with sweat and all the aches gone but the best of them.

I'll never, no matter how long I live or how often I love, feel like that again.

"I didn't know I was built to be this happy," I said to him once.

He just smiled.

But I was right. I wasn't built for it. Two, perhaps three months after we began, the horizon started calling out to me. I stopped loving the way Theresa's chubby hands would pat at the edge of my chin when I picked her up. I stopped feeling like my heart would break from being happy and started feeling like my heart was broken already.

So that's that.

Sometimes I dream about him, but not much. I hope he doesn't dream about me.

Not feeling so hungry anymore, I gesture to the front door of the house.

"Let's take a look around the block, eh? See what there is to see around here."

Amy shrugs, not seeming to care either way. She must've eaten with the mysterious Pia earlier.

The sunlight's not as bad as I'd feared, and I don't even need to squint to keep my headache at bay. I glance around the street, taking in the orderly houses, the neat gardens. I don't see this sort of world often.

"There must be a fair in town," Amy says, gesturing to a forlorn bundle of paper ribbons left in the muddy gutter. "These look like they were won at a sideshow last night."

"Yeah," I agree, nodding to a pair of girls across the street. "They're playing with a Kewpie doll. Kids only get those at fairs, most times."

The hand holding my sketchbook begins to itch. I don't usually draw when I'm badly hung over — the pictures turn out rotten — but today doesn't feel like an ordinary hangover, and the pull to make a picture is stronger than usual.

"C'mon, I want to go over."

Amy trails after me as I approach the pair. One of them is dark, much too dark to pass, and the other's small and brown-haired. Remarkably small, no bigger than Theresa was but obviously years older. They both look nine or ten.

"Can I draw you playing with your doll?" I ask. They nod, obviously impressed that they can draw two grown-up girls like us to their game.

Amy hangs back, hands dipping into her pockets for her carving again. She looks uncomfortable.

"What're your names?" I ask as I begin to sketch. I like the way their grubby hands look against the glitter of the Kewpie's gaudy costume.

"I'm Fran," says the little one. Her eyes are a cloudy green, and her miniature face is speckled with moles, making her sharp chin look smaller and even sharper.

"I'm Ev. Evelyn," the Aboriginal one introduces herself. "Do you live here?"

"In the town?" I ask.

"Yeah."

"No. We're just passing through."

"Same as us. Just passing through," Fran echoes, trying my words out in her mouth.

"We're with the fair," Evelyn explains. "Frannie's got a booth in the Freak-show Alley, and my Mum and Dad do the rides."

I look at Fran in surprise. She's little, but that's hardly remarkable enough to warrant display. She sees my unspoken question and shrugs, looking defensive and cross.

"I'll be worth more when I'm older. I tap-dance now. Wasn't any money at home, so Mum said we should make something outta my smallness."

"Don't mind her," Evelyn says breezily as I glance down at my hands on the paper. "She's always like this. I'm gonna have a spot in the Alley when I'm older, too. Mum and Dad won't let me do it yet, even though I know I can."

Fran sniffs. "Can't."

"Can," Evelyn retorts, then turns to me again. "I'm going to dress up traditional and tell the old stories. I seen it done in other shows. People'll pay top for the chance to see a real savage."

I don't know which of the girls I feel sorrier for. Amy would kick me if she knew; I get the feeling she doesn't like sorries any more than she likes bargains.

"Want to hear one of my stories?" Evelyn asks.

I concentrate on capturing the way the light hits her knuckle and nod. I won't think about them as real kids anymore. They're just part of my picture, just storytellers. It'll make it easier not to feel.

"*Out in the wild, the far-away wild where only the hunters go to get their game, the Mamu live. They're tall, taller than any person ever was, and their heads are pointed, and the men carry giant clubs to beat people to death with. Their teeth are sharper than knives and always bloody, and they can change themselves to look like anything they want.*

"*One day a hunter carries a 'roo he's speared back towards his tribe and meets a man sitting on a sand-hill. The man says to the hunter, 'I've got some meat here. Come eat it with me, and we'll walk back together.' So the hunter sits down and puts the 'roo down and takes the meat off the man and eats it.*

"*But really, the man's a Mamu — they can change to look like anything they want, remember. Sometimes they're knives buried in the sand, waiting for someone to pick them up. Then they jump up and cut your throat right across and gobble up your blood.*"

Her eyes are lit up with the feral joy that only kids get.

"*So this man was a Mamu, and the hunter tries to jump to his feet to grab his spear to kill it. But then, inside* him, the meat he ate twists and laughs, and the Mamu says 'That's my wife in there.' And she bites down on the hunter's heart. CHOMP."

Evelyn clicks her teeth together, clapping her hands at the same time to make a crack of noise.

"And that's the end of the hunter. The only way to ward off a Mamu is to stay closer to the fire at night. Dogs can tell when they're near, too. That's why it's good for hunters to have a pet dog with them all the time."

"I wish we had pets," Fran pipes up, her voice gone from defensive to petulant. "I want a pretty little kitten to cuddle, but Mum says no."

"Cats are never pets," corrects Amy, joining the conversation for the first time. Her own cat, carved in the wood, is almost finished. "Dogs are pets, with their monstrous loyalty and slavish love. Cats are familiars."

I put the final line to my picture as Amy and the girls debate the finer points of animal ownership. I've worked in close, framing tightly around their hands and the shape of the doll, but now that I look at it, the whole effect is strange and unsettling. The girls' hands look huge, engulfing and manipulating the tiny form of the toy. Its wide blue eyes, rimmed with painted-on spiky black lashes, look wide and afraid. I didn't mean to make it scary, but it is.

We bid the girls goodbye and return to our room, drawing back the curtains to let more light in. My headache's almost gone now, but my drawing hand still trembles for the want of creation. I turn to a fresh page in my book, taking up residence in the chair Amy was sitting in when I woke up. She perches on the edge of the unmade bed, still putting the finishing touches on her carving.

Faces are difficult for me. I can't get them right unless I've got a guide. But my lines are making the shape of a chin, the slant of an eye. A shock of hair. This is nobody I've met, no form I'm copying. I add an eyepatch.

Feeling very strange, I slam the covers of the book together and throw it to the ground. Amy's wandered over to the window while my attention was distracted and is staring up at the darkening blue above. The evenings are long this time of summer and can feel like a stretch of forever.

"People tell the future with stars because they need to believe in a pattern," she says, almost to herself. "In destiny. Why would the stars care? Why do people think that we're important enough to shape the sky? Astrology's the easiest lie of all. Stare up and say what people want to hear and blame the stars for being untrue if it doesn't quite happen in the end."

"People need to believe in something," I venture. She shakes her head.

"People are afraid of how free they'd be if they stopped. If the stars don't have our future planned, we have to make it happen ourselves."

The front door creaks as it opens on the level below, and Amy's introspective mood vanishes like a summer storm. "Come meet Pia. You'll like her."

Pia has broad shoulders and freckles and faded black hair that's mostly grey. She slices up the lamb from the cold-box and makes us thick sandwiches of it, then pours herself a drink of apple cider. Amy looks squeamish at the sight of the meat but takes a careful bite anyway.

"You girls are on the wallaby, aren't you?" she asks as we eat. I swallow a ravenous mouthful and nod. I wonder how the term got started. Do wallabies migrate?

"Would've liked to give that a go myself. Not that girls did it when I was young, but then there ain't that many of you giving it a shot even now, are there? But no, never got the chance. I was just a kid when me Dad came back from the war — the first one, not this one that's just been — and we both knew he didn't have long to last. Got shrapnel in his lung over on some beach on the other side of the world. Mum died when I was born, so I didn't have any brothers or nothing. Me and Dad knew I'd have to get married quick smart if I wanted a hope of keeping this place. My Harold was a good guy. Did right by me, especially after I gave him a son. Called the boy Ray, though he were more like a cyclone than a ray of sunshine in our lives, I'll tell you that.

"They both got done in, in the war that's just been. Ray went first, which is the real pity of it. Nobody should ever have to tell a man his son's been killed." She draws in a deep breath. "But listen to me go on. Girls like you don't want to hear prattle from an old fool like me."

Amy's got a hesitant, squeamish look about her face again, same as before we tucked into the food that's lying in remnants before us now. There's something feverish in her dark, exhausted eyes, and she looks away from me like she hopes I won't see it. She puts her hand on Pia's, like she's trying to comfort her.

"I'd like to hear more, if it won't upset you," she says, a gleam in her eyes.

It reminds me of nothing so much as the way a cat looks when it catches a glimpse of a mouse. I feel like shaking her. Of course it'll upset the poor woman! She's barely holding her tears in as it is! Surely, Amy can see that?

I stand up, collecting our empty plates. "I'm just popping upstairs for a tick," I say, fleeing the table as quickly as I can. Pia has begun to tell Amy about Ray's favourite songs.

I go to the window in our room, looking up at the sky. It's dark now, and the stars are out. I want some answer, some truth. The astrology Amy doesn't believe in.

But the only thing I can think of is an old Land Army song Nell taught me those afternoons when I'd help her pick the beans and silver beet. It's a long song, full of patriots and guns, but there are four lines I remember clearest.

"They fight the silent battle," I murmur to myself there at the window. "On the front behind the front. And their combat just as vital, though it's girls who bear the brunt."

I used to daydream about how awful it would have been for girls like Nell, like Pia. To be left behind, with all their loved ones off and fighting. But I never imagined that I was a sweetheart left behind, singing and working and hoping, hoping, hoping. My imaginings were how terrible I'd feel if I had to leave a girl and go to fight. How guilty I'd feel to put her in the distance as I went.

The stars look so endless, and I feel as if I'm going to fall into them. I grip onto the window frame, hoping that the feel of it will stop my vertigo. It doesn't.

CHARLOTTE

From *Reign in Hell: Two Weeks in the Life of HUSH*, by Charlotte Waterhouse, Amplify Press, Australia, 2011:

"I sometimes…" Ben stops, bites his lip, takes a breath. His hair falls forward in his eyes as he moves his head, making his thin and delicate-featured face look even younger than he is. He's had just as many knocks and bruises in his life as any of the other band members, but his bleak times have left less of a mark on his appearance than those of the women around him have on theirs. In many ways, he's the band's baby brother.

Ben's clearly considering the best way to phrase his next words. "I often worry that some kid in the crowd will be pushed over the edge by something in one of our songs. How self-important is that, right? To assume we have that much power. But I'm super-conscious of that potential situation, self-important though it may be.

"I've talked to the others about it, of course. Everyone's got different perspectives on it. Like, Jo thinks that's just the way it goes, that you can't step up and demand that people pay attention to you, that people follow you, without being willing to wear what that might mean. If you can't cope with that, you shouldn't speak in the first place, she says.

"Jacq grew up seeing the power of her grandfather's photography. She knows how world-changing art can be. But she also grew up with a front-row seat to how random and unfair and fucked-up life and death are, with what happened to Marie. That left her with... not a fatalism, exactly, but a belief that we can't ever brace ourselves against tragedy. It'll come no matter what we do, and art will never change the world enough to change *that*.

"Cherry and Tash think it's a waste of time to worry about the aftermath you might create. They don't like talking about it much.

"But for myself... there was this girl I knew at school. We weren't all that close, but there were a couple of times, when... I used to do volunteer work at a teen health center in the neighborhood where this girl lived, and she came in sometimes. To get the morning after pill or free condoms. Her boyfriend used to get violent when he was drunk, so sometimes she needed stitches. Once, an abortion. Another time, a cast for a broken wrist.

"I'd get her coffee or an apple and sit with her while she waited to see the doctor or for her cab ride home. She had an eating disorder, so I knew never to get her a muffin or a bagel or anything.

"God, when I list out all the shit she had to deal with it sounds over-the-top, doesn't it? But it really happened. She wasn't just a litany of clichéd teen disasters. She was a real person, and I knew her, and I liked her, and she killed herself.

"When that happens... it makes you think of all the things you did, or didn't do, or could have done a different way. I didn't know her that well, but... could I have saved her, if I'd somehow... somehow given a different set of gestures and words to the world she inhabited?

"And with crowds, with concerts, that's multiplied a thousand-fold. There are so many kids out there each night. And I feel like I owe it to that girl, the one who was alive and then murdered herself one day, to try as hard as I can to be the light that saves, instead of the dark that drags you under.

"But who knows, right? Who knows what reactions the actions we make will cause?" Ben shakes his head, hair falling in his eyes yet again. "When we give something away to the world, it's out of our hands."

ELLA

Dear Tash,

Girl A, also known as Natsumi Tsuji and Nevada-tan, was eleven years old in 2004 when she took a box cutter into an empty classroom during lunch hour at her elementary school. Her twelve-year-old classmate Satomi Mitarai was with her.

Girl A and Satomi Mitarai both liked the internet. Satomi Mitarai had called Girl A names online, teasing her about her weight and calling her a goody-goody.

Girl A used the box cutter to slice up Satomi Mitarai's arms and throat. Then, covered in her blood, Girl A returned to class and sat down.

The police, trying to conceal her identity, called her 'Girl A' whenever they mentioned her in the media. But people found out that her name as Natsumi Tsuji anyway. They always find out the names in the end. Then they give us new ones.

The nickname Nevada-tan was an internet invention. Someone found a photo of Girl A wearing a hoodie that said 'Nevada.' The 'tan' suffix is a mark of affection and friendliness.

There is a lot of lovingly drawn, gory pornography of Nevada-tan on the internet now.

Only eleven percent of female serial killers murder by stabbing. Shooting accounts for twenty percent. The most common method is poisoning. Even Lady Gaga and

Beyoncé use poisoning in that Telephone video they did. They kill a diner full of people and then drive off in a van donated to the video by Quentin Tarantino. Mickey and Mallory Knox really did end up as pop idols.

X E

Tash,

I've been killing time (no pun) thinking more about sayings and stock phrases. Repetition gives things a sort of power, as does recitation. That's part of why the rules are different for saints.

(I'm sure Jo would interrupt at this point and scornfully say that I don't know anything about anything. That's an advantage of the written word: there's nobody here for me to argue with except myself and the idea of you, my phantom audience. Abstract listener. Reader, really, though I tend to think of everything that you absorb as things you pricked up your ears to catch a whisper of. Even before the music, long before it, the world was already a song for you.)

So, sayings: the one I'm thinking of right now is the one about how, if you save someone's life, then you're responsible for them forever. You kept 'em breathing, so now it's up to you to find the oxygen.

Maybe there's truth in that. Maybe there isn't. Maybe Darcy can answer one way or another.

But what I keep thinking, as I turn that saying over in my head like a jagged rock in my palms, is that the one which sounds truer to me is the one on signs in stores selling fragile things:

All breakages must be paid for.

Or, the variant:
You break it, you bought it.

X
Ella

Dear Tash,

I have started the process of letting go of the little girl you used to be, the one I said goodbye to on that morning. I have started to accept that you didn't just stay static in that moment when I turned and couldn't see you anymore.

You aren't still sitting there, oblivious and young, unaware that I'm gone forever.

I think a lot about what I said. Or, no. What I didn't say. The million, million things I didn't say that last time we spoke. You were just a child. I know in my head that children's understanding — their ability to comprehend — is limited. The things I said to you were limited by how young you were.

But in my heart I wish and wish that I'd said so many things. I wish I'd told you about Irvine Welsh novels and about chat rooms and about MTV and about pizza and 3 a.m. and kissing and algebra and *A Clockwork Orange* and video games.

But I didn't, and now all I've got are these letters I write to you that you aren't ever going to read.

Leslie Van Houton was a member of the Manson Family. She once said, "You really have to love someone to kill them." I left you alive, but I really do love you, Natasha-who-isn't-Nattie-anymore. I really promise that I do.

Sylvia Seegrist, who stabbed her psychologist and strangled her mother and went spree-killing in a crowded mall, said that what she did was a form of public service.

Maybe it was, but mine wasn't. I wanted to destroy the world, not service it. Motive has never mattered as much as action, but perhaps it matters a little bit.

Valerie Solanas was a writer and homeless. She shot Andy Warhol because he lost her manuscript. She wrote the SCUM manifesto: Society for Cutting Up Men.

Cobweb never had a manifesto. If you were a part of it, that meant you got it. If you didn't get it, you weren't part of it. No manifesto needed.

My name is on lists with all these women on websites and in crime books. I'm scared that the fact that you and I were sisters is simply the past, while these women are my sisters in history. I don't want any sister who isn't you, Natasha. Even if you have one now who isn't me.

xx
Ella

Dear Tash,

Time doesn't pass the same way here of course, but we quickly fall into the habit of keeping one eye on Earth. We watch news anchors and presidents and parents wring their hands and stammer platitudes. Rock stars disclaim influence. Schools panic and install metal detectors when they get suspicious and terrified at the sight of children who look different.

Being here is like being young at Christmas, gazing into lighted windows at little clockwork railroads.

xE

Dear Tash,

I want to tell you about Vivi. She was one of the first people I met when I got here. I like her. If I had grown up, I would have wanted to be a woman like her. I feel like I'd have done a better job of it than most of the teenage girls who dream of being the next Vivi.

Then again, psychopaths make up four percent of the general population. I'm not as unique as I'd like to think I am. There are plenty of people out there equally equipped.

You'd probably recognize her if you saw her, if she had her real face on at the time. Vivi Verdun. She's as famous now as she ever was when she was alive.

There's at least one Verdun store in any city that's worth talking about, and there's not a starlet around who hasn't got a pair of earrings or a quilted leather shoulder-bag emblazoned with the interlocked double-V insignia of the brand.

The smell of Vivi, the Verdun perfume named Vivi I mean, still takes me back to my childhood whenever I smell it. It's one of those opium-y eighties smells that permeated all the closets and makeup tables of upper-middle-class women for all of the decade. I was an only child in those days. You hadn't been born yet.

I used to sneak in and try on the matte brown lipsticks our mother loved, which looked like smeared chocolate on my lips. I'd loop her long dangling earrings over the shells of my small, unpierced ears. I'd clomp around in her high, skinny heels. And all of it would smell like Vivi.

Vivi's own childhood was as lonely as mine, though far less cushioned. I think that might be why we get along as well as we do. We... we aren't friends. Vivi doesn't have friends, and I have a very select few.

She'd grown up left to her own daydreams and plans,

just as I did, but where I'd decided to burn the world, she'd built herself a high-walled castle with one occupant. The core of it was the same for us both: we felt painfully isolated yet had nothing but poisonous contempt for the people we might have let into our hearts.

The few confidantes we did manage to have were people as evil and selfish as we were ourselves. They were the only ones we understood and who understood us.

The teenage spree-killer and the world-renowned fashion designer.

Just two little girls, playing alone.

After her mother died and her father abandoned her to be raised by his two prickly, miserly sisters sometime around 1895, Vivienne Verdun began to play in graveyards. She liked the quiet and that there was nobody to answer back when she made pronouncements to the air.

One of her few joys in those years was riding the horses her aunts owned. When the aunts invited a local rich man to come and buy some of the horses, Vivi prepared for his arrival by riding the horses full-tilt across the cobblestone courtyards without shoes, ruining their hooves, making them worthless. She'd rather break a thing than lose what she loved.

When she was sixteen years old, she ran away and became a nightclub singer and a whore. She wasn't a very good singer, but she was a very good whore. It wasn't long before a rich man came along and swept her off to be a pretty, fuckable little pet at one of his country houses. Vivi didn't mind. There were horses to ride and people to talk to. Then one day she fell in love.

In case I haven't made my point clear by now, after so many letters, there are few things in the world more dangerous than a teenager who falls in love.

His name was Arthur, and he went by Art because

sometimes God is painfully unsubtle. He was English and would eventually have to marry someone suitable (and therefore not a skinny French whore), but he loved her back. Oh, it would all have been so much easier if he hadn't loved her back. But he did. They were perfect together. Vivi hadn't known she was built to be so happy.

To make up for the fact that he would never marry her and would instead marry a plump sensible girl named Alexandra who was neither French nor a whore, Art bought Vivi a hat shop. She'd wanted to be a hat-maker when she'd run away from home, but singing badly and fucking well was an easier job to get for a young runaway who'd grown up in graveyards.

Vivi was a good hat-maker. That might have been all she ever was if not for the First World War. The War meant fabric rationing, and that meant there were legions of spoiled, rich women who wanted new dresses, though there was no cloth to make them from. But Vivi had cloth. The ration rules for hat-makers were different. She began making dresses. She was a good dressmaker.

Art died. Not in the war. He died in an ordinary car accident. Every life is vitally important to the people who love it, but not everyone gets an important death. Not everyone leaves a legend in their wake. Some people just swerve the wrong direction on an icy road.

Strangely enough, in the immediate aftermath of Art's death, Alexandra and her new baby son went to live with Vivi. It was a pattern that would repeat later; during her affair with Igor Stravinsky, Vivi lived with the composer and his wife and all of their children. She'd once asked him, early in the affair, if his wife knew about the two of them.

"Of course," Stravinsky answered. "She's my best friend. We tell each other everything."

Vivi never had a best friend, not really. After Art died, she didn't want anybody she could love in her life. Her one brush with the emotion had proved too painful to bear repeating — nothing about his love had been worth the feeling of his loss as far as Vivi could see. She had people she called friends, but they were more like competitors and often closer to enemies. She wanted to be challenged, not adored.

Her dressmaking business became more and more and more successful. She went into business with a Jewish family who made perfumes. They sold the scents in austere glass bottles. Vivi didn't like decoration. She didn't like distraction.

During the Second World War, Vivi's lover — she always had at least one and often more if she could be bothered and they didn't irritate her too much — was an officer in the SS. She didn't care. She'd burned away all the parts of her that cared. Caring was useless. It was better to play alone in graveyards; you could hear your own voice without interruption that way.

In fact, Vivi decided she didn't even like having business partners. And here was a perfect opportunity to get rid of them. She told her SS officer about the perfume family. About how they were Jews.

It didn't work in the end. The perfume family had enough German friends that they could transfer their shares of the company into safe Aryan hands rather than have them confiscated and given over to Vivi. She'd forgotten to factor in the possibility that they'd have friends. She always forgot details like that.

In the end, they bought her out. When you buy Verdun perfume now, or lipsticks, or dresses, or hats, or earrings or bags or any of the rest, your money is going to the Jewish family that Vivi tried to destroy.

But it's still her name on the storefronts. It's her

photograph in articles about the history of fashion. It's her love affairs on cinema screens. She's the iconography, the figurehead.

Style and morality never had anything to do with one another in the first place anyway.

xe

AMY

By the time I awoke, shortly before dawn, the burn was healed enough for me to unwind and discard the bandage. There was still a shallow blister on the ball of my thumb, but that would fade before Sally scrambled out of her own dreaming.

I'd opened my eyes to find myself tangled in her again, as I had on the two other mornings prior. My thigh pushed into the delicate crook of her knee, my face buried in the sweat-damp weight of her hair. When out of my control, my body craved touch. It made me curious and a little unnerved.

My own hair, wild and coarse as ever, took me a long time to wash in the small rose-patterned jug and basin set Pia had place in the room. I combed all the tangles I could find, wrung the droplets free, and crept downstairs on bare feet to dry out under the early sun.

I took the patchwork with me from the bed, leaving Sally with the warmth of the red flannel under-sheet and the humid ghosts of our breath. The pattern was ancient; the colours of the scraps faded to uniform grey all over, save the seams. Where one colour joined another, deep veins of the old dyes ran along the neat stitches. Royal blue, copper green, apricot yellow like old secrets.

Pia was awake already, pruning the shrubs lining the edges of her garden. In the chill early light, a blue wash seemed to settle over the stretch of the trees and the pale, sun-brittled leaves. A bird took off overhead, making the branches crackle against each other.

The smile Pia greeted me with was fresh as a bride's. She looked as if years had been lifted from her kind, toughened face. Girls, like the one she'd once been, have a very fast flowering; they are the butterflies that live only a day. Sally was in the catch of it, sleeping upstairs, but I knew that soon enough disappointment and hardship would strip the bloom off her, too.

The fiction everyone pretends is that the rich are naturally more beautiful past a certain age, and I suppose that's true enough: few things are more natural to human nature than injustice.

I sat on the stoop and pulled my carving from the pocket of my dress, wondering idly if Richard and that new whelp of his would still chase me like a hare if they could hear the new careless life in Pia's tune. Probably. Hunters rarely care to know what good their prey offers to the world. Such details complicate their chase.

Probably, I decided. Their kind tended to absolutes.

"You're taking your time with that," Pia remarked, gesturing to the forming shape and the knife in my hand. "The path of needles, we used to call it."

I looked down at the smooth haunches, the powerful jaw. More like a panther than anything domestic, though I hadn't bothered to give it claws. Its eyes were too big for realism, but it needed realism even less than it needed claws.

"People used to say that there were two paths a girl could take when she set out to do a thing. The path of needles or the path of pins. For sewing, you see? You can sew a hem up and have it hold, and that's the path of needles. Tacking it with pins is faster but doesn't hold. You'll be prickled and stung with every step on that road."

As fables went, it lacked finesse, but I liked the imagery of sharp points and small flashes of steel.

The door at my back opened, and Sally sat down beside me. She draped the patchwork across her shoulders, bumping her arm companionably against mine. She'd washed her hair, too, and the wet dye looked ruddy and rich like fresh clay.

She had her drawing book in her hands, thumb tracing over one battered edge of the cover. I hadn't meant to do that, to put the little flame in her, but I'd known it was a risk. You can't cut a memory out of someone without something of yourself rushing in to fill the hole, even when the memory is relatively inconsequential.

Making Sally forget about Richard and his follower had left me worn out and nauseated, even after the two fruitful expeditions I'd just had. Without them, I might not have been up to it at all.

"I'm sorry if we upset you last night," Sally said to Pia, giving me a pointed look.

Pia smiled again, waving a hand as if Sally's worry was smoke to be dispersed. "No, no, 'course not. The past is the past."

Sally's eyebrows knitted together, a question forming in her eyes.

I cleared my throat with a loud cough.

"Do you know the best place for us to go to hitch a ride for Sydney?" I asked and didn't look at Sally again until Pia had given us a detailed answer.

CHARLOTTE

From *Reign in Hell: Two Weeks in the Life of HUSH*, by Charlotte Waterhouse, Amplify Press, Australia, 2011:

In the end Cherry, not Tash, comes down with the dreaded 'plane flu,' and by Adelaide she looks as miserable as any sick person I've ever seen who was still ambulatory. Her skin is clammy and grey, her eyes dull and her nose red from constant application of tissues. She refuses to see a doctor.

"I know you're not as cult-of-big-pharma over here as we are, but it's still ridiculous to pay a trained professional to prescribe bed rest and lemon tea." But she is clearly in no condition to play the show that night.

The rest of the band recruits Gabe to fill her spot, leading Cherry to threaten weakly against Jacqui "going all Bowie onstage and fellating my Epiphone; I will end you and all that you hold dear."

While everyone else is off at sound-check, Cherry offers to do a one-on-one interview with me, despite my protestations that there's really no need, and she can rest if she wants.

"I don't know *how* to rest. I have the attention span of a hyperactive puppy. I'll let you look at the new album," she tempts in groggy sing-song.

I relent, sitting down opposite her.

She's curled up in one of the plush armchairs in her hotel room, a blanket around her shoulders and an oversized HUSH shirt stolen from the band's merch supplies standing in as an emergency nightshirt.

"The tee and boxers I usually sleep in are getting decontaminated with the rest of our laundry," Cherry says. "This band is made up of five of the grossest people in the world. You need a hazmat suit to deal with our dirty clothes even when I'm not a snot factory. It's kind of tragic."

The band's communal laptop is decorated much like their instruments and equipment cases are, with a scattering of decals and shiny stickers. Cherry switches it on and loads up a pdf of the new album's art.

"The booklets aren't printed yet, but unless something comes up this is the final look. You're one of the first to get a peek. Be gentle!" she says, sniffling her way through a new box of tissues.

The cover image is one of Jo's stark chiaroscuro photographs, a pair of little girls playing with a doll. The picture would be sweet and perhaps even a little banal if it wasn't rendered in such sharp blacks and whites, which lend it an uneasy air. Small, neat letters in a serif font spell out the title in one corner:

HUSH | the devil's mixtape

The art for the inside of the CD case is equally simple and monochromatic.

"This reminds me of zine art. It almost looks photocopied," I remark. Cherry nods excitedly.

"Yeah, yeah, exactly. We drew a lot of inspiration from that look. Like, here, this part." She points to the section of artwork which will lie underneath the CD, revealed only when the listener removes the album from the case. In shaky, hand-drawn letters, it says A GIRL WENT TO HELL TO BRING BACK A STORY. "That's based on Scarlet Slaughterhouse's stuff. Gabe's got almost a full collection of her zines. She was pretty amazing. HUSH will never be half as punk rock as her."

I bite my lip and don't say anything, the fingertips of my right hand brushing against one of the small scars on my left wrist.

Scarlet Slaughterhouse wrote her initials in sharp angles, like a Nazi SS, because that was ugly and offensive and terrible. Profane.

She wrote stories where tiny blind kittens, drowned in sacks weighed with bricks, returned from the lakes in waterlogged prides and tore out the soft sleeping throats of sweet small children, and of torn-throated children who roamed the night with gleaming teeth and high, ruined laughs.

She wrote dark and awful stories set in bloodied libraries of boys kissing slick and open-mouthed as they shoved the blunt heads of their guns against each other's stomachs.

She wrote angry, passionless, filthy pornography and sold it to publishers and spent the money on tacky useless crap she didn't need that was made in airless factories pumping poisons into the Pearl River Delta and paying a pittance to its rows of tired and sleepless workers, then wrote out long public letters to herself eviscerating those same actions.

She made collages about love and hate and death and horror and global warming and the end of the world. She pasted down whole articles about how it was up to each one of us to save the environment, then blacked out every word except a sentence in the center about how birds had begun to sing at a different pitch to fight against the sounds of traffic.

Scarlet Slaughterhouse knew, years before she took a taxi ride with Jacqui Caramano, that there was no point in trying, there was no hope, because the belching shitting monster of humanity would never cease its rotten-toothed chewing, its devouring, and the only moment of control or coherency that Scarlet Slaughterhouse ever felt was when she sliced into the flesh of her legs and arms and breasts and hips and stomach with the cheap, sharp razor blades she bought and had to replace constantly because the blood made them rust and blunted off the edge she needed in order to feel anything at all.

Scarlet Slaughterhouse vanished one day. Disappeared, dormant and disillusioned and exhausted, behind a façade of adulthood. She stopped calling herself Scarlet and went back to being plain old Charlotte.

She had no idea that her angry vomit of art had any kind of legacy. That anyone had been paying attention at all, let alone remembered.

"Who wrote the line?" I ask finally, gesturing at the words on the screen. A GIRL WENT TO HELL TO BRING BACK A STORY.

"That was me," Cherry admits.

"It's a whole hero's journey in one sentence," I say. "It's got a protagonist, a quest, a middle act in the underworld, and a resolution. Joseph Campbell would be impressed as hell."

There was a time when I thought complete and closed-up stories were something only bourgeois sell-outs wanted. Now I'm a little kinder. Some of my brittle edges were worn away by adult life, perhaps. Or I just grew weary enough to see the value in endings.

Cherry smirks. "You're so sure she gets the story, then? That she brings it back? The sentence doesn't say that. Just that she went. Maybe she failed."

"The album exists, doesn't it?" I counter, not fooled at all by her attempt at cynicism. Nobody who's survived as much as Cherry has could ever manage it if they weren't an optimist.

She laughs, the sound breaking off into a harsh cough.

"Ow, don't make me do that!" Cherry drinks more lemon tea, scrolling down through the rest of the pages of the pdf.

"I write quite a bit, you know. Some of it's published, under different names I made up. Just short stuff; I did a kind of novel-length thing once, but the three or four publishers I sent it to all politely declined.

"One of them said I had a lot of talent but that I needed to learn to get my thoughts in order before I'd be ready for publication. Which I think is a pretty fair appraisal — like I said, I have the attention span of a hyperactive puppy. Maybe I'll try again one day. I don't really have time while the band's so busy.

"When this thing you're writing comes out I'm gonna have to face a few determined callers, I bet. There're already two or three publishers back home who've been shoving contracts under my nose. They'd take anything I gave them — notes, novels, my teenage diary. *Especially* my teenage diary, I'm sure.

"I've never capitalized on any of those offers even if they come from the Ministries, and I know it's about motivations other than a quick buck. I do want to be a writer, but as myself. Not as Stacey's little sister."

'The Ministries', are the Stacey's Gift Ministries. They publish a range of inspirational books in cooperation with an Evangelical publishing house. It's hard to imagine anything from Cherry's skewed, sharply perceptive imagination sharing shelf space with their titles. The bestseller of the bunch is, of course, Stacey's diary from the year leading up to her shooting.

Cherry's tattoo, *Only love*, is a partial quote from this diary. The full quote is *Of all the tools before us, we need only love*. When the diary was published as a book, the book was titled *We Need Only Love*. With each successive paring-down, the original, somewhat clumsy teenage sentiment becomes more elegant.

The diary was published with the cooperation of Stacey and Cherry's mother, Abigail Reardon, who gives motivational talks and appears on talk shows. Stacey's Gift Ministries runs a nationwide school outreach program for the prevention of teen violence, as well as programs to feed the hungry. Their annual budget of $3.5 million is almost all paid through fees from schools for presentations and seminars run by Abigail.

Beyond Stacey's formalized legacy through the Ministries, there is a larger legend that has grown up around her. The number of teenagers who began attending regular church services after her death was so great that Stacey was given the nickname Saint Stacey. Chuck Norris dedicated his autobiography to her.

"Sometimes I think that's why I ended up in a band," Cherry says of the Norris connection. "The crazy stuff that happens on tour cannot *possibly* compare to the surreal reality of my home life. Well, not my actual home life — that's, thankfully, very normal most of the time. But my mother's world is much stranger than the world of rock and roll."

Tash joined the family as a foster child less than a year after the events of Cobweb, having been left with no living relatives by the shootings. Abigail and Zack Reardon separated a few years after Stacey's death. The girls were raised by Zack following the split.

When she talks about her mother's work, Cherry's mouth presses down into a frown, momentarily thinning her full lips. She looks sick, but she also looks very tired and older than her young age.

"I don't think any child, no matter what the circumstances of her birth, could ever have competed with Stacey in my mother's mind after the shootings."

Is she referring to the persistent rumors that Cherry was Stacey's biological child, not her sister?

"I don't think about that much," Cherry tells me with a shake of her head.

She picks at the polish on her nails — a red of roughly her namesake shade — and sounds matter-of-fact, sensitive but sensible.

"You have to understand that I wasn't even six years old when Stacey was killed. That means that I have only a handful of memories of her. Those memories are very precious to me. I can't risk corrupting what few recollections I have of the big sister I adored by searching for subtexts after the fact.

"I had no awareness then of... I had no sense that she was hiding a deep sadness about the true nature of our bond. If I were to think about the possibility of her hiding something like that, then the real memories would get warped with imagination and embellishments.

"As far as I'm concerned, she was my sister. I was her sister. That's who we were. That's how my father raised us afterward.

"I'm resistant to all the Saint Stacey stuff for the same reason. I can't engage with it because that Stacey isn't *my* Stacey. I can't risk losing sight of the real person behind the iconography.

"What I meant earlier about no other child being able to compete with Stacey in my mother's heart after Cobweb... I think that everyone has a point at which the amount of sadness they face is larger than their ability to face that sadness.

"It isn't anyone's fault that my mother couldn't cope with Stacey dying. Some people have an almost infinite ability to handle what life throws at them, and some don't. Some people never have anything particularly sad happen to them, and some do. You can't anticipate how things are going to happen; just deal with them once they've occurred."

I can't help but remark that this is an incredibly philosophical position for Cherry to take. Her calm face quirks up into a brief smirk before she answers.

"Oh, I'm not talking about *forgiveness*. I don't think I have the right to offer any kind of forgiveness. Not on behalf of anybody but myself, certainly, and I've never felt especially forgiving for my own sake. The person I loved the most in the world was murdered; who'd forgive *that*?

"Acceptance is a different thing. It's even harder than forgiveness, really, because at least with forgiveness you can pretend your feelings, one way or another, matter.

"*Accepting*, on the other hand — when you look at reality right in the face and just keep going, even though you know nothing is ever going to make your pain better or fix the wrongs done against you — that's hard."

AMY

By the time we'd had breakfast and a pot of tea, packed what little there was for us to pack, and said our goodbyes, Sally's silence was beginning to prickle the length of my spine. I didn't want to break the quiet, knowing I'd be the worse for it, but I missed her voice prattling beside me as we walked.

Finally, as we reached the road out of town, she opened her mouth.

"You stand. I want to draw."

So I stood on the edge of the unpaved path, waiting to hail down passing cars, while she sat in the sparse shade of the nearby trees and sketched. I considered climbing into the first offered ride alone and leaving her there. I imagined how lucky it would be for her, for the both of us. Far less complicated, at the very least. Travel with someone like me was never going to remain simple for very long, and the presence of someone like Sally wasn't going to make things any smoother either.

But I don't believe in luck, and I didn't want to leave her, no matter how much better off I'd be from an objective perspective.

So there we stayed, each in our own little world, as the day grew hotter and our shadows shorter. Finally, as my arms began to ache with the familiar scorch of the sun, she came back over to join me at the roadside. There was no apology in her stride, but I hoped that there was at least an offering of peace.

"Can't we leave it?" I wanted to ask her. Just for now. No questions, just for now. Because we'll be happier that way, I promise. But I didn't say anything.

She opened her book to a page, and two faces, as different as the two sides of Janus, both framed by errant locks of hair, looked up from the page. One expression was smirking, sarcastic and sharp, the other looking at something unseen off the margin, thoughtful and forthright, a pragmatic set to the corner of her smile.

"They were meant to be you," she explained, as if it was my fault her pen had betrayed her. "The two parts of you I can't work whole out of. But I think they turned into other people while I drew."

"Sisters?" I asked, unsure if I was asking about the picture.

"Sisters," she confirmed, and I was no surer of her reply than of my question.

But, regardless, that was the end of the argument, such as it was. Whether she'd decided to forget or was waiting for a better moment to end our comfortable companionship once and for all, we were in a truce.

A truck with a whining engine carrying a load of potato sacks on its back bed stopped for us. We squashed into the small cabin beside the driver, an Aboriginal man with one of his index fingers missing beyond the first knuckle. Paul, he told us his name was. With Sally in the middle, we made a spectrum of shades. Black, brown, white, from one door to the other.

I didn't know yet that I was the first to guess the secret of her skin, but I was there when Paul became the second. People who have been discarded by society are good at noticing details that others would miss — some call it intuition or a keen eye. Sally's relatively fair skin had let her pass in the eyes of most, but there were other details in the cast of her features and the hue of her tan which told the truth of the matter to those who gave her more than a glance.

"You heading for Redfern, eh? Most blacks I know who stay in Sydney head for there. Ain't so unfriendly in Redfern."

Sally ducked her head, obviously completely at a loss as to what she should say. I didn't help her; the question hadn't been for me.

"I don't, I mean, I've never... I don't know much about it."

"Should give it a look. They've just built themselves an all blacks football club last season. All us Koories go along and have a cheer, and nobody much cares if you're halfway like you are. It's good fun."

Looking up again, staring out at the bush road reaching out before us, Sally shook her head. "I'm not Koori. My Mum, she was... well, she was nothing, really, 'cause they took her before she was old enough to understand, but she woulda been Murri."

"Queensland, eh?" The man laughed, like Sally'd suddenly become a marvelous joke.

"Kind of far from home, aren't ya?"

"Less distance than me," I said, and that got him laughing all over again.

"True enough, true enough. So you're one Brit —"

"I'm not from Britain," I interrupted.

"One Yank, then," he went on. I didn't correct him a second time. "And one who'd be Murri if her Mum hadn't been snatched. Bet neither of you have the faintest clue about the way things got started, am I right?"

Neither of us answered.

He took that as a yes, and maybe that's how we'd meant it.

"Well, this land we're getting to now, it's all ups and downs, you see? That's Rainbow Snake's doing. Rainbow

Snake was bigger'n all the other creatures in the world when the world began. Rainbow Snake'd wind himself across the flat world and make valleys and mountains all over. Rainbow Snake is red and yellow, all in stripes. You ain't never gonna see reds and yellows like the ones on Rainbow Snake.

"When Rainbow Snake was done making all the valleys and the mountains, he curled up with his missus in a waterhole for a rest. They's the biggest in the world, but the world's still big around 'em, and they were tired enough to sleep forever.

"All the animals were careful at the waterhole, so they wouldn't wake the snakes lying down together at the bottom. Only time they ever wake up is when rain comes down on them and drums on their heads. Then they stretch up high in the sky and come back down at a different waterhole, so they can get back to sleeping. Bet you've seen 'em up there and not known, huh?"

Sally nodded.

I copied her.

"Gotta be careful of Rainbow Snake, though. If you're hungry, he don't mind you spearing a fish in his waterhole for dinner. But if you're catching just for sport, or to get one bigger than all your mates have got, Rainbow Snake's gonna catch you up and drag you down so all the fish can eat you.

"Rainbow Snake knows how to keep you from drowning down there, so it's not over quick."

When he finished, Sally spoke in a small, shamed voice. "I was baptised. Had communion, too. Kinda. Wasn't much to make me dress from."

It intrigued me how different her voice would become, depending on who she was talking to. I wondered if she even realised or if it was instinct. *Blend in, be the same, don't draw attention.* I'd learned it so studiously and with such difficulty that to see her do it without effort sent a pang of hot, green, envy up my nerves.

"You think one thing means the other can't be true, right?" Paul asked. Sally nodded. "Way I see it, kid, is that it's all as true as the rest of it. Same as how some're black, and some are white and you're somewhere in the middle, eh? I can't see a reason why Rainbow Snake and those angels and saints can't make a brown between them too."

"But the middle isn't anywhere," Sally protested.

Nobody answered her.

CHARLOTTE

From *Reign in Hell: Two Weeks in the Life of HUSH*, by Charlotte Waterhouse, Amplify Press, Australia, 2011:

Stacey Reardon's modern martyrdom occurred in this way: Stacey was a senior at John Wallace High School, a popular girl with ambitions to one day become an actress. She was in the same after-school drama club as Dean Summerset. He helped with lighting and sound; she strutted her stuff on the stage. Though not close enough to be called friends, the two were friendly enough in their interactions. One videotape of a rehearsal shows them playing Hackey Sack together.

On the morning of April 9, 1999, Stacey skipped her usual geography class in order to avoid a pop quiz she hadn't studied for. Instead she went to the school library to work on a social studies assignment.

When panic spread through the school grounds, rumors of a shooting, Stacey and the other students hid under their desks. The teacher who had ordered them to do so hid in a storage cabinet. This teacher survived the massacre unharmed.

At 10:17 a.m., Dean, along with Chris Morrison and Ella Vrenna, entered the library. They already had twelve kills between them. Dean had shot four people, Chris five, and Ella three. Their combined count would be twenty just six minutes later.

Stacey was the third of the eight students who lost their lives in the library. Crouched beneath her desk, she quietly prayed as the carnage began. Vashty Chowdhury, another student, had 911 on the line on her cellphone.

The recording of this call leaked to the media in the immediate aftermath of the Cobweb massacre. Umberto Eco once described it as the first mass-produced saint's relic, and this is an apt description. The death of Stacey Reardon was played over and over and over on the news and other media in the weeks and months following the end of her life.

The recording captures the ragged breathing of Vashty and, quieter, Stacey's own panicked gasps from the next desk over. It captures the sound of Chris's footsteps drawing closer and the sudden sharp crack of sound as he slaps his palm down on the top of Stacey's desk. Vashty gives a yelp of horror and fear, but Chris ignores her, speaking instead to Stacey in a cheerful tone.

"Boo!" Chris says, leaning down so he can look Stacey directly in the eye, his gun pointed directly at her face.

"Oh, God," Stacey says in reply, her voice trembling and audibly terrified. "Please don't kill me."

"You really have faith in God?" Chris asks. He sounds curious rather than mocking; the mildness of his tone makes the words all the more chilling.

Stacey does not instantly reply. The seconds are endless and painful to listen to no matter how many times the recording has been heard before. Then Stacey speaks, her voice calmer than it was moments before. It's a wise, brave voice.

"Yes," Stacey says. And Chris pulls the trigger.

During the band's Adelaide show, Cherry and I use the laptop to watch the Twitter hashtag #HUSH, which members of the audience are updating from the crowd.

Everyone seems to be having a fabulous time.

When one Twitter user by the name SkylinerEyeliner posts the message *I miss Cherry :(#HUSH*, Cherry uses the band's official account to send back a message saying *@SkylinerEyeliner Cherry wishes she could be there! xxx Enjoy the show!*

The SkylinerEyeliner twitter promptly explodes into delighted 'holy shit' and 'omfg' tweets.

"I want to be someone real, not any kind of 'celebrity'," Cherry says to me, her fingers making the air quotes. "Sometimes I'm not who people want me to be. I disappoint them, but I think honesty's better.

"I'd rather know the real person than some slick marketing ideal. I feel a little uncomfortable when fans get so excited when I say something to them. Like, guys, I'm just a person, calm down please!

"But if I keep it up, if I talk to them enough, I'll start to be real. They'll stop seeing the shadow, the idea of me, and see the real me instead.

"It's better to deal with the real thing than the dream. Always."

Later in the conversation, Cherry returns to the topic of the song 'Limp,' from the first album, the song inspired by the film *Heathers*. She and Tash shared an adolescent obsession with the film.

"The thing you have to understand about how me and Tash grew up is that Cobweb was... was just *there*.

"We once decided that the best way to explain it is with Harry Potter and his lightning-bolt scar. Or maybe like someone with serious burns on their arms, like Jo. Something that's a part of who you are, that basically everyone you meet knows about you. You can't shake it off, so you have to just acknowledge it and cope with it and get on with life.

"For us, saying 'Cobweb' is kind of like saying 'Voldemort'

is for Harry Potter. Everyone else gasps and looks uneasy, but you don't get that luxury. You're the one who has to live with the reality of it, not just the boogeyman idea. And so you never learn to romanticize it. It never gains power as a concept for you, the way it does for other people. It remains exactly what it is. No more and no less.

"So yes, we watched *Heathers*. And even *Natural Born Killers*. I think Tarantino's written much better movies than *Natural Born Killers*, to be honest. I like *Inglourious Basterds* the best. Excellent use of David Bowie on the soundtrack. God, when *RPM* compared our first album to Bowie, I was in definite danger of an aneurysm. Oh, wait, I have the best idea."

She loads Twitter again. *Anyone in Adelaide who has a copy of* Inglourious Basterds *want to lend it to me in my time of plague? #HUSH*

"Clearly, I know how to live the rock star life," she remarks wryly, and sips her tea again.

ELLA

Dear Tash,

I wonder what you made of the fact that you were alive when all the rest of our family wasn't. Did you think I did it to punish you?

I hope Darcy disabused you of that idea, at least. I hope he was there for you and made you see that I left the two of you alive because even if I burned the whole world, I didn't want to burn you. Someone had to remember me. Someone had to remember that there was an Ella before there was an *ellavrenna*.

Darcy... why did I let Darcy live? After all of it, after our shitty breakup, after his parents tattling to the school about the website Chris and I made, after he told all his friends that I was a necrophiliac and a nymphomaniac and made him lie in ice before we fucked so he'd be cold and clammy as a corpse... after all that. After all of it, why did I let him live?

He's told his side of it a hundred times, in documentaries and in magazines and in books. (He has become an expert at talking about me. I guess you all have.) Nobody will ever read this, but I am going to write it down anyway. Because no matter how much of an expert he is, he'll never know why I let him live. And maybe I'll never know for sure either, but my idea about it is closer to the truth than anyone else's. I am the only one inside my head.

I was walking through the parking lot. The gun on my hip still smelled like fireworks from when I'd shot Mom and Dad and Dody. My coat itched a little at my collar, because my T-shirt's neckline was lower than the shirt I'd worn when I tried on the coat at the store. That was the only variable I hadn't planned for. The only thing that went wrong that whole day. The back of my neck itched.

Darcy was smoking by one of the fire doors in the back of the building. We'd been talking a little. Not really back to being friends like we'd been before we tried dating, but we were talking a little. Enough to say 'Hi," or "How's it going?," or in this case "We had a pop quiz in History."

I shrugged. My itchy coat was heavy on my shoulders. My gun smelled like the Fourth of July, like sparklers, like kids playing cowboys with pistols full of caps. "Doesn't matter."

"I know we're about to graduate, El, but they can still suspend you if you're truant all the time."

He ground the butt of his cigarette under his boot, and I decided that he shouldn't die. He shouldn't be one of the ones who died that day. Because he had nice boots, maybe. Or because he still called me El even after I'd made a website that listed all the ways I wanted him to die. Or because I didn't want you to be alone in remembering me. I wanted someone else to help you carry that.

"Go home, Darcy. Get out of here. We're square, okay?" I said. He looked confused, asked what I meant.

"Just go," I said again, and I don't know why he did. I don't know why he listened. I don't know if he guessed, or if he suspected, or if he thought I was just being an asshole, and he was sick of me and wanted to get away from where I was. I don't know.

But he went, and now there's two of you who remember me. Someone once said that three can keep a secret if two are dead. I wonder if three people can keep a not-secret if two are alive?

If not, I guess I'm nothing more than *ellavrenna*, now.

xx
E.

AMY

Eventually, we reached the city. The light was fading again, and clouds were rolling in to threaten rain. Paul dropped us at the central railway station since we didn't know where else to direct him and gave us a jolly wave in farewell as we climbed out of his truck. I'd never known how friendly people could be before I travelled with Sally. She was much better at conversation than I'd ever learned the trick for.

"I don't want to barge in on the folk I know right at dinner time," Sally explained. "I'll go in the morning. We don't have to stay long — just a couple of days, so I can help with anything they've need of extra hands for."

Sydney is oldest of all the country's cities and, as such, home to more dark crannies than most places. I could amuse myself for a year without repeating a single outing. "That's fine." I glanced around at the streets of Sydney. "Looks like the Rainbow Snake was wriggling a lot here, doesn't it? So many hills."

We ended up wandering along to the Australian Hall building as the lamps around us came on and the traffic swelled with workers heading home. I'd forgotten the way a city could swallow everyone down into a single seething crowd. I missed the solitude of the open land.

I have never been a creature of foresight or planning, and so I have always had a tendency to dismiss fears related to potential future problems as irrelevant. But I couldn't shake a thin sharp sense of worry that Richard might manage to catch up with me again. No matter how carefully I covered my trail, there was always a chance that he'd be able to track me. My pulse fluttered a little faster than usual, tension knotting up my spine.

I shook the feeling off as best I could and looked around us.

Fourteen years before we stood there, uncomfortable from long hours in Paul's truck and hungry for a bite and a bed, a crowd of a hundred had gathered in that hall and declared a Day of Mourning for all that the white settlers had taken from them . As far as I could see, the battle had a long way left to go before it would be done. But every fight needs a first shot.

"I don't feel black," Sally mused to herself, inspecting the outline of the Hall against the sky as if there were answers hiding in that shape. "Or white. I don't feel Irish or Murri or anything."

"Do you have to? Can't you be yourself, without any people or country to belong to?"

She made a face. "I dunno. That'd be lonely."

"Free," I countered, my voice firm.

"You're a queer one, you know that?" Sally smiled, putting affection in the words.

"I'm a lot of things," I answered, linking my arm in hers. "Come on, let's go find a church that's serving soup to the starving."

We found one in no time. The menu for the night was gamy ham and very stale dinner rolls, but we didn't care. As we sat eating, a hard jab poked me in the shoulder. I turned, cursing myself for letting the weight of a meal in my belly throw me off my guard.

He was tanned and freckled, hair darker and finer than mine. We had the same eyes, but his smile wasn't much at all like my mouth has sometimes looked. My brother was much less interested in appearing unremarkable. He never made any effort to hide the sardonic curl, the vicious bitterness behind his gleaming teeth.

I was speechless, time stretching out until the moment felt eternal.

I knew he was somewhere in the country; the only other one of my family apart from me to choose this land as home. But I never expected our paths would cross, especially not with the persistent Richard-wasp buzzing at the edges of our lives.

Stay quiet, stay apart, stay alone. That was how my family survived. But seeing him again pulled all those vital defences down.

"Blackbird," I managed, my throat dry. I swallowed, and tried again. "Caim, what are you..."

"Nice to see you too, little sister," he interrupted, giving me another smile that was as honest as a blade. Caim was born with a trickster's grin, and the expression had only grown in nuance over time. The only other member of our family who ever looked as dangerous and charming as Caim was Murmur.

I climbed over the bench that lined one side of the church's long makeshift table and hugged him. He smelled like the ocean, like cove caves where water rests in the dark through low tides. It wasn't a particularly human scent. It made me homesick.

He chuckled, patting me on the back with one graceful hand. "The climate's been good to you. I never thought you'd embrace me by choice, much less out of sentimental impulse."

"Shut up," I snapped, clinging tighter for a moment before releasing him.

He laughed again. His laugh reminded me of the sound of birds in the early morning.

"I've missed the poetry you bring to every conversation, Amy."

"I thought you were on the Western coast," I said, ignoring the tease.

"I was. Got bored," he answered, turning to beckon someone over. "This is Anabel."

She had light brown hair that curled against her cheeks and eyes that might have been a pretty grey-blue if there'd hadn't been such misery behind the surface. She made me think of an abandoned doll, beautiful and glazed and shot through with hairline cracks threatening to make her whole form crumble in.

She was about six months pregnant, the waist of her dress stretched as far as it would go.

I hoped and hoped that Sally's instincts would keep her sitting and out of Caim's notice. She was entangled enough just by knowing me, and I have never had the same talent for trouble that my brother has always possessed.

The trouble with not believing in wishes, however, is how rarely your wishes will come true thereafter. Sally stood up and turned to join us.

"Hi," she said, holding out a hand.

Caim took her hand in his and shook it. "An artist?" he asked, gaze flickering to me for a split-second. I couldn't read the expression on his face. "I can feel the pencil-calluses."

Sally nodded, still uncharacteristically wary in her stance. She could draw a story out of anyone we met but seemed to know enough to feel skittish around my brother. If only she'd had the sense to feel that about me when we'd first met and kept herself out of the mess of trouble my family always brought along with us.

"I suppose we all get that itch, the creative instinct, when we hit a certain age," Caim said slyly with a tiny nod at Anabel's belly. I knew it was a dig at me, at the almost-vanished burn I'd sustained. It wasn't pencil-calluses he'd felt at all; it was the little fire of inspiration I'd left burning in her heart without meaning to. "Some of us use lead and paper, and some go straight for flesh."

He winked, which was uncharacteristically blatant for him as far as gestures went. It must have been especially important to him to make Sally and I feel as grimy and uncomfortable as possible in his presence. Caim never missed a chance to gain the upper hand, if he thought it was there for the taking.

In less than a heartbeat, Sally's hand had snapped back and struck his cheek, hard. It was comical to see the bright hazel of his eyes darken in surprise. Anabel shrank back, afraid at the sudden violence.

"You can go to hell," Sally spat.

Something strange and proud rose up in me; I didn't have a name for it then.

"Blackbird." My warning was sharp, bitten off by the click of my teeth. All around us, the dining hall went on, disregarding us completely. We were hardly the first urchins to get in a scrap there, I'm sure.

"Haven't you heard?" Caim asked Sally, cruel-edged smile blooming back into place on his mouth. "Hell's empty, and all the devils are here."

"Yeah, I did Shakespeare at school too," Sally spat, a sneer of her own on her face. "So fuck off."

"Stop," I cut them off before Caim could counter. "Caim, I'll meet you tomorrow, all right? At the central railway station at nine."

He gave Sally a final look, then took one of Anabel's thin hands in his own and moved to walk away. "Fine. See you then, little sister."

Sally and I had no appetite after that, so we went to wait outside under the stars until the church started making up beds for transients. I tried to think of something to say, some way to take back Caim's words on his behalf.

Before I thought of anything, Sally spoke. "Your

brother's a boofhead."

Laughter bubbled up in me. "Yeah." I stared up at the sky. The stars were telling stories I didn't care to hear, futures I'd rather leave unknown. "I didn't know you knew Shakespeare."

"Yeah. They did the big stuff young, 'cause they knew most of us would end up leaving soon as we were needed on our farms. We did a bunch of the plays when I was twelve. My teacher was a right bitch. I used to get the cane for everything you can think of. Once she gave me three stripes across my palm for coming to school with a black eye, if you'll credit it. Between Dad at home and her at school, I was just about ready to do bloody murder on someone." Her words were without malice, but a little sadness crept in. She sighed. "Always liked *The Tempest* best. Guess that's why I got so riled when your brother went and threw it at me like that."

I put my hand on her arm, feeling how fast her heart still raced. "Don't let him take it away from you."

Her other hand came down on mine, still resting on her arm. "Ain't the kind of thing anyone can own, really, is it?"

I squeezed her arm, once, then slipped my hand from where she held it close.

"Most things aren't," I answered.

ELLA

Dear Tash,

Except for characters in books, people mostly don't remember the exact details of the vital moments in their lives. When the event happens, they don't know it's going to be important — foresight is very fucking far from 20/20 — and so they don't memorize the tiny facets of the moment that would allow it to be conjured back to life and replayed later.

But we knew. We were babysitting you. It was late and you'd gone to bed already. You'd demanded that Chris be the one to read you your bedtime story. Dean's voice was always too weary, and my flat tones didn't have nearly enough inflection for your liking. So Chris read to you. I think the book was *Min-Min Lights*, but I don't remember that for certain. I wasn't in the room.

After Chris read to you and you were asleep, we watched *Event Horizon* because we all loved the gnarly, gory nihilism of it. Hell in motion. When the video was finished and rewound and back in the box (we hated wasting our meager money on late fees), Chris went down on Dean. Dean played with my tits and then jerked off on Chris's back while Chris fucked me because Dean always got off hardest just touching himself and watching. Chris and I made a game of seeing who could make the other come first. I almost always won because even freaks like him are totally slutty if they're teenage boys. I won that time and told him his payment was to do my History of Government homework.

We ordered a pizza because I got my allowance early, and I got extra on account of babysitting you. Dean and I let Chris pick the toppings because he was the pickiest, and we always figured that pizza was kind of like horror movies — even shitty ones were great if you were drunk or stoned or happy enough. We got drunk a lot, stoned less. We didn't pay attention to it much, but we knew that we were almost never happy. We were so unhappy.

Seemed like there were open wounds on all our chests that only the three of us could see. That's how we knew we loved each other. Love is being able to see the invisible blood. To put your palm on the pulse of it and stand there eye to eye.

After we ate the pizza and Dean and I ragged on Chris for a while because his voice was all hoarse and fucked-out from the blowjob, we watched *Natural Born Killers* for a while but got worried that you'd wake up and get exposed to gratuitous violence and adult themes. So we stopped the video and flicked around the different shows that were on TV. I remember that we were watching music videos when I got the idea. Madonna's video was on. One of the really early ones. 'Holiday.'

I was picking at the slivers of cheese clinging to a crust of pizza on my plate, and Chris and Dean were talking about the new *Doom* level that Chris was designing and how fucking awesome it would be to have that as a job, to design games for a living.

I tried to imagine Chris as an adult, grown up, making games and maybe married and maybe having kids and a house and all that shit, that grown-up responsible mature boring shit. He wouldn't blow Dean or fuck me or eat pizza or anything else ever again. He wouldn't even want to or miss it, and neither would me or Dean because we'd be just the same; we'd be adults and wouldn't remember. It would be gone, and when our own teenage kids were hurting or happy and fucking *feeling*, we'd do just like every other grown-up always did to us and smile indulgently and say something patronizing about how everything was always the end of the world to kids.

And I couldn't bear it, I couldn't. Becoming that. I'd rather have been dead.

I put down the pizza crust and said, "We should go Mickey and Mallory on the school"

They were so beautiful in that moment as they looked at me. The moment they nodded and agreed. Tied their fates to mine. I never thought I could love anything as much as I loved them both in that moment, their eyes bright and their bodies trembling with fear and excitement.

Dean fucked me while he jerked off Chris with one shaking hand, and I came so hard and fast that Chris made me do my own homework for History of Government after all. We watched *The Blues Brothers*, and we were all so quiet that you never woke up, not once. That's why Mom and Dad paid me as much as they did for looking after you; I was so good at it and so careful.

xE

Dear Tash,

Jacqui's grandmother and grandfather were one of those couples who were in love almost from when they were born. It was magnetic, lightning-struck metal in their bones. The orbit of the Earth isn't something that you question. Me and Dean and Chris were like that, so I speak from experience. And from talking to Nicolas.

So there was Nell and David, Jacqui's grandparents, and they were destined for each other. And there was Nicky who was different. But all of them were family, in a way beyond blood. Beyond even love. Family is a different thing altogether.

But maybe you know more about that subject than I do in the end.

I wish I could tell you that even though he died young, Nicky had a love of his life, or at least that he got laid a whole damn lot. Truth is that most of the sex he had in his short, shitty life was in cramped, furtive shards of time, cracked brittle little stolen moments with other young, terrified, and horny soldiers. Nicky had beautiful hands, you see. Graceful fingers. It was what gave him his musical talent, and it's what made him an object of affection and convenience for those even slightly so inclined. His lovely clever hands, his gasping wanting mouth. You want so much from life when you can feel the unfathomable looming of death just beyond the periphery of your vision.

I don't know why I'm even fucking writing any of this. I don't want to tell you about war, and I don't want to tell you about Hell. I don't want to fucking talk about any of it, and I don't want to tell you about violent girls and killer women and dead children and guns and knives and how you were there the first time we set off one of our little homemade shrapnel grenades with nails and bits of junk shoved into a casing along with gunpowder and then a fuse coming out. You thought it was fireworks, even when it ripped the leaves of the trees in the yard to shreds and tatters. You thought we'd made fireworks, and you laughed and clapped your hands.

xe

Dear Tash,

A bunch of the theater kids all planned this big trip together to go see *The Matrix*. They bought tickets in advance and everything. They were going on a Saturday. That Saturday was after the date we'd picked for Cobweb, but Dean bought a ticket anyway. When Chris and I asked him why he did that since he knew he'd be dead by then, Dean just shrugged. Why not? What difference did it make? Chris and I didn't like that. Something about it made us uneasy. Like maybe Dean's heart wasn't in this. Like a part of him was still thinking of Saturdays and movies and shit in the future even though we knew exactly when the future was going to stop.

Dean and Chris fought about everything around that time. They both did heaps of work in the school computer lab because they were such fucking nerds, and the teacher in charge thought they were great and was nice to them. Not many teachers bothered being nice to us. But then Dean broke a disk by accident that had some of Chris's stuff on it, and Chris went fucking crazy screaming at him and calling him all sorts of nasty shit. It was pretty bad.

In a climate like that, Dean buying the ticket made me feel shitty as hell. What chance did we have if not even impending death could keep us from drifting apart?

Cobweb was our only hope.

xE

CHARLOTTE

From Reign in Hell: Two Weeks in the Life of HUSH, by Charlotte Waterhouse, Amplify Press, Australia, 2011:

The band returns triumphant after their Adelaide show, crashing into Cherry's room in a tumult of noise and color. Tash, grumbling with disgust about how sweaty she is, peels off her shirt and tosses it aside. Ben raids the minibar, tossing a bottle of chilled green tea over Tash's head to Jacqui. She catches it awkwardly, hitting Gabe in the face with the back of her hand, but he just rubs at the red mark blooming on his cheek and laughs at her clumsiness.

Cherry props herself up in bed and interrogates them on the strengths and weaknesses of the show. She demands to know if Gabe treated her guitars with due respect.

Jacqui deposits a canvas bag on Cherry's legs. "A gift from one of the kids at the show. She texted her mom during the set and had her mom bring it to the venue, then gave it to us at the backstage door."

There is a stack of eight DVD cases inside the bag along with a hastily scribbled note telling Cherry to get well soon. The letter goes on to say the fan loves the band very much and that the movies can be mailed back to her at the enclosed address.

"People are so awesome," Cherry says, the delight obvious on her face. "If I'm not violently contagious and halfway dead tomorrow, I'm going over to this girl's house before we go to the airport."

"With self-preservation skills like that, how do you ever

end up sick?" Tash asks with a roll of her eyes. She shoves Cherry's legs aside to sit on the bed and shuffles through the DVDs.

After considerable debate — the squabble is all the more remarkable for how harmonious the band's interactions typically are — they finally agree on David Fincher's *The Social Network*. As soon as they make the choice, Ben declares that he's going out to get them pizza. He asks me if I want to come along for the walk.

Adelaide at night, like the Brisbane of my childhood, is so quiet and still that it barely feels like a city at all. There's no sense of cohesion between the individual lives being played out by its residents, no shared identity as citizens of the place where they live. When I was a child, I thought the fact that I didn't feel like I belonged in Brisbane was a flaw in me. Later, when I grew up and ran away, I began to understand that wasn't the case at all. There hadn't been anything for me to belong *to*, there.

"I knew they'd pick that one," Ben says as we walk toward a late-night pizza place. "The movie, I mean. Right now they're all debating what the best part is: Tash is saying the music is the best, Cherry likes the dialogue, and Jo's arguing that the best thing about the movie is the character's ruthlessness and ability to stay true to what they know is right, even if they're just kids and the people with the power say they're stupid and wrong. Jacqui and Gabe are probably reading comics and not even paying attention."

Before I can ask him why he didn't want to stay and watch the movie as well, we find the restaurant. Compared to the darkened, shut-up stores on the block on either side of it, the well-lit little shop, worn though it may be, is very inviting.

"I legitimately could not name a single smell that's more inviting after midnight in an unfamiliar town than a pizza place," Ben says as we head inside. He orders two large pizzas — one with mushrooms, one without — and a can of ginger ale, which he drinks immediately.

"Ginger settles the stomach. Helps me when we're travelling so much," Ben explains.

The restaurant is mostly empty. The only movement comes from a broken television frozen on the jumpy image of a man holding a fish hooked to his line. Without warning, the sound comes on, juxtaposing a commentary about stock market movements with the picture of the fish.

"I don't stick around when there's a movie that upsets me on TV," Ben says as we sit down to wait for the order, answering my unasked question. "When I was a kid, I couldn't be in the house during the part of *The Neverending Story* where the horse drowns. I'd make my dad take me out in the car and drive me around the block. I wasn't satisfied just to turn it off or fast-forward it; I needed to be away."

It's the sort of small, sweet story that the children of loving parents can tell. To hear it from someone who was thrown out of his home is disquieting. How could a loving parent do something like that? Or, perhaps more to the point, how could a love like that prove to be so conditional?

Ben draws his foot up onto the seat, resting his chin on his knee and playing idly with the frayed cuff of his jeans. "Sometimes I feel like maybe that's why he threw me out."

I'd ask him what he means, but the pause after the words is clearly that of Ben collecting his thoughts, not an end to the statement.

" Or... no. Not exactly. I think maybe I deserved to be thrown out because if I run away from things that suck, why shouldn't my dad do the same when I turned out to be a fag? There wasn't any obligation to stick around for the bad parts, get it?"

He sighs and shakes his head. "But I'm okay with what

happened now. Gabe's always trying to make me, like, hate my dad. But that's Gabe's shit, not mine. I don't hate my dad.

"It'd probably be easier if I did hate him. You can't feel abandoned by somebody you hate. You can't feel betrayed. You can't feel like it was your fault, your failing. If I hated him, I wouldn't care that he didn't love me as much as I loved him. I wouldn't care that I needed him more than he needed me."

Ben rubs his thumb across the ink on his wrist, tracing the lines of the tattoo with the edge of his thumbnail. He repeats the small movement throughout the rest of the conversation.

"Things worked out for the best in the end. I got Jacq and Lena and David as my family. I got the band. I got this whole life that's perfect for me. I might never have even dreamed of this life if I hadn't been thrown out and forced to find it for myself. I'm sad it happened the way it happened, but I'm not sorry it happened. Does that make sense?"

I nod.

Ben smiles.

"Cool. I love it when I make sense. Doesn't happen very often," he says jokingly, not halting his chatter for long enough that I can get in a contradiction. "Anyway, that's why I came out on the pizza run. Because I can't cope with movies that make me sad.

"My boyfriend's used to getting phone calls from me whenever we're on the road, and I'm hiding out in my bunk in the back of the bus. The others are all watching *Dancer in the Dark* or *Moulin Rouge* or *Pan's Labyrinth* or something like that. I can't exactly run away when I'm stuck on a tour bus. He talks random crap at me until the movie's over.

"Back there in the hotel room, I couldn't exactly lock

myself in the bathroom and call him because it's only about seven in the morning in LA right now."

Speculation has been circulating in the music press for several months that Ben is dating Louis Kupanaha of the straight edge hardcore band Trace Mutinies. I ask him if he's willing to comment on the rumors.

He rolls his eyes. "I can't believe anyone gives a shit about who people in bands are dating. Cherry and I bitch about this all the time. Just because she and Andrew are both public figures, people think that makes their relationship public, too.

"It's like, if I don't say something, I'm being coy, though, you know? That's just as bad, in a way, because it makes the secrecy a big deal. So yeah, okay, I'll say it. Lou and I are together. And that's all I'm saying about it."

Ben snorts with quiet, wry laughter all of a sudden. "When we go back to the hotel I'll give him a call — it'll be late enough by then — and tell him we should change our Facebook relationship statuses. He's addicted to the internet, so it'll make him really happy to announce it that way. Plus, it's a good antidote to getting bummed out over the sad stuff in the movie we just ran away from. Adding a little bit of love back to the social network."

He finishes his cola and tosses the can. He rests his chin on the knee of his jeans again, face in a slightly weary, thoughtful set.

"Do you think, with something like Facebook, it's like blaming the school, or like blaming the gun, or like blaming the album on the kid's CD player? Does it fit into the same category as any of those things?"

"With rampage shootings?" I ask. He nods, sitting a little straighter as he warms to his argument.

"Yeah. Because, if blaming Facebook is like blaming the school where a shooting happened, then you're looking at social networking as a cultural framework for the interactions between people. Being at school means you interact a particular way with the people around you, and the same's true online. The context of the interaction always alters the interaction, even if only slightly.

"And putting tighter controls on the bullying and dangerous behavior that goes on may well have an impact on the amount of bad shit that happens, but it's not going to go away completely. Nothing can make bad shit go away completely, trust me. I've seen enough of it to know. You can't stop people from being people."

"Or," Ben goes on, "some people choose to say that Facebook is like a gun. It's the tool that enables the violence to happen. They say 'Facebook doesn't kill people, people kill people,' same as they do about guns. And yet, there are a lot of very valid, very sane, arguments in favor of gun control. Semi-automatic weapons don't have any practical application in daily civilian life even if you're a hunter or a farmer. And look how quickly and quietly you Australians managed to adjust your laws after the Port Arthur Massacre; your quality of life, your freedom, wasn't compromised at all by not being able to kill farmland pests with a machine gun, you know?

"If the people who go on shooting sprees don't have access to guns, they wouldn't be able to go on shooting sprees, right? But then you look at news reports from China about people who can't get guns. When they snap they take machetes and axes and knives into kindergartens and cause horrific carnage.

"If you take away the tool, some people are just going to find another tool. Yeah, sure, there have been a bunch of people who somehow incorporated Facebook into their crimes, but let's be honest — if they weren't 'Facebook killers,' they'd be 'Twitter killers' or 'Tumblr killers' or whatever other social networks there were.

"Then, you know, they say an album can be a contributing

factor when it comes to violence. That's a cultural influence rather than a tool. I guess that's the problem I struggle with most: how much bad am I willing to risk in order to let the good happen? Because music can be such a huge, positive, life-changing, inspiring thing. It can do so much good in so many lives Does that good outweigh whatever evil or tragedy it might cause?

"I feel like it's the same kind of thing with Facebook. There've been a bunch of murders all over the world because of Facebook. The most infamous deaths are probably the ones from that Colombian 'death list' that got posted, along with the warning for the kids to get out of town or die. Nobody paid any attention, and they started dying.

"But see, that all happened because they were tied up with this big criminal organization that has a lot of power in Colombia, FARC. Facebook didn't kill those people; FARC did. And Facebook's also been used by groups organizing against and protesting FARC—those groups had marches all over the world with like 12 million people standing against the tyranny.

"If the murders are 'Facebook murders,' then we also have to acknowledge 'Facebook revolutions' like in Libya and Egypt, where important and positive things happen because of the platform.

"Social networking is a huge amount of good with a little portion of evil. I guess everyone has to decide for themselves if they think the scales balance."

CAROLINE

Transcript of *Australian Story: Caroline Gubura*, ABC TV, July 2006:

Caroline [v.o]: Some days are bad, of course. That's what everyone always asks me when they first hear where I work.

[Footage of Caroline with several students, working on a bar-graph diagram together on a white board]

Caroline [v.o]: "You work at the Flexible School?! How do you handle it?!?" Like they think I'm taming lions all day!

[Footage of the class gathered under a tree in Brisbane's Albert Park, hanging out and chatting. Some of the students are smoking, others are pregnant. Several are clearly homeless, and of those, some have the haggard, dart-eyed look of hard drug users. Caroline is handing out wrapped sandwiches to those who approach her.]

Caroline [v.o]: But honestly, there's nothing about any of these kids that's any different from the kids in mainstream high schools, except that mainstream high schools have let them down. They're not evil or difficult, no more so than other teenagers. I was no different to them when I was a kid — I ran away from home at fourteen. I was homeless for years. Doesn't mean I magically stopped being a kid, just because I had it rough.

[Footage of Caroline demonstrating long division to the class]

Caroline [v.o]: People seem to... people seem to think that writing a book that kids love lets me off the hook. Like that's *enough*, so I don't need to be doing this work with these kids.

[Footage of Caroline and a scruffy, punky looking young girl with a bruised face painting a mural on the side of the school building with aerosol cans. The pair laughs together.]

Caroline [v.o]: But I was just the same. There were people... I was lucky. I was given a chance. I want to do the same for other kids now.

[Footage of the class, heads bowed over their exercise books, at work on an assignment.]

Caroline [v.o]: I do it because one of them will be the one who writes the next *Min-Min Lights*. And what kind of Australian literary icon would I be if I didn't nurture that?

[Cut to a kindergarten classroom at a standard state school. The teacher is reading to a circle of tiny students. Copies of Mem Fox's *Possum Magic* and Shaun Tan's *The Red Tree* are piled neatly on the floor beside the teacher. She is reading from *Min-Min Lights*.]

SALLY

After bad dreams I wake up tired. My teeth feel slick, my head aches. Amy's awake already, a bright shape of cheery cotton and warm skin sitting cross-legged on the bedroll beside mine. She offers me a limp-looking sandwich.

Ham. I chew, swallow, gag.

"Awful, aren't they?" she says cheerfully, her face all lit up with happiness. Kinda makes me wish I had someone out there to run into unexpectedly. Though if that someone turned out anything like Amy's brother, I'm better off without.

The thing that really bothered me wasn't that tosser — I've known his type before, all smirks and better-than-yous just because he's a bloke, no other reason — but the girl tagging around with him. I've been up and down the country more than a couple of times these last years, and I've seen her in a dozen faces and a dozen stories.

She gets herself a fella because she wants a fella, but then she gets the notion in her head that she wants to stay close to him even after the lightning's done sparking in her thighs. It's dumb, but no crime. Girl like that, on her own, doesn't have to worry about her dad laying down the strap to teach her not to fall in love.

Then she isn't careful, doesn't keep one eye on the calendar. Gets herself in trouble. Starts drinking to distract her brain from how fast she's losing grip and doesn't think about how it might make her baby simple. A man like Caim'll start striking her after a kid like that's out, if he's not already now. She'll be more careful with the next one and the one after. Give him kids he can love, so he'll stay.

It's easy for me to see why Mum liked fairy tales so much. There aren't too many real stories with a happily ever after at the end.

Amy's giving me another of her needle-looks, like she can break my thoughts open like an egg yolk. I shake thoughts of Caim's grog-dumb girl Anabel out of my head and try to bite the sandwich again.

"You were storytelling," Amy says, "Weren't you? In your head."

I shrug and give up on eating. "Suppose. Just thinking about your brother's girl. I feel sorry for her."

Amy's sunburn-pink forehead crinkles in confusion. "Why? She looked happy."

She's such a funny duck. Even after days and miles in her company, I can't choose whether she's dear or infuriating. It's like she learned how to be a person from a book that was missing the end of every chapter.

"Couldn't you see her eyes? Drunk as a lord, baby on the way, trusting that shit of a brother of yours to take care of her. That's no kind of happy I know, not trapped like that."

Blinking wide, just as her brother did when I slapped him, Amy stands up.

I follow, my legs and back aching. The rover's life's not kind to bones.

"Not trapped. She's not. Having no cares, that's freedom," Amy protests. It's too early for a fight, so I don't reply as we leave the church.

"It's sort of sweet — quaint — that they still open it up for drifters," I say as we make it out the big front doors. "Like they missed the announcement that most churches treat kids like us like dirt these days, 'specially in a place like Sydney. It's so hard and bright here. Everyone's always on a hustle."

Amy's not listening; her eyes are on a skinny marmalade stray winding its way along the wrought iron fence dividing courtyard from footpath. Its short tail kinks at a permanent sharp angle. She plucks the uneaten ham sandwich from my hands and crouches down, clicking her tongue to draw it close.

Yellow eyes wary, the cat edges near enough to bite at the thin pink filling. Amy lets it take its prize and stays crouched, watching it tear and gulp.

"Cats need meat," Amy says. The stray gobbles the slice of salty flesh. "Did you know that? Dogs can survive on other things. They manage. But cats just die without it. They can't help it."

My mother used to talk about her cat that she'd had before she got married. She said she'd loved it and that it made her happy, but all I'd remember later were her tales of unwanted kittens and a sack to drown them in. I used to have nightmares about it, about their faces down in the dark water, baby eyes glued shut forever.

I walk with Amy back to the train station where she's to meet her brother, and then I part with a coin to get a ticket out to where the Mellens live.

Against one of the morning-damp brick walls, bundled in a ragged blanket, an Aboriginal woman is begging. Her face is uneven, the flesh looking waxy and inflexible on half of it. She's had fits and lost the movement, I think.

I'm down to nearly nothing in my purse-pouch, just as always, but I look at her, and I see who my mother could have been, who my grandmother might have been, who I still might be. Is that bad? To only care about someone's pain when you can imagine it as your own?

A penny's not much to part with. I put it in her palm, and she repays me with a grin. Her teeth are broken and missing, a smile of gaps. My tongue finds the missing spots near the back of my own mouth.

"I'll give ya a story, eh?" she offers. The dead side of her face makes the words slur together. There's still a while before my train, so I nod.

"*The moon makes the girl babies. Lizard makes the boys, and sometimes tries to steal the girl babies to turn into boys. The moon stops him. Sometimes, when the moon is late coming up, it's because girl babies take longer to make,*" the woman tells me, in a quiet voice like it's a secret. "*Crow makes girl babies, too. The girls that Crow makes are stubborn and don't make good wives. Crow wants to wake up the dead instead of making new babies, but the moon says no.*

"*The moon doesn't let the dead back in, 'cept for children. Dead children can go back to their mothers again or choose someone who was kind to them to be their mother this time. If the dead children don't remember their mother, they hide in a coolabah tree until a woman walks underneath.*"

When she's finished, I thank her and leave her be. Further down the platform, I get out my sketchbook and begin to make another face. It doesn't frighten me as much anymore how easy lines and curves have become. It's not like it'll go away just because I'm afraid of it, so I might as well make the best of the situation.

I draw dark hair, of course. A girl made by Crow should have dark hair. And a strong jaw, too. Black clothing, a long sweeping coat. It almost looks like a cloak, furling out behind her in the wind. A gun-shape almost invisible beneath the bulk of her coat. Boots, sturdy as the ones Amy wears.

It's the first full figure I've tried without a reference, and she stares out from the paper with such a look to her that I'm almost convinced she can see me there on the platform with my frizzy red hair and old clothes.

I've just put the book back in my apple-bag and am

about to stand up when Amy steps beside me.

"I've got hours yet until he'll be here," she says. "Figure I'll come on the trip out with you and see where you're going. That way I can come out and meet you later when I'm done."

There's a hopeful smile on her face to go with the words. Her smiles never look all that easy, which I think makes them worth a little more when they turn up. I grin back.

"All right."

I met the Mellens on my first trip through Sydney. Their eldest girl, Maggie, was trying to nick an orange from a fruit cart and was about ten seconds away from getting caught at it, so I made myself a distraction by asking the vendor about tomatoes. Maggie caught up with me two streets later and brought me home for supper as a thank-you. She's barely ten years old now, but we're good mates. She says she wants to be just like me when she's older. I can only hope she gets enough sense in the meantime to change her mind.

Maggie's got two older brothers, or did have. Bill's gone and got himself dead in Korea, so that just leaves Martin, who's a bit older than me. There were others between Martin and Maggie, but none lived long, so now there's just a gap of years.

After Maggie there're two more, both girls: Brenda, who's seven, and Aster, who must be... strewth... must be almost four now. Sometimes the way time flies frightens me, makes me think about how fast the world is whirling around in the march of days.

Their dad's Jim, and he works at a bank. Their mum's Vicky, and she's got a better smile and a kinder soul than most I've met. It breaks my heart to think she lost Bill before he was more'n twenty.

I heard about Bill from Heck and Joke, who live and work in the shop next door to the Mellens' house. Heck and me write letters sometimes. He sends them to the post offices of the places I say I'm going. Sooner or later I get them.

The world's still waking up when we get to their neighbourhood. There're two corner stores only a few blocks apart — Heck and Joke's, and then the other newer one, with a sign propped out the front with SHOP HERE BEFORE THE DAY GOES written in bold block letters.

"Shop here before the dagos," Amy says aloud, voice dry on the pun. "I thought you said your friends were Greek?"

"One wog's as bad as another, I guess," I suggest.

The store with the sign has a crate of milk, still cold and fresh from the morning cart, waiting on their step. We take a bottle each and gulp down greedily. I take another to give to Vicky, and a little of my anger at the sign goes. Even petty revenges are satisfying in their way.

CHARLOTTE

From Reign in Hell: Two Weeks in the Life of HUSH, by Charlotte Waterhouse, Amplify Press, Australia, 2011:

Cherry has — understandably — never been much for diary-keeping. Instead, she regularly creates collages of images and words, like a very rough version of the zines that are behind the aesthetics of the new album.

She uses 110gsm foolscap sketchbooks and has, over the years since she began, filled "probably forty or fifty, maybe more. It only takes me a month or two to fill them."

Because of the personal nature of the contents, Cherry doesn't let anyone look into her notebooks without carefully selecting what they'll get to see beforehand. For me, she chooses a double page created during the writing and recording of the new album.

Every edge and corner is tiled with photographs of young blonde girls and women. Some are anonymous snapshots, maybe from Cherry's own home album–smiling girls, thoughtful girls, dreamy girls, frowning girls. Cousins and friends.

Stacey is present; her picture was taken before Cherry was born. The young Stacey Reardon is dressed up, smiling a gap-toothed childhood smile in front of a Christmas tree.

The other images in the mix are clipped from magazines and print-outs. Equally young and equally blonde, these faces are more recognizable. Courtney Love, JonBenet Ramsey, Natascha Kampusch.

"She was held captive in a cellar for eight years before she managed to escape," Cherry says of Kampusch. "He beat her with a crowbar and starved her and abused her. She got away. He was making her weed his garden, wearing a short dress and no underpants. Trying to humiliate her. But she ran away. An animal will chew off its leg to get out of a trap. What's a little shame compared to that?

"But a lot of people hate her. Did you know that? They don't know what to make of her because she isn't what they think she should be. She isn't the victim they demand. She's too clever, too sharp.

"That's what these pictures are about. They make me think of this quote from Courtney Love." Cherry touches her fingertips to the picture of Love, as if to call up additional information from within the photo. "About how, for the people who were cruel to her, and to Yoko Ono, and to all the others who are still here despite it all… for those people the nice ending to Hamlet is when Ophelia drowns."

Cherry takes the collage book back from me, paging through the fragments she's collected and arranged. "The world can't stand a heroine who lives. They want the quiet and passive girl. Snow White's *dead*, and that's how she gets a prince. Sleeping Beauty's in a coma.

"Do you think the princes were sad when their silent, still girls woke up?"

ELLA

Dear Tash,

    I guess I have at least one more violent girl to tell you about. Jeanne d'Arc, The Maid of Orleans. Joan of Arc.
    Or just Jo, like she is in the liner notes of your CDs.
    Did you know she only became a saint in 1920? She was burned to death, tied to a stake, in 1431. She was nineteen.
    Her father was in the local watch, and she grew up on a farm. At 12 years old, she'd begun to fathom, just a little, how small and pointless her life was probably going to be, no matter how brilliant her mind. But her brilliance was the rare and crafty kind that knows unshakably that there's always a way to get what you want, no matter what smaller and duller minds might say to the contrary.
    Jo wanted to win wars, to puzzle out tactics on the chessboard of the world and hold a pennant high at the head of legions of her soldiers. She knew that she could do it. She felt as if she had been born to do it.
    So she went to her family and told them that she had seen visions of saints, and at sixteen she convinced her cousin that the saints had demanded that she go to see the king.
    Everyone knows the rest of the story: the battles she won, the plans she made, the way she turned the tide of defeat with her clever blade-sharp brain.
    The witch trial, the bonfire.
    Everyone knows that story. But the part that not everyone knows is that she made up the saints because they

were the excuse that could get her where she needed to be. A girl born on a farm has very few ways to become a figure of potency and power, to capture the hearts and minds of thousands upon thousands.

Getting that kind of attention is extremely difficult but not impossible. Some soldiers returned from the Civil War to live long, successful lives. They married their sweethearts, had dozens of friends, and shocked the undertakers who discovered they had been hiding a female body beneath their clothes all along. And those are just the ones we know about; who knows how many were permitted to take their secret along with them into death?

But Jo didn't do that. Maybe it would have worked, maybe not. Working up through the ranks, a farm boy with little more obvious merit than a farm girl would have had, that would have taken too long. She had no patience for the tried and tested methods of the world. She knew what she could do, and she knew that she could do it *now*.

And she did. She was perfect. She was glorious.

But God has little time for the perfect and the glorious if they aren't afraid.

Pope Callixtus III declared her innocent 25 years after her death. I think a lot of people would be disappointed if they knew the truth, that God didn't consider her innocent at all. I wonder who they'd be disappointed in, God or Jo. Not that it would make any difference.

And so now she's no different from me, just another dead teenage killer in Hell. Or she's playing rock star at her drum kit on Earth and capturing new hearts, new minds. She doesn't have to invent visions of saints anymore. She just has to touch her fingers to the glass of mirrors and grasp her own hand through the barrier.

xxxElla

Dear Tash,

I knew Dean was sad a lot. He was the saddest of the three of us maybe, if you measure sadness in frequency rather than depth. (I think Chris had the sharpest sadness, the deepest pain, though it flared rarely and quickly. And as for me, I felt almost nothing.)

I saw Dean cry sometimes, but not all that often considering he probably cried a lot. He must have done it when he was alone. I didn't like the idea of that. I didn't like the idea that there was a part of him hidden away from me and from Chris.

I remembered seeing him cry once, when he was twelve maybe. He and Chris argued at school — Chris was dating Bridget Hamilton, and Dean didn't like her for some reason. The two of them were alike in lots of ways, and Dean should have been fine with Chris dating whoever. But for some reason, Dean was miserable he and Chris fought. I ended up going back to Dean's place with him after school that day. We had a math exam coming up and needed to study for it.

Instead of studying, Dean went up to his room and went to his closet. Later, years later, we'd hide a shotgun in that closet. That was before we sawed it short and kept it in my drawer instead. Back then the closet mostly had random crap in it, winter coats and sports stuff and cartons of stuffed animals Dean kept even after he outgrew them. He got all those stuffed animals out, dumped them on his bed, kind of burrowed down underneath them, and just stayed under there quietly crying for forty minutes.

I sat at his desk and did my math homework, singing along with the radio and pretending I didn't even know he was in the same room as me. Then, when he was done crying, he washed his face and put the stuffed animals away, and we went downstairs and made peanut butter and jelly sandwiches. After that we watched TV for a while until his mom got home and checked our homework answers for us. I'd done Dean's math homework, too, since it was the same as mine, and it wasn't a big deal for me to write the answers out twice.

The day that Chris was an asshole about the disk, Dean cried then as well. Not in a baby way like he had when he was younger. We were seventeen, almost eighteen. Too old for stuffed animals and sobbing. These were quiet tears, but he blinked a lot so I think they were stinging his eyes. Quiet tears can do that sometimes.

He was crying while we had sex, and he was underneath so the tears slipped down sideways from the corners of his eyes towards his temples. I kissed them because I wanted to see if they tasted the same as my own did. Sort of, they did. Mostly. Everyone tastes like everyone else, and nobody tastes like anybody else. Things can be true and contradictory sometimes.

He tasted like quiet tears and I was on top, which was exhausting. We didn't bother with a condom because Cobweb was soon, and it didn't matter if we gave each other anything, not anymore. There was still a tiny swell of puppy fat on his stomach, soft below his skinny ribs. We would never have the adult bodies we might have grown into. We would never be any older than we were then.

"Everything ends," I told him while he was inside me, while we were stuck together like one mechanism, a clock of two cogs. Tick, tick, squeaky bedsprings and a poster about different kinds of booze above the bed. "Romeo and Juliet. Kurt and Courtney. Hamlet and Ophelia. They all fucking end, Dean. If they don't end one way, they end the other. Do you want us to burn out or fade away?

"Chris'll leave us. You know he will. He'll get a job making games and marry someone just like Bridget Hamilton, and they'll have babies and a house and a car. He'll break your heart and leave you and live happily ever after. That's what happens without Cobweb. Everything ends. But if we do this, if the three of us die together, it'll be like we're together forever. Our names will never get mentioned apart from one another ever again.

"That's why we have to do it, Dean. That's why we need to do Cobweb. Cobweb'll be like killing Bridget Hamilton, even though she moved to Utah back in tenth grade. It's crashing the car and blowing up the house and drowning every single one of the perfect 2.4 children she won't ever have.

"I was fucking Chris yesterday," I told Dean. "And we didn't use a condom. Maybe I've got his kid inside me now, growing like a tumor. Or maybe I'm getting knocked up right now from your cock up inside me. Think about that. When you blow my head off at the end of Cobweb, that'll be like killing all the futures you and Chris were gonna have without each other. I won't ever have to be anyone's mommy; I can just be Ella Vrenna forever. You and Chris will be you and Chris forever, with no fucking bullshit coming between you and fucking it all up.

"Cobweb is our insurance against a future."

We came, almost at the same time, but more and more as I got older, coming didn't even seem like the important part of sex. I liked being together, really together, with Dean and Chris, in a way that only seemed to happen when we were having sex. I didn't even feel it when we were out doing target shooting or planning Cobweb, despite what I said to Dean. Just being with them, skin on skin and breath on breath, was my favorite thing in the world. I loved them both so fucking much.

I was so scared of it ending. I was so scared of the world

intruding, of things coming between us. Of there someday being an end to our little world of three.

Better to burn it than to watch it fade and wither.

Exxx

AMY

On the train ride back into the city, I remembered a saying my mother used to impart when she was in a whimsical mood. This wasn't an especially frequent occurrence, so the small child I'd once been had paid close attention to her words.

My mother, I'd studied because she had required careful study in order for me to catch the nuances of her meanings. My father, I'd studied because each lesson he offered me demanded study, and he expected nothing less that total attention from me. Myself, I'd studied because to be ignorant was to be vulnerable, and I have never been in a position to afford such a luxury.

Elsa, in her English toned and hued with Germany and France and loss, used to say 'Justice was invented by the innocent, mercy by the guilty.'

When I was young, I loved the thought of these things as inventions, as some clockwork mechanism with cogs and pendulums. Justice would have sharp metal teeth lacing together in the spin of the machine while mercy's tick would be a softer, fainter, darker rhythm. The sound of wounds no stitch could spare the scar from.

Elsa had a sister when she was a child. Aimee, for 'beloved.' I'm sure she thought it was a kindness on my father's part when he suggested I should be Amy. We never explained the joke of the coincidence to her.

Justice was invented by the innocent, mercy by the guilty. I sat on the train and wondered at how irrevocably human that shard of wisdom was. I've never liked those words, not since I first learned their meanings — innocence and guilt, as if ignorance and knowledge had anything to do with the capacity for compassion. If I'd been the one to coin the phrase, I'd have chosen different words: Punishment was contrived by the righteous, forgiveness by the imperfect.

Back at the central station, I wandered the platforms in search of some distraction. A beggar sat against a wall, and I could feel the stories swirling around her. I gave her a shilling; I could always find another if I needed one.

This is the story she told me:

> *When the world was young, Emu and Turkey were rivals. Emu was the queen of the birds, and Turkey hated the way Emu would circle gracefully across the sky on her huge, beautiful wings.*
>
> *One day, Turkey thought up a plan. It was a cruel plan, but in her blinding envy, she didn't stop to care.*
>
> *Turkey tucked her wings underneath herself and sat contentedly out in the open where Emu would see.*
>
> *"Hello!" Turkey called as Emu drew near. "Oh, how happy I am! Now I'll be queen of the birds!"*
>
> *"What do you mean?" asked Emu. For Emu was queen of the birds, not Turkey, and did not want that to change.*
>
> *"I have cut off my wings!" Turkey said. "All the common birds have wings, but not I!*

Oh, how happy I am!"

So Emu went back to her nest and cut her wings off with an axe made of stone. Now she would never circle gracefully across the sky on her huge, beautiful wings again.

"But I will still be queen," Emu told herself and decided that was more important.

When she went walking across the plain the next day, however, Emu could see that Turkey still had her wings. And so Emu thought up a revenge she would take for Turkey's cruel trick. It was a terrible revenge, but in her deafening anger, she didn't stop to mind.

Emu hid ten of her babies deep in her nest and took the two fattest and prettiest ones out walking with her on the plain.

"Hello!" Emu called as they walked past Turkey's nest of babies. "Oh, how happy I am! My babies are the biggest and the fattest, and they'll be queen of the birds some day! What a shame it is you have so many babies, Turkey! You'll never find enough food to feed them all like I feed mine! That's why my babies are so big and yours are so small!"

So Turkey led her babies into a dark part of the world and killed them one by one, save for two she spared. Now her dead children would never grow up and laugh and play.

"But my two daughters will be as big as Emu's," Turkey *told herself and decided that that was more important.*

But when she went walking across the plain the next day, however, Turkey could see that Emu's babies were all alive and happy. And then Turkey knew that every trick they played would be worse than those that had come before until there was nothing left. Some say they are still playing tricks, and some day their fight will get so bad that all the world will die from it. And this is why Turkey lays only two eggs, and Emu cannot fly.

Caim had swapped his absurd ragged-prince costume for an ordinary shirt and trousers for our meeting. I was wearing the third of the three dresses I carried, a red shift patterned with small flowers, and my boots. I kept the cat-carving in my pocket.

We looked like any other pair in a crowd. I didn't hug him this time. He'd only be unkind about it if I tried. We set off together to find somewhere darker, out of the haze of the city's early smoke.

CHARLOTTE

From *Reign in Hell: Two Weeks in the Life of HUSH*, by Charlotte Waterhouse, Amplify Press, Australia, 2011:

On the way to Brisbane, the band's flight is delayed by hours. Tash handles this setback with less grace than her travelling companions, quickly growing bored with the selection of games on her phone and demanding that I come along for company while she explores the shopping options in the terminal.

She buys a giant coffee, despite her already keyed-up mood, and doesn't temper it with milk or sugar.

"I've got an iron-clad stomach," she says, a bitter edge to her smile. "These days."

It's common knowledge that, on the morning of the Cobweb Massacre, Ella Vrenna gave her baby sister a cup of mustard water and demanded that she drink it all.

Tash immediately became violently ill, and Ella convinced their mother to keep Tash home from school for the day with a babysitter.

"Of course I knew something was wrong," snaps Tash, her voice scathing. "I was six, not *stupid*. Ella was nine years older than I was, but she was my best friend. And she makes me drink a cup of this shit that tastes like poison, and it makes me spew everywhere? Of course I knew something was wrong. Of course I did.

"I had no fucking idea what was coming. None of us did. But I knew she had to have a good reason for making me stay home, so I didn't say anything to Mom about the mustard water.

"Some people hate me for that. Mothers of kids who died have screamed at me that it was my fault because if I'd told Mom, then Ella would have been stopped.

"Which is complete fucking bullshit on a couple of different levels, not to mention a shitty-ass thing to say to a little kid. I don't care how wrenched with grief you are; you don't tell a fucking seven-year-old that it's her fault that forty-eight people are dead. That's fucked up.

"Besides, it wouldn't have made much of a difference if Ella had been taken off the board that morning, 'you know? If I'd ratted her out, the whole rest of her plan still would have played out just the same. She only killed three people directly. So unless that woman who screamed at me was the mom of one of those three, then it doesn't make a difference to her. It doesn't change a thing. Ella set it up so that she was almost secondary once everything started. The whole point of the Cobweb was that there wasn't a single thread for everything to hang or fall by."

Tash's rants commonly fall into a rhythm of this sort, where a note of savage pride creeps into her tone as she speaks of her sister. Forced to grow up in a world that has made the name Ella Vrenna synonymous with the lurking evils in the heartland of the American family, Tash's oftentimes disquieting loyalty to her older sister is the only method she has of salvaging the remnants of that eviscerated institution.

Because of Tash's apparent nausea, the next-door neighbor came around to stay with her while Gregory Vrenna drove his elder daughter to school and his wife, Arlene Vrenna, to work before going on to his own workplace. Only Ella ever reached her destination that morning; she shot both her parents in the backs of their heads at point-blank range when the car pulled up outside her school.

Her only other direct victim, a sophomore named Dody Schillinger, was arriving at the same time and had the misfortune to be within sight as Ella climbed out of her father's car.

"It was such a fucking shitty thing to say," Tash says more than once, still speaking of the stricken parent who blamed her for the atrocities orchestrated by her sister. "It stuck in my head for years, you know? The idea that it was my fault. I was convinced for the longest time that it must be true."

Tash wanders over to the newsagent-bookstore that dominates the scatter of shops, going to the extensive True Crime section.

"Economics, chick lit, and true crime. Why the fuck are these three so over-represented in airport bookstores? I've been in about a zillion of these things, and it's always the same," Tash says as she rearranges several books on the shelves, hiding copies of one title out of view and bringing another forward to prominence.

"I hate that one," she says of the now-obscured book. She tells me she doesn't mind if I disclose what book it is in my own writing; it's Samson Pattison's bestseller *Cobweb*, published ten years to the day after the killings.

"It's so fucking crafty," Tash says with venom in her voice, scowling. "In tiny ways that almost nobody is going to recognize. Like when he recounts the shootings, right, he uses active voice when writing about Ella and passive voice for Chris and Dean. So then by the time he starts declaring shit about how she was a psychopath and they were just poor depressed manipulated schmucks, you find yourself nodding along and seeing his point *because he has manipulated you into it.*"

"How a story gets told changes what the story is. I wish people knew that. I wish it so much."

I find one of the Australian publications in the

section, a compendium of notorious 20th century crimes in this country. Sure enough, there it is, between Lindy Chamberlain and the Port Arthur Massacre: the Lesbian Vampire Murderers.

"That's my father," I tell Tash, pointing to the name of one of the lawyers involved in the criminal trial. "His client was the only one of the girls who didn't go to jail."

She gives me a crooked smile. "I know *that* tone of voice. The *proud-even-though-I-don't-think-I-should-be* voice. My shrink's been living off the fact that I get that tone in this section of book stores since I was six years old."

I give her a crooked smile of my own right back. "I started at seven. That's when Dad did this trial."

"But he wasn't a killer. He was an attorney," she says, sitting down on the carpet of the aisle and gesturing for me to sit beside her.

I do so.

"My dad was my hero," I reply. "I wanted to be a lawyer when I grew up. I loved logic puzzles — you know, that one where you have to get the grain and the chicken and the fox all over the river in the boat, and tangrams, and everything like that. I thought being a lawyer was a grown-up version of that. Solving logic puzzles. When my dad came home from work each evening, I'd sit next to him on the back porch while he smoked and read legal briefs and told me about his cases. Drug lords, murders — he told me all of it, and I gobbled it up.

"Then, when I was seven, he took on the Lesbian Vampire Murderers case. It... the part of it he told me then, the only part I knew until years later, was really only the second and third acts of the whole thing.

"He told me about how this group of girls, these uni students, they lured this older guy into their car. He was drunk. They stabbed him 27 times and cut his head nearly off, and then they drank his blood."

Tash is the first person I've ever told this story to who doesn't recoil at the thought of my father telling the tiny seven-year-old me these grisly details. Her own life contained far worse by that age, after all.

"My dad brainstormed out his whole strategy, sitting there night after night with his daughter, me there in my dressing gown and pink pajamas." I smile at the memory. "His plan was to make the girl, the one he was representing, move back in with her mother. He said that people act differently when they're being taken care of. When they're loved. It makes them softer.

"He made her dress softer, too. So she'd look... well, so she wouldn't look like a Lesbian Vampire Murderer, I guess. So he could point to her in court and instead of a member of a pack of killers, the jury would see a vulnerable girl. A kid who was taken care of and loved. And then my dad could say to the jury that the only reason she'd been there, seduced into hanging with those other, bad girls, was because they'd wanted a backup victim. He told the jury that if the girls hadn't found the drunk man, it would have been her, this soft loved girl, with 27 stab wounds and her head nearly severed.

"They found her not guilty. My dad won the case. But... but I stopped sitting with him on the back porch. I stopped saying that I wanted to be a lawyer when I grew up. And three years later, my father left my mother. I didn't see him again for a long, long time. I still believe it was mostly my fault he left. Because I stopped sitting with him. It must have hurt his feelings when I did that. It wasn't his fault that I didn't understand what being a lawyer really meant."

SALLY

Despair happens in the eyes, it feels like to me, somewhere in the goo between the arch of the bone socket and the little black pupil-dot I peer at the world through. When I'm sad, my eyes ache with it. It makes perfect sense to me that crying is how people show that they're blue.

I'm not crying now. I don't have time to cry. I'm up to my elbows in tepid, greasy water, scrubbing furiously at old smears of food on chipped china plates. I used to think the chips on the rims of these dishes were dear, that wiping them dry with a cloth was the height of simple pleasure. Ordinary, cared-for, battered little plates. Now I want to strike them against the floor and watch them shatter. I want to run my scrubby hands through my hair and pull, and more than everything I want to cry.

I've sent the girls next door to see if they can fetch Heck or Joke, and I've pulled the curtains wide to let as much light in as will come, but the room still feels as dead and dull as it did when I arrived an hour ago. Vicky's curled up in her bed, under blankets like it's winter. Maggie seems to have taken over caring for her sisters, for the most of it. If there was any part of growing up to be like me I wanted to spare the girl from, it's this.

Life on the road's got its ups and downs — never knowing where your next meal might come from, struggling through the bad and lonely days — but I love it more with every day I live it. Maggie could do a hell of a lot worse than to dream herself into that kind of future. But this, this is a thing I remember too well. This is a thing that breaks a girl in ways she can never quite fix.

I run the pad of my thumb over one of the bigger, more jagged chips on the rim of the plate I'm washing. God dammit. No kid deserves this. I didn't when Dad missed Mum and gave me the strap for still being alive when she wasn't. And Maggie doesn't deserve it now that her parents have lost her brother.

They're not striking her, far as I can tell. I didn't get a look at her all over, but she's got no bruises on her arms or legs. What's being done to her is a different sort of wounding, without a name.

I'm not crying. I don't have time to cry. I sniff and wipe my eyes with the back of my hand and get back to scrubbing.

"Hey there, fire brain," Heck says from the open doorway. He's lost a bit of weight and gained a little height and feels bony when I hug him. "Hey, hey! No soapsuds on me, girl! Gotta work in this shirt later."

"Hector, did you know about this? About what's happened since Bill died?"

Released from my hug, he looks around the room. At the dirty floor and the stack of plates, the dusty air and the smell of old milk, the rubbish piled in the corners. "Oh, hell. Those poor kiddies. We've been so busy trying to drum up business at the shop, what with those ratbags down the road and their fucking sign. I've barely seen my own reflection since the New Year, much less kept an eye next door. I thought... I didn't know," he says.

I can tell it's the truth.

"Can you help me out today? Until Jocasta needs you at the store?" I ask.

He nods. "Where're the kids now?"

"Left 'em with Joke. She's got them sorting the different mixed candies into jars."

"What's happened here, Sal? Did their mumma and pop run off?"

I shake my head. "No. Just Jim, Maggie says. He stopped coming home in stages, like. Worked later, went in earlier. Then just buggered off one day. Vicky might as well be gone, though. Stupid bitch is lying in bed while her children —"

"Hey, hey." Heck cuts me off with a sharp shake of his head. "Lower your voice."

My anger wilts a little. "I don't know what to do. It's too much."

He unbuttons the cuffs at his wrists and rolls his sleeves up. "Then let's get started, right? You wash, I'll dry."

It's easier with two, because Heck keeps me distracted from the dark bubbling mess in my head. Heck came over to Australia with his older sister when he was seven and she was twenty. That was back in '42, and as far as I've ever been able to tell, they might as well have sprung from the thin air then. Heck doesn't remember anything from when he was a little kid, and Joke's not the chatty sort. She's tall and wears long black dresses with chinking necklaces made of shells. Her hair's always in a bun, and the first time I met her, I had all these day-dreams about wanting to grow up just like her someday, so cool and calm and strong. I imagined getting married to Heck and running the store with him, wearing my hair smoothed back and tight, slim shoes that made my feet look elegant.

Now that I'm older, I've given up on silly things like that. Me and Heck aren't ever gonna marry, but we're good mates.

When we're done with the dishes, we set to on the little stacks of rubbish dotted about the place. Newspapers and scraps, mostly. I bundle them up, to use to stoke the copper. Heck finds a stack of comics under a couple of old baby dolls and starts to bundle them too. I stop him and glance through the pile as I carry it to Bill and Martin's room. Martin's off in the wild somewhere, Maggie said. He'll be eighteen soon, so he'll be called up for service before long. He didn't think Vicky could handle losing another boy like she lost Bill, so he's nicked off to dodge it.

I want to be angry at him like I'm angry at Jim and Vicky, but I can't be. Martin and Bill were a double act, and I bet it's a hit like no other to lose somebody who's the other part of you.

The comics are a mix of all sorts. There're the old ones from the War, the same ones every kid had a bunch of — Captain America, Superman, Batman and Robin. Some Aussie ones, too, the dumb stuff like Ginger Meggs and Boofhead. I snort. Boofhead — that just makes me think of Amy's brother and wonder what they're up to. It feels like a million years since I said goodbye to her, even though it can't be more than two or three hours. Something about seeing Maggie answer the door with her little sister on her hip and her hair in knots, inviting me in like she was the mistress of the house… something about that made me get a bit older, I think.

I put the comics down on the little desk between Bill and Martin's beds, then go to the small cupboard against the far wall. There're a few shirts and pairs of pants still folded on the shelves, and I change quickly. I have to make a new hole to pull the belt tight enough, but once I'm done, I feel more suited to the day's tasks. The pants aren't even too long. Bill was always a short guy.

CHARLOTTE

From *Reign in Hell: Two Weeks in the Life of HUSH*, by Charlotte Waterhouse, Amplify Press, Australia, 2011:

"I like your necklace," Jacqui says, looking at our reflections side-by-side in the backstage mirror as she applies her makeup. She's painted the lids of her eyes a vivid sunset-crimson. It makes her look like an exotic coastal bird. We look like creatures from different worlds to one another, her with her dramatic rock-star getup and me in my T-shirt and jeans, a million freckles on my face and slightly frizzy red hair pulled back into a bun.

"Thank you," I say, touching my fingertips against the pendant, seeing my mirror-self copy the action. Jacqui's not wearing any jewelry around her own neck but has written words in liquid eyeliner across the bare skin of her collarbones. The message for tonight's crowd is *rock stars break your heart.*

"It's a compass rose, like in your song," I say redundantly. Of course Jacqui knows what the design is; 'The Sharpest Rose,' is one of HUSH's best known and most loved tracks.

"That's our Ella song," Jacqui answers, painting careful swirls of darker red within the crimson above her lashes. "We don't say that in interviews much, but I don't think Tash will mind if I tell you. Ella wasn't a diary-keeper like Stacey was, but she wrote in her journal from time to time. Tash burned it after she died, so nobody would see it.

"Tash tried to memorize it first, before destroying it, but she forgot most of it right away. She was only a little girl.

Shit." Jacqui blots at a make-up mistake on her cheek with a tissue. "The only line Tash could remember was from near the end, when everything was getting kind of incoherent and fucked-up in Ella's head. Poor kid. Ella, I mean. They're both poor kids, of course, but Ella… people have made her into this monster, so they don't remember that she was really just a kid who did a stupid, evil thing. All kids do stupid, evil things. We just mostly have a chance to grow beyond them, and she didn't. That's all.

"The part of the journal that Tash could remember just said *I want to burn the world, I want the most of all things, I want the fire, I want the sharpest of the roses*."

The lyrics to the HUSH song, a haunting melody that closes *Jazz Funeral*'s short running order, are as follows:

> North West East South
> the simplest of stars
>
> the moth is better off
> without your pins and jars
>
> you call it a compass rose
> a compass star for me
>
> the sharpest of directions
> waiting out across the sea
>
> let's watch the sun burn down the waves
> and swear we'll live forever

"Is it bone?" Jacqui asks, nodding again to my pendant. I resist the urge to touch it again, to treat it like a lucky relic.

"Yeah. It was my father's. A family heirloom, I guess. I liked the idea of that. Something beautiful coming out of the wreckage." I don't know if I mean the bone or my family. Jacqui doesn't ask me to specify.

I was seventeen in 1999, less than a year younger than Ella Vrenna. I wore black, hated everything. My father had finally initiated divorce proceedings against my mother, and I had taken into slicing into the flesh of my wrists with the little twin-blade mint-green razors I shoplifted from the supermarket in order to shave my pale puppy-fat schoolgirl legs. I dreamt bad dreams, of Jack the Ripper.

Some part of me, the part of us that will chew off a foot if caught in a trap, knew that I had to find something to believe in, something to catch me from this free-fall. I lived in Australia and so it couldn't be a gun. Guns were too difficult to get ever since what happened at Port Arthur. So instead, I picked up a pen and a pair of scissors and a glue stick and began to make zines.

Scarlet Slaughterhouse was my vigilante mask, a mouthpiece for every angry, fucked-up monster in my head.

While Charlotte studied journalism and did work with charities, striving to bring a little bit more compassion and tolerance and fairness into a world so devoid of them, Scarlet was the snarl of hate.

Scarlet wanted to take a crowbar to the glass of every gleaming high-rise block, letting the wind and rain and pollution in to destroy and sully papers and clean linen of the offices and bedrooms inside. Scarlet screamed for blood, for the limbs of skinny dowagers to be torn from their sockets and grilled over burning oil drums for the mouths of hungry children.

Letting Scarlet feel my madness was all that kept Charlotte sane for a long time.

And then music began to do it, as well. Crowds, concerts, sounds so loud they hurt the ears: those became my dark salvation. A promise of somewhere to belong, even if it was among the lost and the damned. Hell was other people, and so was never lonely.

AMY

The reason crossroads feature in superstition so often is because there's power in places where choices are made. There is immense potential of all kinds in a place that forces decision, invites variables. Suicides used to be buried at crossroads. Popular legend has musicians selling their souls for talent there.

Before Red Riding Hood was written down in books, when it was still a tale told at firesides and spinning wheels, the story used to begin *"Once, a girl met a devil at the crossroads."*

Our walk took Caim and me to a library, situated on the upper level of a building on the corner of an intersection. The traffic grumbled and roared down below us as we sat by the open window, our backs against the rows of books behind us. Occasionally there was a clip-clop of hooves or the bell of a bicycle to break the monotony of car-sounds. Nobody paid us any mind or even noticed we were there.

"Oh, here." Caim reached into his pocket and drew out the curve of a bone, thin as one of my fingers. It was light in my palm, like the bones of fish and dolphins, the bones of birds. "I know you like carving."

It was always hard to tell when he was being sincere and when he was being ironic, but the gesture was a small, kind offering. I could tell he meant to make me happy with it.

"Thank you." I put it in my pocket, planning to decorate the small curve with a dozen tiny faces. Then I screwed my courage up and met his gaze with mine. "Father wrote to me. Murmur brought me the letter." I didn't want to have to tell him, but there was no choice. Better to get it over and done with.

Caim frowned. He had a good mouth for frowning; expressive and petulant. Once upon a time, I'd resented him for that. What did a boy need beauty for? I'd come not to care in the years since, though. I was sixteen and a girl, and everybody who is sixteen and a girl has a special sort of beauty that nobody else can ever achieve, no matter how they might try.

"I don't care," Caim said, and he sounded determined to convince me.

I opened my mouth to try again, but he cut me off before I could speak.

"We're in a library; let's discuss something more interesting than him. Let's talk literature, or fortune-telling, or the ocean, or ham sandwiches."

"I had a ham sandwich this morning. I fed it to a cat."

He had a good mouth for smiling, too. "You and your familiars."

He'd remembered, even after all this time. I smiled back. "Yeah."

"So that's one of our topics discussed. What about literature? Surely you, of all people, have read something interesting?" He skipped his fingers along the spines of the books in the short space of shelf beside us. Leather covers, paper covers, cloth covers. Words in gold and black and white.

"Of all people?" I raised my eyebrows. "Doubtful. I like spoken stories better. I always have. Or drawn ones. Give me a hieroglyph over a newspaper any day."

"The paperboys in your brave new world might have some trouble carrying around a stack of tablets." He quirked one of his sardonic little smiles. "Does that mean you haven't any great works to recommend to me? I'm disappointed."

"I don't care," I answered, parroting his earlier trying-to-be-convincing tone "I haven't had time to read."

"There is always time to read." He grabbed a hardback off the shelf at random, a yellow-papered one with a lurid ink design. "Here. I want a full report the next time our paths cross."

I shoved the book in my bag without paying it any attention. "Our paths shouldn't be crossing at all. You shouldn't be here. It's not safe for two of us to be in the same place."

"Not safe? Amy, this whole country's a keg with a match above it. Everyone's a *red* or an *abbo* or a *shirtlifter* or a *catholic*. Everyone hates someone else, everyone wants someone else dead. Paranoia's a waste of time when you're in a place like this."

"But it's not paranoia." My voice came out a sharp whisper, so I wouldn't shout in the library. "Caim, listen. Richard almost caught me, and he's got a helper now…"

He held up a palm, fingers splayed, between us. When I'd acknowledged the gesture by shutting up, he curled the middle two fingers down. "That's literature and ham sandwiches done. Want me to tell your fortune?"

I rolled my eyes. Outside, down on the street below, a child cried out for Mummy at the top of its lungs, then started sobbing. The child was quickly hushed, leaving the air blank and empty.

When I was eight and Caim was twelve, we spent several months in France. The few memories we had of Germany and our mothers were shot through with the sickly weight of sadness, and I think we ended up in Orleans in the hopes of catching sight of the ghosts of little Elsa and sturdy Gretel. We'd steal and lie and cheat to get the money we needed because a hungry child is pragmatic enough for any misbehaviour.

Sometimes we'd plant ourselves on thoroughfares, and Caim would offer fortune-telling to passers-by. He was very bad at it. People, as a rule, want a lot more delusion and illusion than we had the knack of offering. I remember one woman slapped him and took her coin back after he told her that one of her daughters would die young, and the other would never marry. I wonder what she thought when she finally gave birth to the twins she was carrying. Did she regret the slap? Did she wish she'd strangled Caim, killing the fortune by killing the teller?

I pushed his hand down. "No. You can't tell my fortune, Blackbird," I reminded him quietly. "Never."

He sniffed. "Bring your friend with you next time, then. She's got fortune hanging off her like a wet net. I'll tell hers with no trouble."

"Don't." My frown wasn't as pretty as his, but I could find good use for it. "Leave her out of it."

"You're the one who brought her into it," Caim said. "Do you want to know where she is now? What she's doing? She's stopped crying. I'll give you that for nothing."

Sally, crying? I wanted to ask for more, and felt my eyebrows pinching together in worry. But Caim's answers might have been tricky, hurtful things, skewed deliberately dark in an attempt to punish me for keeping her from him. I shook my head, my hand still atop his.

"One subject left," I said. "Tell me about the ocean."

Caim and Anabel had been in Tasmania for months, and no wonder.

"I've been to my share of bruised places, sister," he said to me, eyes so bright and glittering that in anyone else I'd diagnose a fever. "But never anywhere like Port Arthur. You should come with me when I return. We could glut ourselves on echoes for a lifetime's worth of years there, both of us. The only reason I'm not still there now is because of Anabel's condition. If the baby's mine, giving it so much to feed on before it's born might hurt the mother. And if it's not mine, who knows what being steeped in that much misery would do to a child? Its blood will likely be bad enough without adding extra poison to the mix."

I shrugged. I didn't care a jot about babies, or what was and wasn't good for them, or about the sad scrap of humanity that Caim had clearly decided to take under his crow-dark wing.

"Tell me about where you lived. Tell me about Port Arthur," I prompted, bored with his talk of the impending son or daughter. Caim stretched his legs out lazily, looking more cat than blackbird behind his human guise. He smiled a contented, sated smile, like a man fondly recalling a favourite lover.

"The jail there was a panopticon. Spokes built out from a central guard post, so the prisoners never knew if they were being watched. Has it ever struck you how like the panopticon the current notions of Heaven are? Everyone assumes that God could be watching them at any given moment, even though they know that with so many other inmates to watch as well as them, God's attention must be almost always on someone else. But they can never be *sure*. He *could* be watching them. So they're always afraid to get caught breaking rules. The whole of the twentieth century and all its faiths are one oversized experimental prison.

"At Port Arthur, when it was a jail, those who were caught by that random watching eye were made to stay silent, their faces hooded. The lack of light and sound drove many of the prisoners mad. That wasn't as troublesome as it might have been; the asylum was just next door.

"The isthmus to the mainland of Tasmania from the port is less than a hundred feet wide. The guards peppered it with traps and soldiers and half-starved dogs, just in case the prisoners grew mad enough to try for freedom.

"Boys as young as nine were brought to the Port, under arrest for the crime of stealing toys. Boys and men alike were given hard labour to do, cutting stones and building walls. Know what they built, those kids and madmen? The jailers made them build a fucking church and made the Sunday services compulsory. Just another bit of proof that humanity's capacity for cruelty exceeds even God's. He'd never even think of demanding that the fallen build him shrines within their Hell or that they sing of his mercies as they burn.

"That's the buildings. Beyond those, there's the Isle of the Dead..."

The last day I spent with my brother, we sat together in a library, and he told me fairy tales of prison graveyards.

ELLA

Dear Tash,

Pilgrims didn't just want finger bones. They wanted to visit holy places.

Everyone believes in haunted houses, at least a little. Invite an atheist to use a Ouija board, and you'll see just how fast superstition overwhelms rationality. People know there is some stuff you just do not want to fuck with.

I don't mean to suggest that a haunted place is soil enough to grow a killer. It's not, any more than a video game or a CD or a book or a bully can be held up as the cause of carnage. But there's blame enough to go around; everyone can have a share.

Port Arthur may have been an evil place already, but there are plenty of evil places in the world. Since the industrial revolution, humanity has created many, many factories of human suffering. Port Arthur isn't, and wasn't, unique for that.

In 1996 on the 28th of April, a young blonde man named Martin Bryant drove to Port Arthur in the state of Tasmania at the bottom of Australia with a surfboard on the roof of his yellow car, even though the day was too calm for waves of any significance. He ate lunch at a cafe and then took an AR-15 rifle out of his bag.

After, when the violence of the day was done and the suspect in custody, 85% of Australians agreed that there should be tighter gun controls. A total of 643,000 firearms

— self-loading rifles, pump-action shotguns, and lots of other kinds — were handed in to the government. The loudest protests against the new laws were from a group supported by the US National Rifle Association.

Thirty-five people died in the massacre. The oldest was seventy-two. The youngest was three. A six-year-old girl ran behind a tree as Martin shot at her, so he walked up and pressed the barrel to her throat as she tried to hide from him. She died instantly when he fired.

In prison he's tried to kill himself six times. He's tried to cut his own throat. Other prisoners have tried to kill him, too, so a new special kind of solitary confinement was created to keep him safe. He has more than a thousand years left on his sentence, without possibility of parole.

e.

Dear Tash,

If you die and your death is more famous than your life, that's a kind of sainthood. A martyrdom. I'm not using those words in the ways that most people would. They're just the best words I can think of.

Sam's a saint. A hell-saint. We don't have stained-glass windows for our saints, not like they have on the other side of the tracks. But if we did, Sam's would be as striking as any glass that filtered jewel-hued sun into a church: a scarecrow, face washed clean by the tracks of his own tears.

I'm a hell-saint too, though I've never taken advantage of the fact. Neither have Dean or Chris as far as I know. We hated the world when we were alive; why would we go back by choice?

Nicky doesn't go back either. He just watches and

asks Jo and Murmur to tell him about Jacqui and Ben. His family was the only really good thing that happened to him when he was alive. He doesn't have any reason to care about anything but that family now. That's how he explained it to me, anyway.

Murmur's not a saint. He's in a situation of his own. I'll get to that later.

Jo, Nicky, Sam, me... we can walk through the Dark and return to Earth if we want. We can go back intact with our personalities and faces and memories all still there. Most can't. They get stripped down to the simplest soul-spark. Lights, we call those. Capital L.

Not even demons — except for Murmur — can do much of anything on Earth without paring down to nothing but a Light and being born. That's why being a saint is so special, so envied. A lot of people in Hell hate me, and mostly it's because of Cobweb, but some people hate me because I'm a saint and don't do shit with it. But there are a lot of saints who don't.

Sam doesn't go up to Earth because Caim can't, and Sam loves Caim. Caim is one of the demons locked inside Hell, like Lucifer. They can't go through the Dark all the way. Lucifer's never been able to, but for Caim it's only been a few decades. The closest he can get to Earth is the very edge of death, like when he collected Sam from the fence that day. That's the closest he'll ever get. An exorcist got him in the early 1950s.

Doing that to a demon is basically like burning them at the stake. Worse, because Jo was burned at the stake and, as a genuine definition-of-the-word saint, she can wander in and out of Earth just fine.

So that's saints. I guess the ones from Heaven can visit Earth, too — people report seeing them often enough — but I don't think they do very often. There's nothing down there they'd want.

If demons want to go to Earth, they have to do like any other Light. They have to make it up through the Dark and get born. Can you imagine how shitty that must be? Being a teenager was more than I could handle the first time around, yet some demons have chosen to live over and over again. There are lots of families with demons in their trees, the snakes and harpies from old fairy stories.

That leads me to Murmur's story, actually. I'll tell you the beginning now; it's long enough to need a few letters.

He started off going to Earth the same way all demons do. This was many centuries ago, before it became so necessary for demons to make themselves look as human as possible. They could look however they wished; they could be blackbirds or gryphons or phoenixes or harpies. That's what Murmur was that time: a harpy.

And then, one day, a girl from the village found his nest.

xxxE

CAROLINE

From: "Modern Dreamtimes: Author Profile of Caroline Gubura", *The New Yorker*, April 13, 1987, New York:

Early forays into international publication proved to be an exercise in cultural tightrope-walking. Gubura's U.S. agent pushed for her to change the book's title to *Will-o-the-Wisp*, but Gubura held firm, feeling that the nuances of the Australian Aboriginal myth would be lost if the story was changed to the near-but-not-exact American equivalent.

The elegiac delicacy of *Min-Min Lights* aside, Gubura's work has a darkness to it, a sense of impending threat present even in the more prosaic canvasses. The stark still-life tableaus of her anti-war work (all Gubura's art is anti-war on some level; only the degree to which the protest is overt fluctuates) is reminiscent of the work of Pulitzer-winning photographer David Caramano.

The two artists know one another and are friends of many decades. Caramano's wife Lena spent part of the Second World War as a Land Army volunteer on the Australian outback property where Gubura spent her childhood. Reunited in 1955, when Gubura came to New York for her first international group show, they have been close ever since.

According to rumor, Caramano and his wife are the only ones who have read the manuscripts of Gubura's other prose works.

"If there was a book aside from *Min-Min Lights* — and

I'm not telling you for certain that there is, understand — then I imagine that Caroline is holding off on publishing it for a reason," Lena says. "It might be a lot of things. Perhaps when Caroline and David and I are all dead it'll get out into the world."

Caramano is slightly more forthcoming. "Yeah, there's another book. It's Caroline's *Maurice*, if you wanna put it that way," he says, presumably referring to the E. M. Forster novel, which was held off from publication until after that writer's death.

In Forster's case, it was the homosexual content of *Maurice* that kept the story unseen by all but close friends until its posthumous debut.

"Everyone worth knowing lives with demons," Caramano offers cryptically. "But only some of us ever have the guts to tell the story of how the romance started."

ELLA

Dear Tash,

    The girl in the forest was dressed simply and carried in her arms a struggling, terrified, lamb. Its legs kicked frantically, small hooves black like wet wood. It bleated and bleated.
    She didn't try to soothe it. The girl had heard stories of the harpies in the woods all of her life. She knew it would be easier to find one if the lamb was properly afraid.
    She didn't know the harpy would be beautiful, but it was. Its hair was ragged but looked as soft and white as down. The pupil and sclera of its eyes were darkest black, as dark as the Dark that lingers between nightmares and waking. The feathers on its wings and legs were a deep grey, and the skin of its human parts, its face and neck and breasts and stomach, was the delicate blue of tired shadows beneath eyes, the blue of new bruises.
    "Excuse me, ma'am, I don't mean to disturb you —," the girl began, because she had been raised to be polite to people older than she was, and though the harpy's face was as unlined and young as her own, the girl knew that the harpy was very, very old beneath its form.
    "Yes you do." The harpy's voice was as strange and as lovely as the rest of it. "And I'm not a ma'am. I'm a boy."
    The girl looked doubtfully at the swell of the harpy's hips above its feathered bird-joints and the curve of its lovely bruise-blue breasts. "You have a girl body."

The harpy's eyes narrowed, its mouth a droll line.

The lamb cried.

The girl didn't flinch, even though the harpy looked bored and annoyed, thin frown turning down even harder. Its long, long, talons shifted restlessly on the branch. They looked as sharp as knives. The girl did her best not to feel afraid.

"I didn't say I have a boy body. I said I am a boy."

"Oh. I didn't realize they could be different things," the girl said. She felt bad about making the mistake. "I'm sorry. And you're right; I did mean to disturb you. Do you want this lamb?" She held the struggling, wriggling animal up so that the creature in the tree could get a better look at it.

The harpy closed his wonderful, terrible eyes for a moment and inhaled deeply. The lamb's frantic thrashing slowed and grew weaker and then stopped. It slumped, deeply asleep, in the girl's arms. She put it down on the leaf litter at her feet. She wondered what its misery and fear tasted like.

"Misery and fear sustain me. It doesn't matter what they taste like," the harpy said, as if he could hear her thoughts. They probably weren't very difficult thoughts to guess at.

"What's your name?" the girl asked.

"My name? Harpies don't have names, not as humans do."

The girl's eyes narrowed, her eyebrows pinching closer together in thought. "How do you tell each other apart?"

The harpy shrugged, wings rustling. Its claws continued shifting restlessly on the branch, tearing at the wood. "We just know."

"Well, I don't want to call you 'harpy,'" said the girl. "And I don't want to just get 'girl' from you, either. My name is Vanya. What do I call you?"

The harpy clawed at the branch again, not looking at Vanya's face. If the harpy had been a person and somebody had asked her, Vanya would have said the harpy seemed shy.

"My name since the Fall has been Murmur."

"Do you want me to call you that?"

Now the harpy met Vanya's gaze. "Yes."

Names have power. Saint Joan, *ellavrenna*, Nattie, Tash... given or chosen, names matter.

Not all demons think so, of course. Caim, for instance, can be found in any book of demonology under the same name you'll see on his library card. Or would, if he had a library card. He's never bothered with an alias.

But Murmur's always been more paranoid than Caim. Murmur doesn't use his real name on Earth, and Murmur has never been caught by demon hunters like Caim and Amy were — You'll find Amy's name easily enough in the *Ars Goetia* or the *Pseudomonarchia Demonum*, too.

Murmur, ever the scavenger, steals other names to use instead. Angel names, usually, just to show how vicious his rebellion against Heaven still is. Selaphiel and Zadkiel and Oriphiel and Ananiel and Barachiel and Gabriel.

But he told Vanya his real name.

Not that Murmur could be exorcised, even if demon hunters caught him as they did Amy and Caim. Not anymore. Because, you see, Vanya went into the woods that day with two things: a lamb and a bargain.

"Are you hungry, too?" he asked her, once they'd exchanged names and so had a small power over one another.

"Yes," Vanya replied.

When Murmur threw her down one of the apples from the tree he perched in, she bit straight into the tart flesh without a moment's hesitation.

If someone had asked, Murmur would have said that the girl didn't seem afraid at all, as if her village hadn't heard the same tales as everyone else. Tales with different names and variations — an Eve here, a Persephone there — but there's one common warning under the words. All the tales are about a girl tempted with fruit by a dark, crooning friend, and when she takes a bite, she must suffer the consequences.

Vanya ate Murmur's apple with impunity, as if untroubled by whatever future cost awaited her. Murmur had never met a human like this, with teasing eyes and a pale, sad cast to her plump pretty cheeks.

"I am the only child of my mother," Vanya told Murmur after she swallowed down her bite of apple. "My father raised me as best he could, but he was young and weak and foolish when my mother died, so I've mostly raised myself.

"Now his new wife has given birth. Twin boys. The birth was bad, and the wounds have fevered.

"I don't want my brothers to grow up as I've grown up. I don't —"

"Why not?" Murmur interrupted her. "You seem to have survived it."

Vanya pursed her lips, then shrugged. She had no wings to rustle with the gesture. "Only because I had no choice."

"And so you've come to beg a favor, to save your stepmother's life."

"No, I haven't." Vanya scowled up at him. "Don't be stupid. I don't beg for anything, and you don't grant favors. Everyone knows that."

"Everyone knows it's unwise to eat fruit given to you by monsters, and yet here you are," Murmur retorted, riled by the snap in Vanya's voice.

"My father needs his wife. My brothers need their mother," Vanya said, not rising to Murmur's taunt. "So you'll cure her fever, and you get my soul in return."

"Human lives are very short," Murmur warned her. "You'll regret spending your soul on such a middling thing. Your stepmother might still die a year from now. And even if you all live past a hundred, that's nothing compared to the eternity you'll have down in the realms of Hell. Sold souls can never come back up to be born again, you know. They're tied down there."

Now fear bloomed in Vanya's eyes. But if this bargain didn't cost her everything, how would she know that it meant anything?

Her voice sounded very sad, sad beyond her years, as she answered. "All children deserve a parent who loves them. That's all."

She'd dropped her gaze down to the sleeping lamb at her feet as she answered, and so the sudden flurry of loud sound as Murmur lighted from his branch and landed beside her was startling. Vanya jumped in surprise.

"Why don't you hate him, for failing you?" Murmur asked.

"My father?"

Murmur nodded his head once, a sharp jerk of his sharp chin.

Vanya shrugged her little plump shoulders.

"What would be the point? The hate would hurt me, not him. And if my stepmother is alive, maybe he will be a good father for my brothers."

"What if he isn't? What if you give him chance after chance, and he fails again and again?"

This time, Vanya smiled along with her shrug. "Then the only sin I'm guilty of is too much optimism, isn't it? I can live with that on my conscience. Better to have been disappointed a thousand times than to have never hoped at all."

"It's odd that you come with such a benign desire," Murmur said. "Remarkable, really. I can't decide what it means."

"I mean exactly what I say. Why wouldn't I?" Vanya asked. She held her palms out, as if to show that they held no secret motive.

"Because it's a selfless request. Disgustingly so." Murmur's voice was heavy with distaste. "Someone who was really as gentle and good as all that wouldn't have gone into the woods to make a deal with a demon or brought along a terrified lamb as an offering.

"Why haven't you come for my sharp claws and cruel teeth? I could tear your whole village apart at a wave of your hand, give your father a slash as deep as a breadknife for every day that you spent sad and lost. I could make you rich. Make you powerful. Make you loved."

Vanya smiled a lopsided, crooked smile, one that looked almost like pity. "You almost had me there. But I'm not stupid. You can't make me loved. I know that for certain.

"And my revenge is my own to find, not a thing for you to offer as an agent on my behalf. Nothing demons do is on anyone's behalf but their own."

xe

AMY

By the time Caim and I had finished our meandering, comfortable discussions of nothing and everything, it was getting late.

"We should meet again tomorrow," he insisted.

I shook my head, sending stubborn strands of my hair every which way as they escaped my braid. "No, we shouldn't, it's —"

"Dangerous?" Caim laughed. "*Life* is dangerous. Stop worrying so much about everything and just *live*. You remember fun, don't you sister? Distantly, in some dim corner of your mind?"

I glared at him. "Stop it."

"No," he countered cheerfully. "Come meet Anabel and me tomorrow morning. Bring Sally along, if you think she and I can behave ourselves."

I frowned. "Sally is already tangled in all this more than enough."

"'More than enough?'" Caim's smirk was condescending but not unkind, as if he pitied me more than anything. "It's all or nothing, Amy. You know that."

If my hunger had been the ordinary, human kind — the kind for food — then my mouth would have watered as I stepped up to the front door of the home where Sally had come to see her friends. As it was, the miasma of shattered hopes and forlorn wishes that overwhelmed my senses made something flip and flutter in my ribcage, made my lips part as if I could inhale it deep along with the air.

I tamped down on the wanting and raised my knuckles to the wood, knocking firmly. After a short wait, a small girl with heavy dark hair and a dress that was a little too tight for her growing frame opened the door. She looked at me with flinty eyes.

"You Sal's friend?" she asked.

I nodded.

With a careless shrug, as if I'd used up all the attention she was willing to apportion me, the girl turned away and wandered off, leaving me to step inside the house under my own direction.

I looked for several moments before I found Sally, who was out in the scrubby, scruffy patch of sun-white grass that passed for a yard behind the house. It bordered a tall, thickly tangled scrubland at the back, a snarl of ghost-pale gum trees and other plants all knotted together in a way that would go up like a tinderbox if the smallest spark struck it.

There was Black Wattle, too. Sally Wattle, it's sometimes called. The flowers look like froth, or clouds, when they bloom. They fill the air with dancing. It spreads and grows like a wild plague after fires. The fires wake the sleeping seeds.

Some things thrive in destruction.

"You have to take it away from her," Sally said. No preamble or greeting. She wasn't even looking at me, her gaze fixed on a haphazard pile of ancient, dried-out, kitchen scraps against the wire of the fence. Lamb bones, bleached white as snow. The skull was caved in with a stone, the blow clumsy enough to be the mark of some violent childish game that the haunted-eyed children of the house had played.

A blunt, inelegant snake-body was curled on the dirt not far from the broken bones, moving lazily into a more comfortable position. Not all serpents are sleek and beautiful. This was a death adder, as ugly as any of the creatures of the world. I was fascinated by it, perhaps even more so because it wasn't pretty. Pretty things, perfect things, I usually found boring.

Sally was looking right at where the ugly snake was sunning itself, but didn't give any indication that she was afraid. Death adders move faster than the flicker of an eye and are the most venomous in the world.

Fearless or stupid. I wasn't sure then and have never decided since which of the two Sally was. Sharing space with predators so casually.

"You need to take it all," Sally said. "All that Vicky's... all of it."

I stared at her, sure that I must be misunderstanding the meaning of her words.

"You also need to blink more often," she muttered, wringing her hands together, still looking away from me, watching the death adder slide lazily through the grass. Her next words came out rapid-fire, a nervous barrage. "I don't know what you are, but I'm not stupid. I seen the Min-Min Lights at night; I know there's things out there that make no sense but are true anyways. I know you took something outta Pia and stopped her being sad, and I reckon you put something in me that's stuffing up my drawing and making it better than it was."

Now she looked at me. Unafraid, but uncertain. "Have I sold my soul?"

"No," I replied, shaking my head. I wanted to reach out and touch her arm, reassure her, but I've never been especially good with social niceties of that kind. "No. I took out a memory, and that left a gap. A little bit of raw creation filled the space."

"What did you take? Don't. Don't do that ever again." Sally's eyebrows were furrowed hard, her mouth a furious frown. "Don't you *dare* do that to me again. I don't care how good you can make me at pictures in return."

"Hunters. We ran into them. They're dangerous. I got us away, but I didn't... I didn't want to have to tell you."

I looked away, breaking contact with the stormy fury of her glare. If I had been ordinary, the feeling in my throat would perhaps have been shame. Maybe it was anyway.

Sally made a noise of anger in the back of her throat, clearly seething with fury. All she said aloud, though, was, "Fix Vicky. Take... take her hurting out of her."

"You want me to do to her what you just demanded I never do to you?"

"Don't try to take a high ground with me," Sally muttered through her teeth. "Just go do it."

"I don't take orders," I snapped, feeling like a cat with bristled fur.

Her glare faltered, began to crumble. "Please, Amy. For her kids."

Pacts with demons rarely feel as grave as they truly are, but somehow this one did, as I nodded at her and sealed our fates together. "All right."

ELLA

Dear Tash,

And so, as I'm sure you've guessed already, the monster and the girl had fallen in love with one another, though neither of them knew it.

Murmur fluttered his wide gray wings. The wind from them blew Vanya's hair back from her cheeks. The breeze smelled surprisingly sweet, like spice and incense and sugared things. Vanya would have admitted, if someone had asked her, that she'd never expected the scent of damnation to be so comforting.

"It's done," the harpy told her. "Your father's wife will recover. Meet me here once every ten years, on this same day. Bring a lamb."

Before Vanya could reply, Murmur was in the air, flying up through the sparse crisscross of branches above the bare forest.

She went home, and it was true, her father's wife had broken through the crisis of the fever. Her brothers wouldn't have to raise themselves.

Sometimes Vanya thought about the fact that she'd sold her soul, but not so often as you might expect. People are mostly too taken up with the everyday business of being alive — tending chickens, helping with the sheep, fetching water from the well — to think very much about death and souls and warm sweet wing-wind.

I understand that now. The way life goes on. I even

appreciate it, sort of. As much as I can from the outside, anyway. But when I was alive I had no idea that getting on with things despite the looming void ahead is what humanity does best. I thought something bad was happening.

A recruiter from the Marines came to talk to the class, to try to talk it up and make kids want to join. Salespitching patriotism and the promise of violence in your future. Chris got really into it, which was no big fucking shock since his dad's been a soldier for about a thousand years. The only reason Chris didn't have a roaming military childhood is because his dad got hurt in a car accident a long time ago. Changed the course of things. If Chris's father had never been hurt, he might never have been at school with me and Dean. That's weird to think about.

Chris got so interested in the Marines that I ended up having a fight with him about it. What the fuck did he think was the point of talking to a recruiter when he'd be dead in a few more weeks? Why was he filling the forms in?

Chris just shrugged. "Doesn't do any harm, right?"

As if I thought that was a positive. As if my sole ambition for the future wasn't to do as much harm as I could.

The fucking *Matrix,* and Marine recruitment forms, and it was all fucked, it was so fucked. I went home and slammed my door and cried hot angry tears into my pillow. How many other kids at other schools were doing the same as Chris and Dean, making small plans for a post-Cobweb life?

I felt like I was being forced to play witness to the foundations of the futures I'd already seeded with tiny time bombs. It didn't matter that the whole fucking thing was going to explode sky-high. I still didn't want to see those few careful bricks added to the cement before the flames rushed up. It hurt. It made me feel like they didn't want Cobweb like I did, that they didn't care as much that we were going to lose everything that was important to us if we let our lives keep on living.

 xe

Dear Tash,

 The first time Vanya and Murmur met again, they spent the afternoon talking about lands far away that Murmur had seen, cities teeming with life, and barren, rocky places almost as desolate as the Dark.
 "I should go look for myself," Vanya said thoughtfully. "I can't put it off if I'm going to Hell when I die. I won't have any other lifetimes but this one in which to take my chance. The paradise in the clouds above might as well be only sky."

 ev
 exxx

Dear Tash,

 The second time that Vanya and Murmur met, the lamb she brought was scrawny and listless and too hungry to be very afraid of the monster.
 "It's been a lean year," she told Murmur. Her voice had gained the lilting accent of the cities, and her clothes were a mix of places far and near.
 "My brothers have wives and babies of their own now," Vanya said. "They're happy. I hope all the travel I've done

makes my soul rich and fat; you deserve a worthy reward for the good you set in motion."

Murmur shrugged; his unchanged wings creaked as they always had. Experience and time didn't paint new aspects to his face as they did to Vanya's. "And you? Do you have a husband, babies?"

Vanya thought there was perhaps a faint catch of jealousy in the words, but maybe she was imagining that.

"How could I?" she asked, as she did her best to keep bitterness away from her words. "I belong to you, remember?"

After that, they exchanged stories of the places and people they'd each seen, the horrors and the joys, the beauty and disgusts. Each of them hid their love for the other deep down in their hearts, nursing it as one might protect a bruise from further harm. Each sure that the wondrous hurt they felt would be worthless to the other, even as it was so precious to them.

xxxE

CHARLOTTE

From *Reign in Hell: Two Weeks in the Life of HUSH*, by Charlotte Waterhouse, Amplify Press, Australia, 2011:

"I promised my grandfather I'd visit the grave of one of his friends who's buried here," Jacqui tells me as the band settles into its Brisbane hotel room. "She died last year, but he wasn't well enough to come to the funeral. I've got directions and everything to get there. Do you know where Toowong Cemetery is?"

The Queensland warmth has left her hair limp, so today she wears it in a haphazard ponytail. It shows off the whiteness of her neck — night-time skin, musician skin. It will burn in minutes in the Brisbane sun.

I reply with a nod, doing my best not to flinch. There are things I do my best never to think about in that cemetery. But if Jacqui wants to go, I'll go.

Before we have a chance to make any plans one way or the other, however, my phone rings. It's a friend from school, one of the few Brisbane-based people I still maintain contact with. She's begging a favour: she's been asked to pull a double-shift at the emergency room where she works, but her three-year-old daughter needs to be picked up from day care.

"Oh man, of course!" Gabe says when I explain the situation. "Kids are the best." His concession to the warm weather is to swap out his jeans for black cargo shorts and forgo shoes entirely. His legs and even the tops of his feet are tattooed, the latter decorated with long, knifelike talons in photorealistic greyscale.

I tell him that I don't expect the band to accommodate for an unexpected toddler. I was just explaining why I wouldn't be around for the evening.

Jacqui snaps her gum and grins. "You can't go back on it now. Gabe's not gonna rest until he plays with the kid."

And so I set off with an international rock star and her baby-mad punk roadie boyfriend to retrieve little Gracie Chang from playgroup.

On the way, I ask about the tattoos on Gabe's feet. "Bird claws, right?"

"Vulture," he confirms, lifting one foot up onto the seat so that he can prod at the ink. "Tattoos over the bone hurt like fuck, by the way. Anyone who tells you otherwise is just trying to make themselves look hardcore."

"Metamorphosis always hurts," Jacqui adds as we arrive at the daycare centre.

"You got here at the perfect time," the pretty young teacher tells us, apparently unfazed by the unconventional entourage. "She's just woken from the afternoon nap."

Gabe immediately crouches in front of her, introducing himself to the pigtailed Grace and proving his credentials as a person worthy of her time by correctly identifying the characters of the television show *Yo Gabba Gabba* in a drawing she'd done that day. When he's perched on the balls of his feet like that, there's something birdlike about Gabe even without taking his tattoos into consideration.

Jacqui watches the interaction with a soft smile. "People in our culture think vultures are evil," she remarks. I wonder if she's been reminded of birds by Gabe's posture too, or if she's still thinking about the conversation from in the car. "But in Tibet, vultures are how they bury the dead. Only it's not really burial at all. Sky burial is what it's called. They lay out the body for the vultures. So that everything stays part of the systems of life.

"In ancient Egypt vultures were the symbol of motherhood. Because of the wide wings, you know? Big protective wingspan. Keep all the babies safe.

"These days people only like cute birds, robins and blackbirds and shit. Violent ones or ugly ones, like magpies and vultures, people act as if they're fuckin' monsters. Why can't monsters be worth knowing and loving, too, is what I want to know?"

The mother of one of the other children in the playgroup steps up beside me, a small, still-napping boy sprawled in the cradle of her arms. She gives me an exhausted smile as if we're both in on the same secret joke.

"I know we're not supposed to admit it," the mother says. "But they're easier to love when they're asleep."

Jacqui and Gabe's gazes both whirl to her, their eyes narrowing into matching hot stares of anger. I'm certain that if I don't get them out of there, a scene will ensue, so I hurry our strange little gang of four out into the low-lying sunlight of evening.

Grace adores the band and draws pictures of all of them, demanding that they recruit her to play violin on their albums as soon as she starts her lessons next year. Ben gravely gives her his word that they will be in touch. She offers one of her plump, marker-smeared little hands out for him to shake to seal the deal.

"Easier to love when they're asleep my fuckin' ass," Gabe mutters darkly at one point. Jacqui pats his arm, comforting and restraining all at once. He's quiet after that.

In the morning, with Grace safely returned to her mother and the concert awaiting us in the evening, Jacqui and Ben and I go to the graveyard.

Most of the things that I learned from my father, I have since rejected. But even though my head knows this, knows that his advice has rarely proved to be wisdom relevant to me, my heart hammers hard and terrified as we step through the cemetery gates. Suddenly I'm sixteen again, beside my father on one of the long, long drives he liked to take to relax his jangled nerves.

This was at a time when we were not close even by the uneven standards of the rest of our history. I hurt. I hated. It would be another year before Cobweb's net spun out across the world from Colorado, before I knew I was not the only lonely angry girl who wanted to set a fire underneath all things precious.

My father cleared his throat and began to tell me a story.

He'd heard that I was winning prizes for my writing at school. A lot of prizes. And that was good, very good, because he and his friend Bradley had a project in need of a writer. They had first recruited Bradley's wife, who was a journalist, but she couldn't do it now.

(I learned later — too late — that in fact Bradley's wife had suffered a nervous breakdown. So did the writer who followed my own shattered footsteps. I've never seen the book that my father and his friend intended to create in all my many visits to bookstores and libraries, so I can only assume that no writer has managed to face down the dragon and live to write it.)

My father cleared his throat and said,

> In Gatton, back around the turn of the century, a boy took his two sisters out in their horse-drawn buggy to go to a dance. Gatton is a small town not far from Brisbane. The brother set off with the two girls and...

Here my memory blurs, the mercy of more than a decade's distance. My father told me the story of a terrible crime;

that much I remember. It was just like those evenings when I was small, except that now I was old enough that words like *raped* and *mutilated* and *eyes cut into, a shape of an M over the features of the face* were more definite in my head, not abstract as they had been when I was small.

I thought I knew the shape of the book he wanted. I could start to see it form.

My father said,

> Nearly all of Brisbane was built with money from the Moorlands family. Lots of the buildings you pass every day on your bus ride to school — hospitals, high-rises, mansions — they're all built with Moorlands money. Queensland University. The hall there is Moorlands Hall. The Moorlands' family home is the old house on the hospital grounds opposite the river. There were three children, two girls and a boy. The father was insane. Back in Ireland, before they came here and built up Brisbane from a town into a city, back in Ireland the father had murdered a man and cut into his face. Carved an M over the features, cut into the eyes.

The day was bright, and the drive was endless. It had been years and years since my father had said this much to me. I began to feel as I had when I was a child, excited by the puzzle of the story he was telling me, as I watched the pieces fall together without noticing the sliced edges and the blood they oozed.

I was stupid. I hadn't learned a thing from the heartbreaks of my childhood. Stupid, so stupid. My father went on.

> The children were insane too. They all died

> unmarried. I think they wanted the family to die with them. James, the son, he was a medical student. The scalpel cuts on that murdered Gatton family, they matched the blades a medical kit would have contained. It was all covered up. The family was very rich.

Oh, I said. Oh.

And then my father kept talking, and the puzzle I thought I'd put together fell apart completely.

> Before Gatton, before the murders started... there were others, but I'll get to that in a moment... before the murders started here, James lived overseas. He lived in London. My friends and I have samples of James's handwriting, my father said. We've had an expert look at it. His Rs are very distinctive. Queensland Rs, they're called. Only schools here taught Rs like that. The handwriting matches that of the 'From Hell' letters. We've found who Jack the Ripper really was. He helped create Brisbane. He's buried in Toowong Cemetery. He didn't stop after those bodies in Whitechapel like everyone thinks. He kept killing here. The mutilations, the cut eyes, the shape of an M made with a scalpel blade on the faces. They're all there.

My heart was hammering. This was huge. Huge. And my father wanted me there as a part of it. Writing the book.

"I could go look at his grave," I said, entranced by the idea that there were tangible relics of my father's wild story, things I could go see with my own eyes. All this was true.

> Never, *never* do that. Promise me you will never go near the grave.

> Do you remember a trial I did when you were young, the Lesbian Vampire Murderers? They were ordinary happy girls, Charlotte. Happy and soft and loved until they did a photography project for university. They went to Toowong Cemetery and photographed some of the graves. They photographed his grave. Part of his headstone was loose, and they took a piece with them to include in their photography display.

> Do you know where the body of that man they killed was found, Charlotte? It was found by the river, near the hospital. Right in view of the Moorlands house.

I tried to write the book. To please my father. But the nightmares began, and the headaches. I started seeing a therapist. She told me I was demonizing a sick man. I assume she was talking about James. Jack.

In the end, I had to leave Brisbane. I couldn't ride the bus past places where the ghosts were known to me. I moved to Melbourne and became a writer, and I'm not happy, not exactly. I don't really remember the last time I was happy. But my life is mine. My ghosts are mine.

My grandmother used to say that if you know the names of the ghosts, you can't stay where the skeletons are buried. It's a weird saying — I come from a weird family — but I know from experience just how very true it is. I know Brisbane's skeletons. That's why I had to leave.

Jacqui leaves roses on the grave of her grandfather's friend, and we leave the grounds. The wattle is in bloom, so the air is full of drifting yellow pollen. It's a warm, sunny day, and once we're on our way again and back within our own story, our own adventures, I can breathe again.

ELLA

Dear Tash,

Eventually Vanya got old. And when she was old, she left the village and went into the forest, searching just as she had years before. Some trees were taller or had fallen, but the forest was the forest nonetheless.

Murmur lighted on a branch. He looked exactly as he always did, and she didn't feel surprised that she loved him just as much as she always had. She would have been shocked if the feeling had changed.

"My heart is yours, after all," the girl said to the monster. Her voice was dry as tinder now, hoarse. Her hair was grey, and her cheeks were wrinkled and thin. She didn't see any reason now to shield the bruise of her love for him.

"And mine yours," he answered.

Choices are simpler, at the end of things.

"I didn't know that demons had hearts," she said.

"Of course we do. Otherwise, what would God have in us to break?"

"Oh," Vanya said, because she didn't know what else to say. She wanted to just stand and stare, to drink in the sight of her love for as long as she could. Her eyes were starving for all of Murmur that she could have.

"I don't want you to go to Hell," Murmur told her. "I love you."

"A bargain is a bargain. You held up your end. If you love me, let me be honorable."

These were the last words Vanya spoke before her life ended and she died. Murmur saw her eyes dim and close. He saw her begin to fall from her still-straight posture down into a sprawl on the leaf litter. He spread his wings and flew up through the sparse branches, and the last thing Vanya felt was the warm sweet wind.

And then, up in the air, Murmur's heart — demon heart, monster heart — broke with grief at the loss of his love, and he died, too, and fell to Earth.

This is when he discovered a curious thing. Like all demons, Murmur went straight back to Hell after he died, yet something was different. A light, a fine gold thread, stretched out before him and up through the Dark. He could walk in and out of the world whenever he wanted, just as saints were able to do. He could pass through the divide between life and death, following that inexplicable golden thread.

Murmur went up into the world and followed the thread until at last it led him to a little girl. She was dark where Vanya had been pale, petulant where Vanya had been placid. Despite these little differences, Murmur recognized the soul of his love in an instant, for he would know her always and anywhere.

He realized then what had happened. Their hearts and souls were plaited. Because he loved her and refused to take her down to Hell, the way to Earth would be open to Murmur for as long as the girl's soul was there. Not even God was cruel enough to break that thread between them.

Not cruel enough, or maybe not strong enough.

The reason probably doesn't matter in the end.

xxElla.

AMY

When I was done with the heavy meal of her grief, Vicky slept for several hours. I spent that time helping Sally with washing and scrubbing and other tasks. Hard work can be a very welcome distraction when the alternative is silence. Maggie, the girl who'd answered the door for me when I'd first arrived, helped us. She seemed determined to prove that she was as old, as worldly, as we were.

Usually, I didn't feel any age at all. My being was eternal, but my current life was young. 'Sixteen years old' was more grown-up in the 1950s than it was later, but it was still far from old. Beside Sally's silence that day, I felt very young and alone.

I wanted to say to her, "see, this is why I took the memory of Richard and his whelp." Because now that she knew what I was, we couldn't be what we were.

After we'd pinned up a load of freshly boiled sheets to dry on the line in the back yard, Sally went back inside to make a pot of tea. I scrounged through the little haphazard graveyard of bones, briefly saddened by the death adder's disappearance. Exiled from my brief home within humanity, it would have been nice to meet a kindred spirit there among the skeletons.

A little bit of looking yielded a flat, fairly smooth curve of bone smaller than my palm, uncooked and free of the little hairline fractures that make scrimshaw difficult to do. I pulled my knife from my pocket and started working, notching out the places where I'd grind the edges down later and sketching the first lines of a design in the centre of the resulting circle.

A compass rose. Something to guide me while I travelled.

Because I knew that was what was going to happen next. I'd leave Sally in this place to make her own choices and set her own future into motion. I'd go see Caim and say goodbye to him. And then I'd go to Port Arthur, to the old ghosts with unremembered names that my brother had told me about, and I'd lie low there for a while.

It wasn't the happiest of endings to this short adventure. But demons aren't built for happy endings, so I tried to let it matter as little as possible.

I slipped away without saying goodbye and walked back to the train. I didn't want to see the flatness, the revulsion, the relief that I was going. I couldn't bear to think of seeing those in Sally's eyes.

Other demons have animal-shapes hiding beneath the human forms they're born to: my brother was a blackbird before he was a boy. Since the invention of cars, blackbirds have changed the pitch at which they sing, so they might hear each other over the traffic. We are nothing if not adaptable creatures.

The philosopher Murmur wears a vulture's skin under that of the man he becomes — a creature once known as much for love as for flight, now reduced to a symbol of scavenging and carrion. These days it often takes other monsters to recognize the beauty of the vulture's form and actions. But that's all right. Monsters are often the only ones who really matter in the lives of demons. Or they should be, at any rate. Demons and monsters still care far too much what other, worthless lives think of them.

I've never had an animal beneath my skin. Perhaps it's because I love having familiars around me. I get all the creature-sense I need through the proxy they provide. Or perhaps my love of familiars grew to compensate for my lack of fur and feathers. I don't remember. It was all so long ago.

Beneath the coarse blonde hair and hazel eyes and European features and lightweight cotton dress and sturdy boots I wore on the train that day, beneath the guise of Amy, I had no animal shape. I was, as always, simply flame, bright and hot and burning. Light and destruction. Sparks and infernos.

I found Caim and Anabel sitting with their backs against the side of the church hall in the narrow space between one building and the next. Sheaves of light from inside the building slanted down on them through the windows above, making a chequered pattern of gold and shadow over them.

They didn't remark on Sally's absence. It stung. It hurt me to think that our separation had been a foregone conclusion to everyone but me, something I'd refused to acknowledge even though it was obviously inevitable.

She'd become so important to me so quickly. I didn't understand.

I stepped past Caim, who was closest to the street, and then past Anabel beside him. I sat myself down deepest in the shadows of the three of us.

"*All About Eve* is playing at the movie house we passed," Anabel said. "Maybe if we do some fortune-telling tomorrow, we can make money and go see it." She turned to me. "I'm better at doing it for crowds than he is. I know how to read people and see what it is they want to hear. Everyone just wants to know that they'll be loved."

"Yeah," I agreed, trying not to be pathetic and self-pitying in response to her words. She was talking about people. It didn't have to apply to me if I didn't let it. "Is anything else playing?"

"*Rope*, the one about murderers."

"That's based on a true story, you know. The real killers

were two University of Chicago students, Leopold and Loeb."

Anabel gave me a crooked smile. "*Everything's* based on *something* true. Even the wildest flight of fancy launched off from the ground somewhere. *Alice in Wonderland* was playing at another theatre I saw. I bet that even that's got *some* truth behind it."

"Well, yes," I agreed. "There really was an Alice —"

That was the moment we heard the Latin. They'd been chanting for a heartbeat or two already. We'd been caught up in our conversation and hadn't heard. But now we did.

As we turned toward the sound, curious, the blood and gunpowder from the shot to Caim's head splattered over our faces and skin. Our ears rang deaf at the crack of the sound. Richard — still wearing his eye-patch, I noted dimly in the endless second — raised the gun a second time, still chanting, to exorcise me along with my brother, and fired.

SALLY

She's gone.

I guess, now that I know, the game's stuffed for her. She could rip my memories out again, but that wouldn't change the fact I'd cracked it once. I can't be a clean mark anymore.

And so now she's gone.

It hurts. It hurts so bloody much I want to cry out from it, but I reckon it's no more than I ever deserved. Because of Chio, and Dad, and everyone else I've ever run away from. Sooner or later it was bound to be my turn to be the one left.

It hurts so much.

Vicky's still sleeping off whatever it is Amy did to her. Heck and Joke helped me throw some tucker together for the kids, a stew of scraps and some bread to fatten it out. Maggie's wrangling them all to bed now. She's got a spitfire spirit, that one. Never stops fighting.

It's a good way to be — I should know — but it makes me blue that she's gotta grow that way. That she's got no other choice. It'd be nice if she could be soft and loved instead. But I guess the world's never been known for being nice.

Now me and Heck are sitting on the back step, sipping at cups of tea with a lotta whiskey added in.

"This isn't your responsibility, you know," Heck says, patting me on the shoulder. "I know you're not the mothering kind. You don't need to feel obligated to stay."

He doesn't know yet, what I asked of Amy. The pain

she ate away from Vicky's heart. Things will be better in the morning. I won't be so needed. But that's not the point.

"Everyone thinks I'm a ratbag," I say. "But I'm not. Not really. It's just that I'm still looking for the place that's home. Maybe it's no place."

Maybe it's people, I think. A person, or something close to one, at any rate. But she's gone now. That's how all stories go if you carry them on long enough.

"You're like the magpies," Heck says. "Most hate you without bothering to know you."

"Mix of white and black in me feathers," I agree, taking another mouthful of tea. "Sounds about right."

"The blackfellas have a real pretty name for them. For magpies. Can't remember it right now," Heck tells me.

Young feet pound through the kitchen to the back door, and Maggie appears behind us, her expression wild. We all go back to being kids when we're afraid enough.

"A man's in the house," she says, breath short, words high and fast. "I found him standing over Mum. She's. She's dead, I think. He's got a knife. I locked the kiddies' room on my run out here."

She holds up one grubby little hand, clutched around the iron key. There's a footfall from behind her, a heavier tread than her own young bare feet. The three of us react to the sound with a flight down the short stairs and onto the grass. We turn to face the approaching figure.

"Go get your gun," I say to Heck without looking over to him. "Take Maggie."

"You, too," he says, grabbing at my arm, but I wrench away from him. After a confused moment he goes over the fence to his own home, Maggie a half-step behind him.

This is for me. I know it. The kids, Heck, Maggie, they're not in danger. Only me, who has that little bit of raw creation-stuff inside. The dark touch of Amy's influence.

Vicky's dead. Maybe Pia, too, and others before her.

Now there's only me left for the hunters to destroy, and everything will be all right.

    I'm going to die.

    But I'm going to die fighting.

AMY

Anabel's reflexes were faster than mine. So much for preternatural speed. She'd prepared for a moment such as this better than I had. My plans had always centered on avoidance and escape, while she'd contemplated the possibility of confrontation. And here we were, hard ground beneath us and hard wall behind us, nowhere to run. Penned like the prey we were.

Her hand grabbed mine between us and squeezed hard enough to grind the little bones together. It was our only chance, our only moment. There was no time to second-guess what harm I might cause her or the child inside. All I could do was breathe it in, like drinking down a hailstorm, battered by the grief panic lossfear*painfury* that Anabel fed me.

I stood, dragging Anabel to half-kneeling by our joined hands. My other arm shot out to splay the flat of my palm across Richard's face. I mashed his lips, still chanting Latin, against his teeth. Surprise made his gun shoot wide, grazing the scant meat of my upper arm, breezing hot and sharp past my shoulder into the dark.

I reached down into his memories. The fire of my inner-self was fed high by the tinder of Anabel's loss, of every hurt that had plagued her since she was the smallest girl. I took it all and sent it into him, burning down every thought or recollection in his head.

This was not the subtle surgery of removing one small memory, leaving errant sparks of inspiration in the wake. This was an inferno, a fireball up my arm, and I was screaming and Richard was screaming.

It hurt like a broken heart.

I didn't even feel it when Anabel pried her hand free from my own and grabbed the gun from his. She fired three times, all point-blank to his head. The recoil threw her backwards into the side of the church. She slid down into a crumpled heap, eyes already closed. With that much stripped out of her heart, I expected her to be asleep for hours.

The fire receded back into me. The blood was sticky and slick and hot on my face and clothes. My arm was horribly burned but already healing fast from all the power in me. So was the gunshot on my arm. I swayed on my feet but didn't faint.

My brother was dead. Exorcised. Trapped beyond the edge of the world forever.

I heard footsteps, the slam of a door. People were coming out of the church. Everything had happened in only a few seconds. In a few seconds more, I would have to explain why Anabel and I were alive and Caim and Richard were not.

I felt grateful that stories were my stock in trade.

SALLY

Tiny frayed strands of memory flutter in my head like they're bits that Amy didn't burn away cleanly. *Pete*, this one's name is. He's the younger of the two hunters who were after her. I wonder if the other is nearby, ready to kill me quick if I manage to get away from this one.

Pete's down the stairs and on me before I can dart out of the way. He knocks me down and stabs at my throat with a long knife, the blade notched and dark with blood. Vicky's blood. This man will kill a grieving mother as she sleeps. I cannot reason with him, cannot argue and talk my way out of this like I have so many other scrapes and problems.

I'm so scared. I'm so goddamned scared. This is the moment in novels and films where Amy would come back and save me, and everything would be all right.

But it never works like that, except in stories.

I block the knife with my forearm, grunting at the pain of it, and bring my knee up to his crotch as hard as I can. In the moment of helpless shock that follows, I roll away from him, too tangled and afraid to stumble upright and run away. My head swims. Blood smears a trail behind me as I crawl, the wound pulsing.

One of the littlies wails from the room right above my head. I'm in the low space beneath the house now, the raised-above-the-floodwater space, like where I used to lie with my radio and my comics when I was a little girl and me mum was still alive. I can hear another young voice shush her.

Those poor kids. What'm I gonna do with those poor kids? What will they do if Pete, whose heavy footfalls are walking the perimeter looking for the best place to duck down and come and finish me off, what will they do if he kills me, and they're left to fend for themselves?

Not that I'll make much of a mum, if I make it out of this. It's not where my talents have ever been. I wasn't built to be happy that way, not forever. Not that anything's really forever, anyway. You just gotta accept that and go on anyways, 'cos the other option's death, and that's no kind of option at all.

Something sleek brushes against my ankle, long and cool. A yelp strangles in my throat because for a second I think it's Pete grabbing at me, and I'm done for. But he's still out in the back yard in the sharp evening air of outdoors. Down here under the house, in the dirt and gravel and small sharp stones and cobwebs, it's just me. Me and the fat, flat body of the death adder sliding against my shin.

It looks at me with reptilian eyes, the tip of its tail twitching in an uncanny little dance. They use those as a lure, somebody once told me. Might have been Nell, who knew a lot about all the unfamiliar poisons lurking in the land around her. Death adders wave their tails like worms to catch the birds that come to feed. A predator playing at being prey.

"Hope you don't have a taste for magpie girls," I mutter, hefting its body with my blood-sticky hands and resting it across my shoulders. My arm is pulsing out blood still. A lot of blood. I'll probably faint soon, and then I'll be finished for certain.

I begin to crawl back out, quiet as I can, toward the open air. If I'm to die, I don't want to do it like a rabbit in a burrow. I lived as free as I could manage, after all. The world owes me an ending to match.

"It's the only way to save your soul!" Pete pleads, his

voice panicked and distraught, facing the darkness as I emerge.

I run at him as fast as I can, stumbling on my shaky legs. As he turns toward me, I throw the death adder at him with as much force as I can muster. It falls short, landing on the grass. Less than an eye-blink later it stretches, striking across the distance I couldn't hurl its weight.

The bite breaks through the fabric of Pete's trousers and into the meat of his leg. He staggers and falls, screaming.

"Nobody asked me if I wanted to be saved," I tell him, and my knees give out from under me.

Shouting. There's shouting behind me, and I turn my head, dizzy. Heck and Maggie and Joke are there with Heck's gun.

Heck's gun in Maggie's small and grubby hands.

Again I flash to Nell, to the little shards of wisdom that she gave me. I remember one drunken, awful night, after she'd got the kind of telegram all the Land Army girls feared like nothing else. A telegram saying that Nicolas, a boy who was Nell's brother in all the ways that mattered, in all the ways but blood, had been killed.

I remember her tears, and I remember something sad and hard and certain in her face as she'd said quietly,

Kids shouldn't have guns.

Looking at Maggie, at her small finger on the gunmetal-black of the trigger, I understand the profound truth of Nell's words in every drop of myself. I cannot let this happen. I must do whatever necessary to save Maggie from this moment, or my own damnation will be worthless.

I want to live, to see the sun come up, to find Nell again someday and meet her husband. I want to tell stories to kids, about Rainbow Snake and the girls from the moon and from Crow and the mystery of the Min-Min lights. I want to see Amy again.

But first I must do whatever necessary to keep Maggie

from firing that gun.

"Wait," I shout, the word feeble as it leaves my lungs.

I crawl across the space between myself and Pete, ignoring the now-departing death adder as it slides away. Pete lies on his back, gasping. I know the death adder's bite can paralyze, but this seems too fast for that. Perhaps it's the pain that's locked him still, which seems strange since I hurt so much and I'm still moving.

Maybe that's all survival is. The ability to go on no matter how bad the hurt.

I take the knife from his unresponsive hand and slice open his throat. His skin is thick, weathered. It's nothing like killing a chicken or a pig. The necessary slaughters of my farm childhood have never felt more distant. What I am doing now would banish anyone from being a kid, no matter how young they were.

I didn't realize I still had so much innocence to lose.

I keep my eyes on his as he dies. It's the least I can do.

I'll never forget it, what he looks like in that last moment. The hate for me in his eyes. The fear. But better that I carry a memory like that than Maggie does. Better me than her.

Joke takes the knife from my hand. I don't know how much later it is. Seconds, minutes, hours. I've been locked on Pete's unstaring eyes, and death is a thing outside of time.

"Come on, sweetheart," Heck says to me softly, guiding me inside the house.

Numbly, I follow.

ELLA

Dear Tash,

I've already said that I don't intend to tell you about Hell, but what about Heaven?

There's not nearly so much to say on the subject as there would be about Hell, of course. Perfection's boring. And just as Hell is other people, Heaven is a private dream for each of its inhabitants.

Actually that's just an idea I stole from the *Matrix*. Really I have no idea what Heaven's like, and I never will. The demons know, of course, but they don't talk about it.

I think it'd have to be like that, though, wouldn't it? Everyone locked in their own happy dreams. Their personal paradise. You couldn't let other people in. People are too likely to hurt one another. It wouldn't be Heaven if there was a way for it to break your heart.

It's easier for God to love people when they're asleep, anyway.

ex

Dear Tash,

Bank robbers living wild and on the run didn't begin with Bonnie and Clyde, of course. From 1878 to 1880, the

Kelly Gang managed an excellent and infamous job of it on horseback in the Australian bush.

Steve Hart was a teenage troublemaker who won horse races and met Dan Kelly during a stint in jail for horse theft. The two were both young, sharp-edged sons of Irish immigrants. They stayed together from when they met until they died.

Out of jail, still teenaged and rebellious and drifting, Dan asked Steve if he wanted to come out to Bullock Creek and pan for gold with Dan, Dan's brother Ned, and their friend Joe. The police were after Dan and Ned for some petty reason or another, much as was always the case. Lying low out in the wild seemed the best way to stay out of trouble.

Steve grinned at Dan and replied, "Here's to a short life and a merry one."

We always remember the first part and not the second when we think of doomed outlaws. Short lives, early deaths, squandered chances. And as more time passes, and I see more and more things I could have done and never did, I understand why the early death of anyone can be seen as tragic.

But the second part of what Steve said is what explains the first. If your objective in the world isn't to as live as long as you can, but to fill your life with as much of what you care about as you can, then a short life isn't a bad thing or a good thing any more than a small bucket or a large bucket is. It's the contents that count, not the size of the container.

The gold-panning expedition hit a problem when the police began to search the bushland for the Kelly brothers. Things all went to shit fast, like they so often do: the gang killed the police and had to slip deeper into hiding.

Then, fueled by the frustration and hopelessness and oppression of their world — much like Bonnie and Clyde would be later, and perhaps, too, like Cobweb would be even later after that — the Kelly gang began to rob banks.

Like Bonnie, Ned Kelly knew the way to make a fable out of truth. He wrote long, thoughtful letters, sometimes dictating them to Joe right there in the banks, and let the world know through his words who he was and how his story went.

Later, a whole lot later, Mick Jagger of the Rolling Stones played Ned in a movie. Rock stars and outlaws. We're never too far apart. Marianne Faithfull, every inch as much a rock star as Mick, was going to play Ned's infamous sister, but drugs got in the way and derailed that plan.

The most important thing to know about Ned's wild outlaw sister, though, is this: she never existed. Or, rather, she did, winning races on her side-saddle and scoping out the lay of streets before the gang moved in to hit a bank. But she wasn't who most thought she was. The slim teenaged riding star decked out in lovely dresses was Steve, not a Kelly at all — at least not a Kelly by any marriage rite known in the ordinary world of that time and of that place.

Because the strangely-shaped, the different, the queer, the monsters — the only place we fit is outside, outlawed, isn't it? It shouldn't be. It isn't fair that we learn to be tough because we have no other choice. It isn't fair we have to cultivate our cultures in ghettos and in Hell. It isn't fair at all, but it's the way it is, for now at least.

Perhaps HUSH and others like you make things a little more even, in small but incremental ways. But for Steve, in that time and in that place, the merry life he carved out for himself could be only this: short and wild, a skirt worn on a side-saddle, a myth of an outlaw girl.

That myth would live on long after the boy behind the legend died a sobbing death in fire. When the flames died down and the police went in, the bodies they found were locked together. Steve and Dan's arms had been wrapped around each other when they burned.

    XE

Tash,

    Being human, being alive, is like being drugged or drunk or asleep. The things we do seem strange in the light of day. We wonder why they mattered, why we reacted as we did. Death is a tragedy as much as growing up is a tragedy, or waking up is a tragedy, or the end of an affair, or the shattering of glass. Energy cannot be created or destroyed, yet once-vital things can cease to have any meaning. Matter is eternal but will not always matter.

    e.

Dear Tash,

    We went for a drive out through the Colorado hills, just the three of us, dwarfed by the scale of the nature all around. We were insignificant and free. The wind roared through the open windows, striking our faces with the force of a slap.
    I wanted to die then, I was so happy. Then I thought *well, close enough.* I'd be dead before the glow faded.
    We got sodas, belched loudly and laughed together, and drove back home so that I could get ready for my parents to take me to school, and so I could give you the cup of mustard water, poison you like the princess in a fairytale

to make sure you'd be safe at home while the monsters had their fun.

But not even Snow White and Sleeping Beauty stayed static forever, and you are far more alive than fictions could be.

I wish I'd comprehended how much wider the world could be than the Colorado plains.

I am so glad you didn't repeat my mistake.

xE

Dear Tash,

One tiny random fact that occasionally gets included in accounts of that day is that the middle finger of one of Stacey's hands was blown off by the gunshot to her head. Forensics teams and authors have concluded that she must have been covering her face with her hands before she got asked the God question and then didn't drop them away as she answered.

None of us who was there has ever said otherwise. Most of us are dead, and those who aren't can see the enormity of the legacy Stacey has left behind. They probably don't want to go up against it in even the slightest way. What good could come from challenging a myth with the truth? And it's such a little truth. It doesn't mean much of anything.

When Stacey said 'yes' she had her middle finger raised, a fuck-you gesture at the three of us. She didn't just die defiant; she died angry.

The nail of her finger was painted messily with bright pink polish and yellow dots. None of her other fingernails were painted, so I knew it had to have been a little girl, her little sister, who did it. You'd done the same to my nails countless times, swirls and smears of candy shades.

And it made me think of you, at home in bed, watching your videos. I looked down at my hands, but there wasn't any polish there. I was going to die with clean fingernails.

I'm sorry.

xxxE

Dear Tash, who was Nattie, and then grew up,

I went to Earth today. A dry run. I'm going to go again tomorrow. That's the important one. But I went today. I went to the school, to the wide park beside it.

There were soccer games playing on all the fields, SUV moms and shrill children, happy screams and sad screams in the late afternoon. And dust motes in the air, little golden pollen flickers that made everything seem heavy and still and slow.

The April heat — in case you don't remember it anymore, in Colorado April is hot and cold all at once, too much of everything, a tangle as complicated and contradictory as a teenage heart — had made the grass into patchy straw, green and wheat-pale in waves and wriggles.

The memorial on the hill is designed in natural curves and swoops, blending into the swells of earth around it so much more elegantly than any other architecture in the suburb.

That seemed funny to me, that the grief and loss was a

part of the landscape here now, blending better than the soccer-screams and schools and houses and stores.

Cobweb was more a part of this place now than any of the things that Cobweb had destroyed.

I followed the looping path through the concentric low walls, past quotes from survivors and a donation box and small trees in a cluster, one for each of the dead. Near and distant casualties all gathered here.

There's a plaque for each victim, too, with quotes from the family or whatever. Dody Schillinger's has the shape of a cross and lines from his dad about how the massacre was caused by legalized abortion and a lack of prayer in schools. I guess people need something to blame, and me and Chris and Dean and the other shooters weren't around. In our absence the grieving had to find other devils.

Stacey's has an excerpt from her diary, of course. I used to think how shitty it would be to be immortalized in words you left behind, to be defined like that, but now I think that it's better than nothing. I'd rather be known through these letters to you than not known at all. Even if these letters could never hope to catch all of me, to convey all the multitudes of who I am. A glimpse is better than nothing.

When I was sitting on a bench higher up the hill from the plaques, I could look out at the view from every direction, the stifling airless sprawl of suburbia stretching to the mountains and the city.

It seems endless, down on street level, but from up here, it's small and easily escaped. Perhaps it wouldn't have looked like that to us when we were alive. But it does to me now, so far distant from my teenage years and the mistakes I littered through them.

I was up there, thinking, when Stacey sat down beside me.

"I can't forgive you," she told me. "It's not my place to forgive on behalf of anyone but myself. And I don't think I want to forgive you on my own behalf. I was a fucking kid, you jackass. I had a whole life ahead of me, and you took it away."

I didn't know what to say, so I didn't say anything.

"I came up here, right after," she said, apparently not needing any input from me in the conversation anyway. "There was like... this stillness. After I died. Like the universe paused and let me slip out of it between one second and the next. It gave me time to come up here, to stand and look around at the world."

"What's Heaven like?" I blurted out.

She ignored me.

"How can you keep loving God?" I asked. "When you know all the things that are *wrong*? When you died so young —"

"When you killed me, you mean," she interrupted.

"When people like Sam Brightwater and Nicky Caramano go to Hell for being gay, how can —"

Stacey interrupted me a second time. "I can love someone even if they're not perfect, even if they make choices I don't agree with. You of all people should be grateful that humans have that ability, Ella Vrenna.

"And you'll have to change some of the names, you know. If you're going to do what I know you're planning to do with those letters. Sam Brightwater, Vivi Verdun. You'll get in trouble, otherwise."

"Because clearly trouble is something I habitually avoid." I snorted, but listened all the same. I went through and changed those two names in all these letters, not because I really see the reason, but because I know that Stacey probably knows better than I do what constitutes a good idea. You'd be able to work out easily enough what the real names are, anyway. I haven't done a very thorough job at hiding anything.

I noticed that Stacey's saint-self and mine were similar:

each of us looked like we had when we were alive, with a single difference. Each of us had tattoos that we hadn't had on our real versions of ourselves. Hers was the same as Cherry's, and mine was like yours.

Only love on her wrist and *only sky* on mine. We were linked to our sisters, linked even though our blood was gone to ash and earth now. We were linked to the women we'd never known, the little girls who'd grown up without us.

Eventually, as night began to fall, we went back down the hill and through the half-maze shapes of the memorial proper.

A camera man and journalist came up to us. They asked if we'd heard about Brazil, where just yesterday this had happened again, another school and another shooter and more dead.

They were here at the memorial to ask why, to try to find some answers.

So Stacey and I were filmed, ghosts on the digital celluloid, saying that maybe there would never be answers. Maybe nobody ever knows why. Maybe music or bullying or illness or sadness or anger or poverty or affluence or ennui or race or anything else isn't where the answers are.

I used to think I knew.

"Sometimes things happen," I said as the camera man filmed me, struggling for a way to explain something too large for words.

Stacey shook her head. "Things don't just happen. People do things. The problem is understanding why."

"Do you think the parents are to blame?" the journalist asked.

Stacey shrugged. "I think the parents probably did the best they could, even if they were old or clueless or strict or didn't understand how the world had changed. They probably didn't help the situation any, but..." She shrugged again, as lost for the perfect words as I was. You'd think that if anyone could offer an answer, it would be us. But we couldn't. "Sorry, I don't know. I guess we're the wrong people for you to ask."

"Do you think it's something you only understand when it touches your own life?"

"Not even then," said Stacey.

Then Stacey and I left Colorado. We moved through the no-space between spaces and came to Australia, to Queensland, to Brisbane, to the little club where your band was stepping onto the stage for their sound check.

You were laughing and chatting, you and Cherry. Sisters together when your sisters were gone. A new life and a new family built out of the wreckage of my youth and hate.

Nothing ever ends. It only changes.

You began to play, and Stacey took my hand, and together we watched the haven you'd created from the dark, from the expectations of heaven and the threat of hell. In the music, there was none of that. There was all of that. There was a story, full of darkness and loss and despair, and maybe, after all the rest, a happy ending. I hoped so.

We stood together, your little ghosts, our hands entwined between us. Only love, only sky.

ella

DAVID

Sometimes there is a small grace between moments, when all the world pauses and stills. David saw it first in the war, not always by any stretch, but on occasion. A bullet hit, and the orderly tick of seconds was breached along with skin as the kid beside him or the kid across on the other side of the lines crumpled and fell.

In those small grace moments, he saw a glimpse of something large and cold and maybe fucking unknowable. David sure as hell didn't know the first thing about how to fathom it.

He didn't feel it, that *thing*, when Nicky died. Not that he looked too hard for it. David Caramano, who spent the rest of his fucking life freezing moments in perfect photographic amber, never touched the memory of his brother's if there wasn't an extremely good fucking reason to do so.

Sometimes that same grace-thing, that stutter in the pulse of the world, happened with photos, too. It happened when he snapped Lena holding Nicky's photo. It happened in little Marie's room at the hospital, the day she cut off Jacq's hair.

Fuck, but he's so fucking proud of those kids. Jacqui and Ben. He loves them so much, with their stupid-ass band that all the kids love so much, that's proving right the challenge Ben set himself to show that music had worth, music had meaning.

David would never tell Ben this — wouldn't know how to even start to say it — but it made something precious bloom up in David's chest that Ben even fucking tried in the first place. That some skinny punk kid believed in song, in *anything,* so much that he thought it could survive against the mayhem and anarchy and horror of war, of seeing Nicky lost, of having to come back and build a life and somehow go on after.

Only a stupid-ass kid ever thought they were that powerful against the world, that they could change it. Only a stupid-ass kid was ever audacious and absurd enough to *manage* it.

David and Nicky and Lena, they'd all been stupid-ass kids, too.

The only way David and Lena had managed to survive, after, was through determination to make the world safer for the ones who came after them. To do whatever they could to keep guns and knives out of hands too young to comprehend their power.

Caroline, she wrote something similar. In her book that's staying secret to the day David dies. She wrote about killing a man so that the kid she was with didn't have to.

Maybe the book's fiction, maybe it's not. David thinks it's probably a mix of both. Whatever it is, Caroline wanted it kept away from the world until all four of them were dead.

And David thinks that maybe that day's coming soon. He's hid his frailty from the kids as best he can — they're touring in fucking Australia, of all places; the last thing they need is an old man complaining about his health — but the day is coming nonetheless.

Amy went first, not even in her sixties. Melanoma. She'd been philosophical about it, saying that she'd always known she'd die by burning.

Lena next, and David still misses her with an ache he can barely breathe around, every fucking morning without fail. He remembers, better than the back of his own hands or the tread of his own feet the way she looked when she danced. The sweetness, the joy. Even after everything, she'd somehow still found joy. She'd believed in music long after David stopped.

Caroline's gone now too, resting in the dirt over in Australia, and so there's only David left to guard the story. He keeps it in a file on his computer's desktop, marked with an explanation of what it is.

But today he thinks he might email it to Jacqui and Ben. Because this morning as he woke up, he felt one of those limitless, cold pauses in the world. He thinks maybe this time it was the end of something. The end of him.

He spends the morning looking through his photographs at the kitchen table. Moments, memories, people. He's done good things, as much as he can. And some stupid things, and things he regrets, and things that went badly. But those things are a part of life, too. Can't remove them without the whole house of cards falling down to shit.

"Hi. Can I talk to you for a second?"

David looks up.

A girl, a bit younger than Jacq or Ben, a teenager, stands at the edge of the table. She looks like that Natasha girl from their band.

Looks like his hunch was right, then.

"Ella, right?" he says, gesturing for her to come in and sit down at the table.

She blinks, like she's surprised. Christ, she's so fucking young, such a stupid-ass fucking kid. The newsreel photos of her have become just a signifier. They don't look like the actual girl. When shown any image too often, people stop actually seeing.

"Most people don't just use my first name," she says. "They use them both, like one word, you know? *Ellavrenna*."

"Most people are dumb fucks," David says, mouth tugging up into a lopsided smirk.

She giggles, shocked, the way kids get shocked when adults swear.

"What's up, Ella?" he asks.

She holds up a thumb drive, the kind kids keep on their key rings to swap movies and music and shit.

"I have... they're letters," she says, a little nervously. "For my sister. I wanted... when you send the email, can you send those, too?"

He thinks of Caroline's story, full of demons and fire and strangeness already. If the kids in Jacq and Ben's band can handle all that, they can probably handle this as well. They're tough, those kids. They've had no choice but to be.

"Sure," David nods. "Let's go send it now."

It's probably some stupid-assed time in Australia. He hopes so. He hopes it's hours before the kids are awake, before they open their inboxes. He wants to be gone already, and for them to know it, before they see the message. That way they'll know he hasn't gone so far at all.

"Want a cigarette, kid?" he asks, offering her the pack after he gets one out for himself. Ella takes one with a small smile, accepting the lighter as well after he's got his own going.

Shutting off the computer, they go back into the kitchen. David thinks he'd like to die looking at his photos, even if the smoking's not good for them.

"Mr. Caramano?"

Another kid stands in the doorway. Not hovering tentatively, as Ella had been. Just standing, still and patient.

This girl's age is harder to define. She's young, but her expression's old, older even than David feels most days. Her hair is spiky-short, white as powder. Personally, David thinks hair like that looks stupid-ass, but he's happy about that. He's glad kids aren't scared of looking like who they are on the inside anymore. The world's a different place to what it was when he and Nicky were that young.

He looks down at the photos again. Snapshots of his family. He's glad they're the last things he'll see. It's been a good life.

"You got a name?" he asks this newcomer, stubbing out his cigarette and standing. "I'm not calling you Death."

"I don't tell my name to many people, sir."

Christ, it's like the kid hasn't even heard that smiling exists. Like the weight of the world's on her shoulders. She's dressed in a long coat of soft blue leather, black pants, and heavy boots. Her eyelids glitter, a paler blue, when she blinks. Her lips are as red as a wound.

"If you don't tell me, I'll just call you 'kid.' And if there's one thing I know about kids, it's that they hate being called 'kid.'"

Still no smile, but there's a grave amusement in her ice-fair eyes.

"It's Lucifer," says the kid.

David blinks, surprised, and then starts to laugh and can't stop. He doesn't mean to be a smartass at the kid, he really doesn't, but goddammit it's been a while since he heard something that funny.

The kid — Lucifer, damn if that doesn't beat everything David's heard before — just waits politely. There's a ghost of something that may be a smile at the corners of her own grave mouth. David notices that Ella has slipped away, vanishing quietly to some other place.

"Sorry," David manages to say when he gets his breath back. "I was thinking I'd maybe have said less shit about God being an asshole if I'd known you guys were for real. Goddamn." He starts laughing again, and this time Lucifer really does smile.

"No, you wouldn't have changed a word," she says to David, and David knows she's right.

"Yeah. Might've even made me angrier, if anything," David agrees. He gives the kid a long look. "So how come a guy like me warrants a visit from a gal like you?"

Lucifer's smile has faded back to her former still, serious expression, but there's warmth in her eyes. "I'm a big fan, sir."

David chokes on another laugh. "I wish I could tell that to a couple of critics I've known. The Devil likes my work."

"Your photographs, and your life as well. I respect a man who throws his doors wide to lost souls, gives them a home."

"Gotta give them somewhere to go when they're kicked out or left behind," David says. "Seems simple enough to me."

"And that's why a guy like you warrants a visit from a gal like me."

David smiles, but his next words are serious.

"I did it all for him, you know. Always for him. I couldn't stand by and let the world go on letting kids like him die for bullshit reasons. I couldn't love a God who didn't want him exactly as he was."

Out of nothing, two more figures step into sight on either side of Lucifer. They're as young and beautiful as they've always been in David's heart.

Nicky is as young and delicate as he was in life, but there's a luminosity to his features now, like a photograph taken with an old, scratched lens. There's a light within him, and in Lena, too.

Lena is just as David has always thought of her, the stubborn and feisty woman with worn palms and a generous, forthright smile. The girl at the picture-theatre every weekend.

"I know," Nicky promises. "I always knew."

"It's time to come home," Lucifer says, and David steps forward and takes her hand.

AMY

I wished that Caim was there to tell our fortunes. To tell me what came next. Even the worst possibilities would have been better than not knowing at all.

But Caim was gone, and we had to go on anyway.

After we awoke in the hospital, we managed to get away — not as difficult as it may sound, since we were poor and clearly worthless, and nobody really cared what we did with ourselves — we set about starting anew.

"I don't know what will happen to the baby," I told Anabel. "What he will grow up to be, after what I did."

She just smiled. Her smiles were easier now than they'd ever been before. The eternal sunshine of the spotless mind, as a poem once put it. I'd taken away all the hurt she carried. Now her heart was as light and free as air.

I wondered if the baby growing inside her was destined to grow up with something missing in his heart. Maybe it wouldn't be so bad for him if that turned out to be the case, anyway. Hearts make us vulnerable.

"If his soul's a little blunted, he can always become a lawyer," she joked.

We bought cheap red dye and rinsed my coarse pale hair with it until the blonde was ruddy and rich and dark. We cut my plait off and threw it into the fire where it stank and curled and blackened and eventually became nothing. I looked like someone new.

Night fell again, and the darkness weakened my resolve to stay away. I was battered and bereaved and wanted nothing more than to fall asleep beside someone I loved dearly.

As evening began, Anabel and I set off to find Sally.

CHARLOTTE

From *Reign in Hell: Two Weeks in the Life of HUSH*, by Charlotte Waterhouse, Amplify Press, Australia, 2011:

Perhaps the catalyst was the visit to the graveyard and the memories it stirred. Whatever the real reason, I find myself telling Cherry and Tash about myself the next time that they ask.

We're sitting out in back of the Melbourne venue, killing time before the last show of the tour. All the members of the band are exhausted but happy, in their element. This is the home they've made themselves, here on the road. It's the home I've made myself, too.

My family... I say. *When I was growing up... I tell people that I'm the eldest of four but it's not strictly true. Or, it is, but there are other answers that're just as true. I'm the eldest of two. I'm the eldest of five.*

When I was growing up, it was me and my mum and my dad. Then I got a baby brother, William. Then a little later I got a baby sister, Kate. She lived seven hours.

In Victorian times, when somebody died they took pictures. Mothers with their dead babies. Those photos are heartbreaking to look at. A few years ago, while I was doing research for an article, I found out that there are photographers who still do the same thing. They go to hospitals and people's homes when a baby's died.

They take pictures, so the family has a way to remember. Has something to mark that these tiny people once existed, even if it was only for a moment.

My parents didn't get photos done. They didn't even... my brother and I stayed with our grandparents the week Kate was born. The week Kate died. We stayed with our grandparents, and they took us to movies and toy stores and pizza restaurants. But never to the hospital. We never met Kate. There are no photos for us to stare at and learn her afterwards. I was eight. Bill was four.

After that, it was like... they tried to pretend it hadn't happened. That Kate hadn't happened. But the space where she wasn't — that space was there — between all of us.

My mother told me once, many years later, that one night nearly a year after Kate died in the hospital, my father awoke from a nightmare and went in to check on his children. I was there, my brother was there, but he turned to my mother in half-asleep confusion and said "Where's the other one?"

Sometimes... I don't know if this is charitable or horrible of me, I can't tell. Sometimes I think my dad's leaving us was just genetics kicking in. The drive to pass down DNA to viable offspring.

Nature's not sentimental. Family units are useful when they support and nurture the viable offspring, but if they can't do that, then they're useless. What's the point in sticking with a mate whose genes mix with yours and cause a dud reaction, a seven-hour alchemy?

Once there's that failed result, well, then the genes begin to wonder about the other two. The girl has a dark disposition, a tendency to melancholy. The boy's temper is trigger-fine. Clearly, Nature thinks, it would be more logical to try a different mate. Mix the genes into another recipe. Find a better alchemy.

I can't decide if I'm being horrible or pragmatic, when I rationalise my father leaving us in this way.

And for whatever it's worth, it worked. My father's

second set of children, Dana and Tamara, are perfect. An extremely successful replication of his DNA. I've met them, of course. They're lovely. I wish I could have spent more time with them.

That's my own fault; I moved to Melbourne while they were still very young.

The last time I saw them before I went, we went to the park. Dana's dress was pink. Tamara's was green. My father had gout in his foot, so we walked slowly. There were these trees in the park, squat and swollen like huge pears. My father said they were full of water but that the water could send you mad.

Doesn't seem like great options to choose between, death or lunacy. Then again, being sane in a barren land wouldn't be any good either, really. Maybe drinking the crazy water is the only way any of us survive. We just changed the name from crazy water to optimism, compassion, religion, family, art, love, connection, civilisation. You swallow it because the alternative is to die of thirst alone in the desert.

I had this one weird moment at the park, though. We were all walking to the top of this hill, up to where the playground was. I got there first and turned back to watch the others after me, the little girls in their pale sugar-shade cotton dresses and white sandals, perfect children far more deserving of love than I in Nature's implacable meritocracy.

Behind the girls, slow on his sore foot, my father followed. And I felt... I felt a lot of things. I felt calm and I felt love, but something even bigger than those as well.

Calm and love weren't new things for me to feel. I was twenty-one that day, and it had been a long time since I'd hated my father. A long time. I loved him again by then, and I loved my sisters.

I loved him, but I'd never forgiven him. It wasn't

my right. I didn't have that power, and even if I had, I wouldn't have used it. How could I forgive him for my mother, whose tender beautiful heart he had broken? How could I forgive him for my brother, a little boy abandoned by his daddy? How could I pretend that I had the right, even, to forgive him on behalf of the little girl I'd once been? It wasn't my place to absolve him for causing her tears.

So, I didn't feel forgiveness. It was more like... acceptance. I couldn't forgive him for the hurt he'd caused, but I didn't have to rage against the injustices of the past. Those injuries can never be healed; they hardened into scars too long ago. But I could stop resenting those scars, stop uselessly proclaiming the injustice that they existed at all. I could accept them and move on with what I had.

When your feet hurt, you have to keep walking anyway. That's the only choice. If you wait for it to stop hurting, you'll never move at all.

Later, I stood beside Gabe in the wings of the stage and watched the lights go down on the seething crowd. The screams rose up, joyful and excited and full of determination to survive.

Ben, Jo, Tash, Cherry, and finally Jacqui filed out, each garnering a new roar of sound from their delighted audience.

A pulse of silence, as if the whole world was holding its breath.

And the rest was music.

SALLY

The huge amount of whiskey I drank while Joke stitched up my arm has mostly worn off by nightfall, and at the sight of Amy and Anabel in the doorway I feel as sober as I've ever been.

I want to shout at her. To be angry on behalf of the dead, or at least furious on behalf of myself. To yell and rage for all the trouble she brought into my life.

But that's the trade-off that comes with love. You get the problems and the trouble, along with the person. It's all or nothing.

So instead of shouting, I grab her tight and cling like I'll never let go. After a moment's uncertainty, a heartbeat's pause, Amy clings back even harder.

"My brother's dead," she says softly, face buried in the crook of my neck. I don't reply, and after a few seconds, she speaks again.

"But we're not. We're alive."

Eventually we pry ourselves apart. It only takes one look at Anabel and Heck and how they're looking at each other, for me and Amy to smirk and roll our eyes. Looks like Maggie's going to have a new mum much better suited to the job than I was gonna be, and that baby in Anabel's belly is going to have the best kind of dad it could ask for.

A nice little happy ending.

It's good. It is. I'm glad things turned out so neat for so many, especially after all the mess we had to go through in the middle.

I just wish, just a little, that things would turn out that simple for me from time to time.

Near to midnight, the three of us end up out on the back step, staring up at the stars scattered above.

All the carnage is gone, cleaned away. Pete and Vicky are buried; I helped Joke dig the graves out in the bushland. We didn't let Heck help. He's the sort who'd never stop thinking about it if he knew.

"You can't stay anywhere if you know where the skeletons are buried underfoot," Anabel remarks after I tell her and Amy about the bodies.

Then she looks up again at the sky. "Though for some, there's ghosts up in the stars, so they can't ever get away. There's a story the Aboriginals tell about those four stars there, see them? What they say is this:

In the beginning, the sun-god made three people, a woman and two men. He showed them how to eat the fruit of all the trees, and then he left them.

"*They ate the fruit, and they were happy, until winter came. And then the fruit was all gone. One of the men and the woman began to kill animals so that they wouldn't starve, but the other man refused. He walked and walked, searching for more fruit, until eventually he was too tired and too hungry, and he lay down in the roots of a tree.*

"*The Yowi, a devil who lived in the tree, reached out and grabbed the man and pulled him inside the trunk, and then the tree flew up and up and up into the sky.*

"Those four stars are their eyes, staring out. Two for the monster, and two for his victim, stuck up there together forever."

"Kill or be killed," Amy says to the night air. She sounds thoughtful. "Be a predator and eat animals for food, or become prey for something worse than yourself."

"No," Anabel replies. "I don't think this kind of story has a moral. Not... not really. Or if it does, it's nothing so simple as that. Sometimes stories are a way for us to remember things about the world. Or to imagine them. And then we share the stories with each other so that we're not the only one. The only one who remembers, or imagines. That's all."

Later, Heck joins us. "I remembered the name for magpies," he tells me. "It's *gubura*."

I like that. Maybe I'll take it for my own name. I think I want a new one, now. Or, if not new, at least a different one. I think Sally's story is over.

"My real name's Caroline," I tell the others. "Before it was Sally, I mean. My mum named me Caroline."

"That's pretty. I like it," Amy says quietly. She's been quiet ever since we got back.

I don't want her to feel rotten about this. It's finished with, and nothing can change it. A whole naked horizon of future is out there in front of us to go explore. Soon as we stop worrying about what came before, we can go off and see what comes after.

"It's all right, that you weren't here," I explain, taking her hand in mine. "I saved myself."

Special Bonus Story

SHOTS AND CUTS

There's almost nothing on this planet that can shove me out of my comfort zone. That was true when I was a snot-nosed kid, and after fifteen years in the homicide unit, it's even truer.

Serves me well on the job, but there's a downside.

Take last Christmas, for example. Sitting around the table after we'd picked the turkey down to scraps on a rib-cage, everyone mellow and chatty, and I realise that the only topics I know anything about are tales of the bleakest places in the human soul. I start telling this one story, about the Maniacs, because that's the one I've been reading up on for a local case. Murder's like any other human interest: if you want to be an expert, you have to stay ahead of the trends.

So I mention something about the case, because I think it's quirky enough to pique at least a little interest, and my sister gives me this look that shut me right the hell up. My sister's as normal and suburban as they come — the opposite of me — and so I've started using her as my yardstick of what it's not okay to talk about at the family Christmas. Turns out the answer is pretty much 'everything I know about.'

Her kids want to hear more, of course. She's got twins, fraternal but both boys, nearly fifteen. Too smart to give much of a shit about school, too dumb to know what to do with themselves otherwise. Old enough to get away with hearing about gory shit and young enough that they can't really comprehend the full meaning of said shit. But maybe I'm not giving them enough credit there; kids grow up early, these days.

Have you been to a concert lately? Doesn't matter the band. Rock, pop, metal — same's true for them all. Next time you're at a show, look away from the stage and around at the crowd.

Little camera screens everywhere, right? Mostly cellphones, some regular cameras. But all of them digital and all of them set to video mode.

Forget any rumours of debauchery and drug use going on backstage; the real danger to the souls of rock and rollers comes from that old chestnut about cameras stealing your spirit when they capture an image. Those poor musicians have been fractured into a thousand thousand YouTube uploads.

The weird part is that most of the kids with the cameras, they aren't watching the stage. Their eyes are on their screens like they're already preparing the memory rather than living the moment. Like my sister's kids, who can't keep their phones out of their hands at the Christmas dinner table or through a movie screening. Always only halfway paying attention to the real world.

Growing up in the age of the Internet has made this younger generation into expert curators of their own lives. They all know how to angle a snapshot to make their faces thinner, how to phrase an update so their day sounds exciting and glamorous. Life stops happening and becomes how they shape the memory of it. Zoom in, jump cut, adjust the audio levels.

So what, right? If kids would rather collect a life than live it then that's their business, isn't it? Okay, sure. But remember this: a generation's monsters reflect the generation. Charles Manson turned free love into free hate. Ted Bundy keeping severed heads in his house like acquisition would lead automatically to fulfillment. Kids in black trench coats thinned locker-room herds.

If the world fears its monsters, what frightens twice as hard is the spectre of a teenage villain. Teenagers, even the non-monstrous variety, do not play by grown-up rules. They care too much about some things and not enough about others. Their emotions simmer constantly, just a degree or two short of boiling over. Even at their most placid, teenagers are scary. My sister's kids are still years away from learning the art of moderation, of subtlety. Everything happens to them with the volume turned up to eleven.

One last thing before I start the story of the Maniacs, something you already know if you've ever watched a crime drama on TV or read a paperback thriller you bought at the airport. One last piece to put on the board before we start the game. It's this: serial killers take trophies from their kills. A lock of hair, a drop of blood, a watchband, a shoe. Something they can keep like a holy relic of their crime. Through this trophy, the killer is able to relive the murder. Sights and sounds and memories, all locked up in one little object, tidy as a YouTube link.

I'm sure you've started to see what sort of situation all these facts could lead to, if properly combined.

In June and July of 2007, twenty-one extremely brutal murders took place in the Ukraine, in a town called Dnipropetrovsk. I'm talking some Jack the Ripper shit here, and even worse than that. Faces bludgeoned with hammers until nothing resembling a face remained. Eyes gouged out of still-living victims. A pregnant woman sliced open to cut out the fetus. Children, the elderly, the drunk and homeless. Multiple bodies turned up every day. Some had their jewellery or phones stolen, though most of them weren't even robbed.

One time, near to the start of the reign of terror — what else is there to call it, honestly — two 14-year-olds were the victims, attacked in broad daylight. One of the kids died, but the other managed to get away. The police denied him access to counsel and then beat him in an effort to make him confess to killing his friend.

Shit like that gets me really steamed. It's shitty police work, and never does anything but work in a defendant's favour when you get to trial — and that's assuming that you've got the right guy to begin with, which in this case they didn't.

Sure, sure, there's reasons like personal liberties and freedom and all that. Violating the rights of another human being is never a good idea. But even purely from a pursuit-of-justice standpoint, it's a shitty methodology to employ. Anything that's gonna muddy the waters dividing the good guys (cops) from the bad guys (mass-murdering scumbag freaks) is poor procedure, in my opinion.

Twenty-one is almost too many people to comprehend as entire individuals, alive or dead. Think of all that you are, all that you hope to be, all that you remember and love and hate. It's unfathomably large. Double that. Then add another. You're still only up to three people. To get to twenty-one, you have to multiply those three infinities by seven. Then take that sublimely huge mass of consciousness, and snuff it out. Use a piece of steel construction pipe, and strike over and over until there's nothing left but red pulp on the ice of a sidewalk.

Authorities recorded a total of twenty-nine attacks. Somewhat miraculously, eight people survived their attempted murders.

But all this is nothing more or less than the usual bloodshed of human history, is it? After all, the recent history of the Ukraine alone has also given us Andrei Chikatilo, who mutilated and murdered more than fifty children and women. Or if you want to get even more specific and stay in Dnipropetrovsk, there's the police investigator Serhiy

Tkach, who confessed to murdering more than a hundred children and women.

Don't think that the Russians have something bad in the water, either. Albert Fish was born and raised in America, and in addition to counting his total victims at over a hundred, he liked to boast that he'd raped and eaten a child in every state of the USA.

To put it bluntly, humanity produces some seriously fucked pieces of shit on a regular basis. So why am I talking about one grubby little string of not quite two dozen kills? Well, the age of the killers, for starters. All this horror and gore was generated by two teenage boys, Viktor Sayenko and Igor Suprunyuck. Nineteen-year-old kids.

They grew up together, their friendship forged by the bullying they both endured and a shared fear of heights. When they were twelve years old, the boys decided to conquer that fear in the same kind of reckless bullshit way that kids try to do all kinds of dumb stuff. They climbed over the railing on the balcony of a 14th-floor apartment and hung on, bare against the wind and gravity.

Igor and Viktor stayed there on that edge for hours, and when they finally went back inside, their fear of heights had vanished.

A third friend, Alexander, had terrors of his own: hemophobia. Crippling fear of blood.

If confronting heights had cured the two boys of their fear, Igor figured that the same logic should apply for Alexander's own terror. Why not torture stray dogs, and get used to blood that way?

I ask you, what kind of fucking logic is that?

So anyway, that's what they did. Over and over. And over. They took photos, posing in silly mustaches beside their kills, drawing graffiti with the blood. Then their rituals evolved, as killers' rituals always do. They moved on to pet cats, and they moved on to video.

The reason why I'm telling you about twenty-one sordid little murders is because these kids shot their kills in just the same way that kids at concerts do. Zoom in, jump cut, adjust the audio levels.

Upload.

Here's another little piece of info about humanity. I should have provided it back at the beginning with the rest of the backgrounding, but like I said a minute ago, if you try to take in too much knowledge at once it all gets a little unreal. Twenty-one murders stops seeming twenty-one times more terrible than one murder. Humanity's capacity for depravity starts to lose its impact. Your nerves get dull from repeated exposure.

So here's a bonus bit of charm: '2 girls 1 cup.' That's the name of a minute-long viral video, also from 2007. Two women shit into a cup, then eat it, then vomit into each other's mouths.

What made the video famous wasn't simply the content. It was the YouTube fad which followed it, in which viewers set their webcams to record their reactions as they watched the video for the first time. Then they'd upload these reactions, showcasing horror and disgust, humor and nonchalance. The fad grew and grew — Esquire magazine did an article about getting George Clooney to do a reaction. Popular cartoon shows included animated gags of characters viewing the video.

A random little piece of scat porn had become the new yardstick by which everyone was measuring how jaded or innocent they were. Surely, this was the worst of the worst, the most base and foul thing anyone would ever have an opportunity to sit through.

Well, okay. Sure. Except that then, one day, a new video started going the rounds. This one quickly got the nickname '3 guys 1 hammer.'

There were Viktor and Igor and a man on the ground. There was the hammer of the title, wrapped in a plastic bag to protect it as it struck the man over and over. His name was Sergei Yatzenko. He'd recently survived throat cancer. He looked after his disabled mother. He had two children and one grandchild.

Viktor and Igor were surprised to find that Sergei was still alive, lapsing in and out of consciousness, even after they'd stabbed a screwdriver into his eye and into exposed parts of his brain.

We know they were surprised because they say so in the video, in mild and calm tones, while they wash their hands and the hammer with bottled water.

Can you even start to look for a motive in a set of actions like those of Viktor and Igor? Can deeds like that ever have an excuse or reason?

During the boys' trial, the fact emerged that Igor had been collecting newspaper clippings about his murders, annotating them in a scrapbook.

Of the videos themselves, one of the Detectives on the case offered this as an explanation: "We think they were doing it as a hobby, to have a collection of memories when they get old."

The abyss at the heart of the human soul is a deep, dark place. It's probably not wise to gaze into it for very long. I try not to, even when I'm working a case and doing my best to get inside the heads of monsters.

But they caught the monsters, so everything's okay now, right? Igor and Viktor are gonna be behind bars for the rest of their days. Their collections, horrifying though they may be, are never going to get any bigger.

Except that in April 2011, authorities arrested two more teenaged kids for six more murders in Siberia, after a video turned up of a woman's death and mutilation. This new pair used the internet to read up on the activities of the kids in Dnipropetrovsk. They were inspired, and so grabbed a mallet and a knife and a camera and set out to start their own collections.

Remember that Nicholas Cage movie from a few years back, 8mm? In it there's a video that looks like it shows a murder, but everyone's sure it must be fake? It isn't just that they want to believe that the film is staged because they have faith in the human spirit or some shit like that — even two-dimensional characters in a gory crime thriller genuinely believe that snuff movies don't ever really exist. It seems too unfathomable, too horrible. Surely, nobody is capable of creating such a thing.

Ever hear that saying about truth being stranger than fiction? I guess we have to add 'infinitely more fucked up' to truth's attributes.

I just typed Sergei Yatzenko's name into Google to make sure I'd spelled it right, and the autocomplete option on the search bar offered me: 'sergei yatzenko video', 'sergei yatzenko death', 'sergei yatzenko killing', 'sergei yatzenko hammer', and 'sergei yatzenko YouTube'.

Forget shady back rooms and underworld deals and clandestine meetings by shadowy figures. Snuff movies are not only real, you can bring 'em up on your home computer at the click of a button.

And remember how those girls and their gross kinky little shock video inspired all those reactions? What's good for the goose turns out to be good for the gander. YouTube is now cluttered with reaction videos of people watching '3 guys 1 hammer.' The edgier message board conversations of the net use animated images of the killing strike to punctuate their banter. Murder, real murder, has become a punch line.

And I'm part of the infection too, sitting there with my family at Christmas, talking about this shit as if it's an acceptable topic of conversation for anyone, anywhere, outside of an investigation or a courtroom. Fuck it, give the world a few more years and people won't bat an eyelash when the chit-chat wanders to the subject of viral-video murder porn.

It started with three guys and a hammer. But now you have to take that three, and start multiplying. Seven times three. Seven times seven times three. Seven times seven times seven by three. Who knows how big and deep and dark that abyss can grow before it swallows everything whole.

Reaction videos will spawn reaction videos, and here and there a kid might get inspired to go a step further and add to the stockpile of the core viral load.

Articles will get written, and articles will get glued into scrapbooks.

Even these words right here that I'm typing to you are adding to the sum total, aren't they?

You and me, right now, we're part of this.

The collection's taken on a life of its own, and it's just going to keep growing and growing.

SO FREE AND SO SMALL

[a devil's mixtape for The Devil's Mixtape]

the paradise in the clouds above might as well be only sky:

THERE'S ALWAYS SOMEONE HURTING { mad world; alex parks }

Children waiting for the day they feel good / Happy Birthday, Happy Birthday / Made to feel the way that every child should / Sit and listen, sit and listen / Went to school and I was very nervous / No one knew me, no one knew me / Hello teacher tell me what's my lesson / Look right through me, look right through me

ELLAVRENNA { the red death ball; hana pestle }

The screams were heard for miles / The sight no one believed / She dreamed that they would bleed / But dreams can much deceive / The scarlet river flowed / Now our villain is free

GOD IS NEVER GUILTY AND THUS IS MERCILESS { the libertine; patrick wolf }

The magician's secrets all revealed / And the preacher's lies are all concealed / And all our heroes lack any conviction / They shout through the bars of cliche and addiction

/ So I've got to go, I've got to go, so here I go / I'm going to run the risk of being free

I WANT THE SHARPEST OF THE ROSES { four winds; bright eyes }

There's bodies decomposing in containers tonight / In an abandoned building where / Squatters made a mural of a Mexican girl / With fifteen cans of spray paint and a chemical swirl / She's standing in the ashes at the end of the world / Four winds blowing through her hair

HUMANITY'S CAPACITY FOR CRUELTY EXCEEDS EVEN GOD'S { 400 miles from darwin; the whitlams }

We pay to shed a sombre tear in the darkness together here / One among the hundreds, crying for the millions / And when the house lights break the trance / Only then unclasp our hands / Compose ourselves and fix our hair / "We would have all been Schindler there" / Drive in silence slowly home / Now horror's more than skin and bone

YOU CAN'T MAKE ME LOVED. I KNOW THAT FOR CERTAIN { tiger mountain peasant song; first aid kit }

Through the forest, down to your grave / Where the birds wait and the tall grasses wave / They do not know you anymore / Dear shadow, alive and well / How can the body die? / You tell me everything, anything true

LOVE IS BEING ABLE TO SEE THE INVISIBLE BLOOD { day glow avenue; alina simone }

I think you needed to be found / And to feel surrounded at every turn / Kissing silhouettes dissolving into smoke /

It's an epic soundtrack for the neon days / It's your revolution and your barricade

I DON'T CARE IF THIS IS HARD FOR YOU { limp; fiona apple }

When I think of it, my fingers turn to fists / I never did anything to you, man / No matter what I try / You beat me with your bitter lies / So call me crazy, hold me down / Make me cry, get off now, baby / It won't be long 'till you'll be lying / Limp in your own hands

AS RED AS YOURS { first lady of rock; the stone coyotes }

She said, I'm not after glory, I'm not after fame / You might not ever know my name / I'm no rock giant, if you know what I mean

I'm 5'6", I weigh 114 / I'll play in the streets, I'll play in the bars / Out on the highways and under the stars / Dreaming the dream I had as a girl / When all I ever wanted was to rock the world

THE WONDROUS HURT { give us a little love; fallulah }

Leave it by its pain, leave it all alone / If I never turn, I will never grow / Keep the door ajar when I'm coming home / I will try, can't you see I'm trying

I DIDN'T KNOW DEMONS HAD HEARTS { love knows how to fight; m.craft }

So if you wanna fuck up with a beer bottle in your hand then so do I / And if you wanna cut up the blueprints and the plans then so do I / You wanna get messed up, and make a final stand? well, so do I / Cause I look around me and I see, nothing can save me now

A MATCH MADE IN HELL { suzanne and i; anne calvi }

Suzanne and I, never will we be apart / But we hold, hold, hold it down / 'Cause the night calls me / When the wind leads behind the world

MATTER IS ETERNAL BUT WILL NOT ALWAYS MATTER { tell me I'm wrong; eskobar }

It's not even making sense, the ground we walk or sky above us / So how to understand the end? I build a shelter under my covers / Where I sit I think of you, my only love / Tell me I'm wrong but I feel / So free and so small at the same time

ONLY LOVE. ONLY SKY { letters from the sky; civil twilight }

One of these days letters are gonna fall from the sky / Telling us all to go free / But until that day I'll find a way to let everybody know / That you're coming back, you're coming back for me / 'Cause even though you left me here I have nothing left to fear / These are only walls that hold me here / You're coming back for me

IT'S ALRIGHT, THAT YOU WEREN'T THERE. I SAVED MYSELF. { abraham's daughter; arcade fire }

And when he saw her, raised for the slaughter / Abraham's daughter raised her bow / How darest you, child, defy your father? / You better let young Isaac go

GLAD KIDS AREN'T SCARED OF LOOKING LIKE WHO THEY ARE ON THE INSIDE { not your kind of people; garbage }

We are not your kind of people / Speak a different language / We see through your lies / We are not your kind of people / Won't be cast as demons / Creatures you despise

AND THE REST IS MUSIC { thriller; fall out boy }

I can take your problems away with a nod and a wave / Of my hand, 'cause that's just the kind of boy that I am / The only thing I haven't done yet is die / And it's me and my plus one at the afterlife / Crowds are won and lost and won again / But our hearts beat for the diehards

The Devil's Mixtape

Fan Art and Illustrations

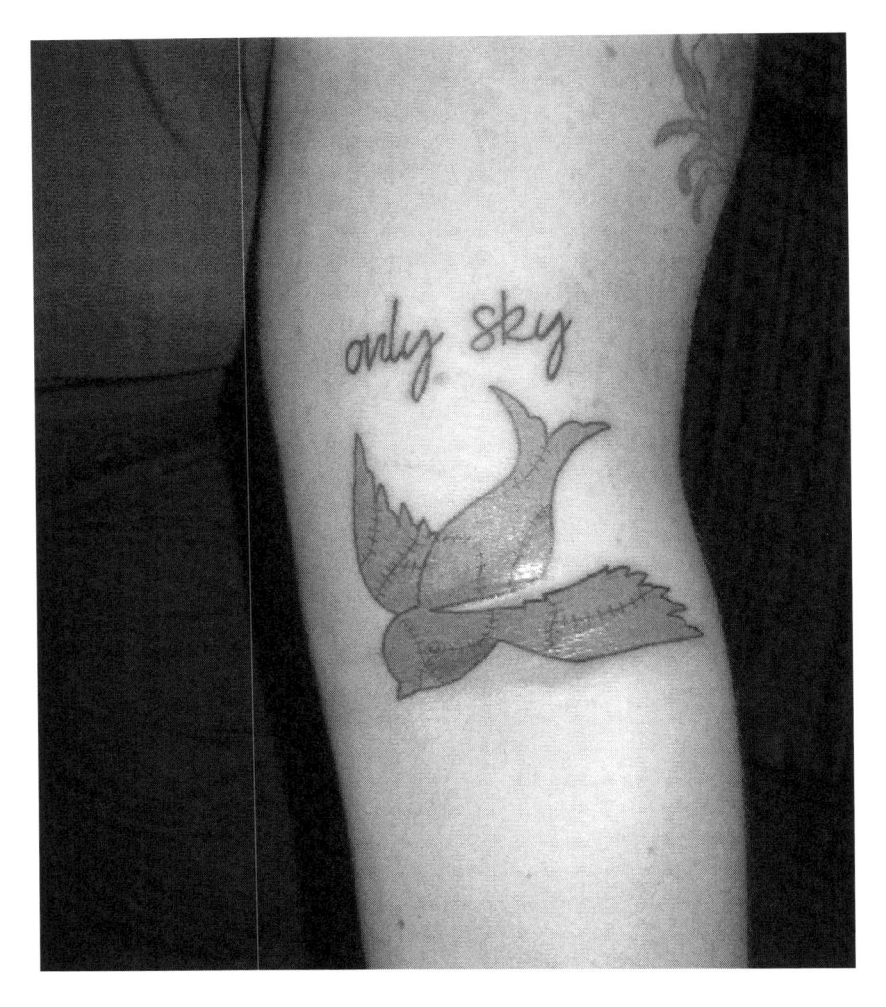

Tattoo - Lauren E. Mitchell's 'only sky' tattoo

Sally Sitting
Artwork by Jing Lan

Sally and Amy
Artwork by Audrey Fox

Sally
Artwork by Audrey Fox

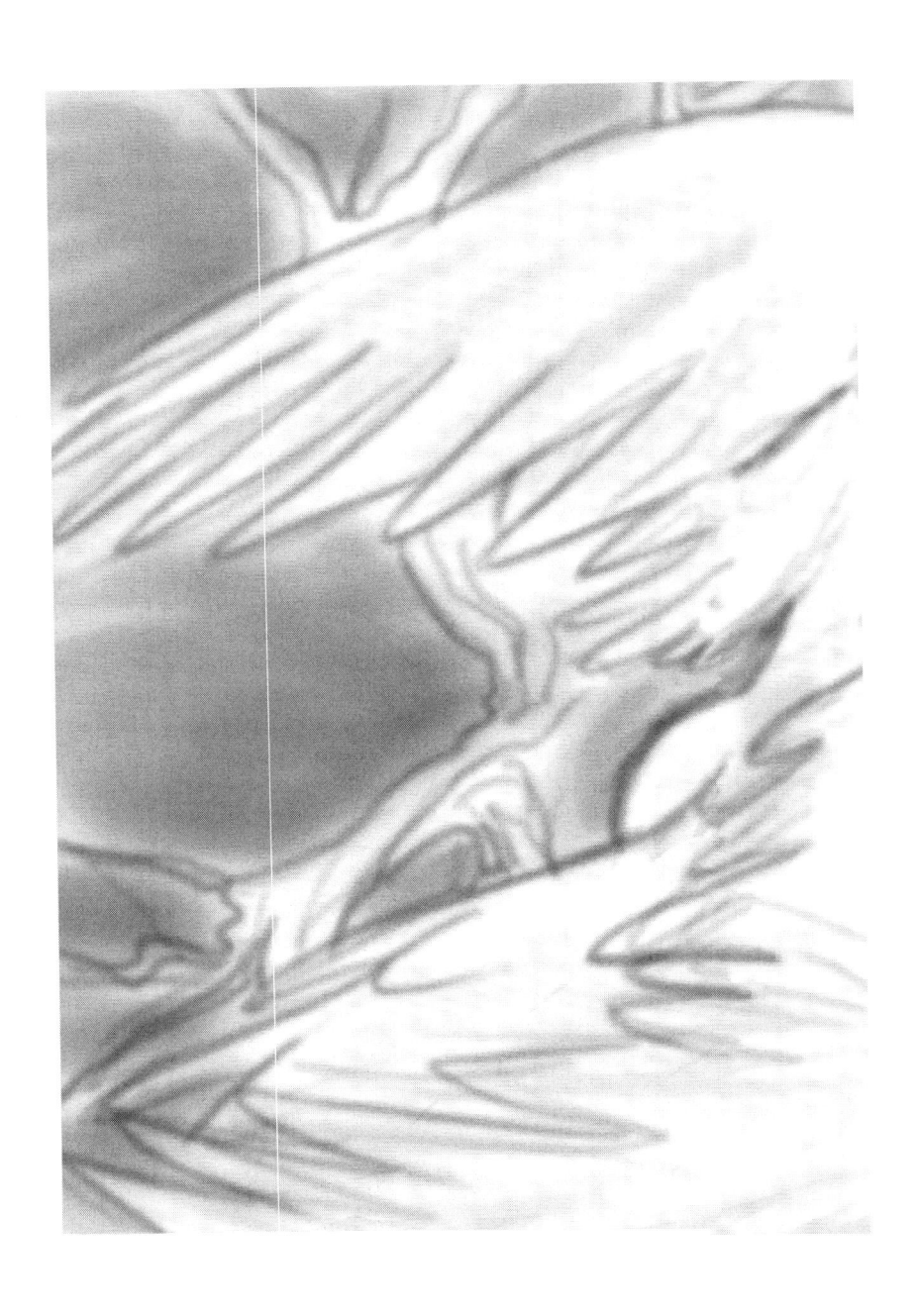

The Devil's Mixtape Cover Cover design by Audrey Fox

the devil's mixtape

mary borsellino

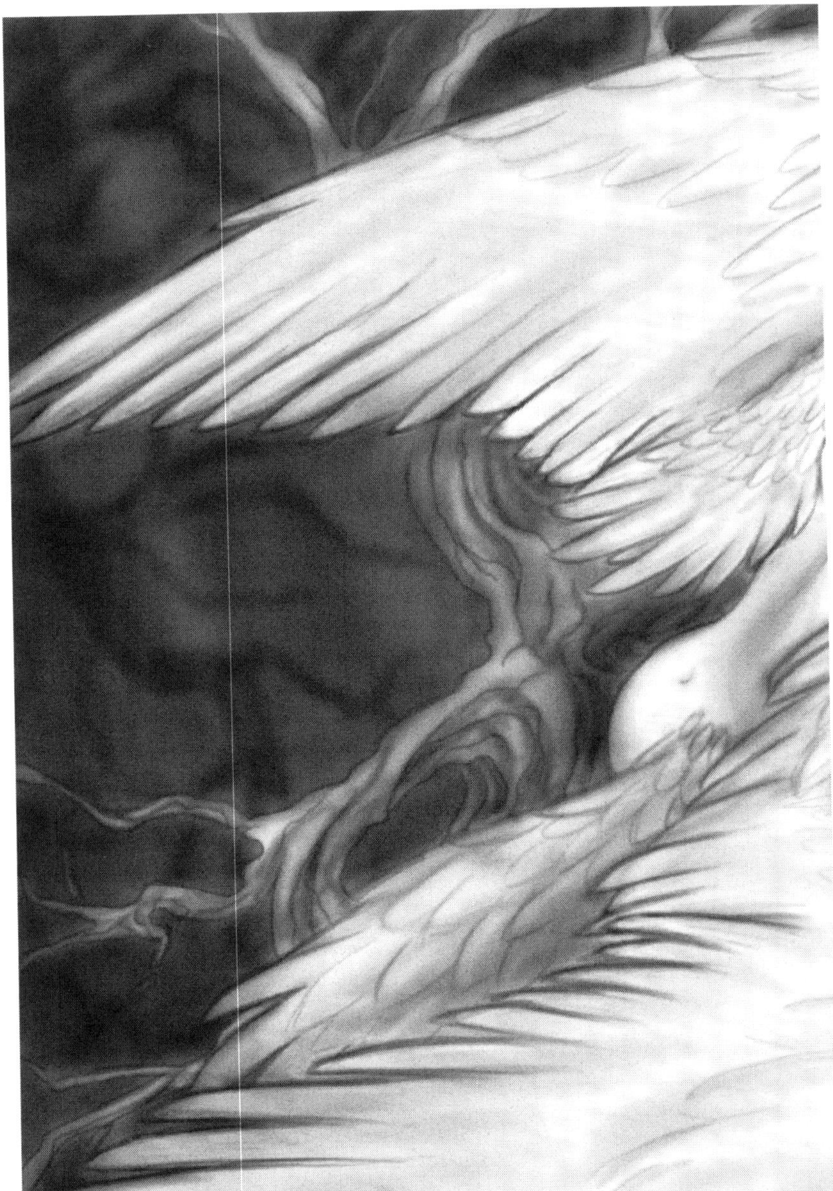

the devil's mixtape

mary borsellino

The Devil's Mixtape Cover
Cover design by Audrey Fox

The Devil's Mixtape Cover
Cover design by Audrey Fox

The Devil's Mixtape Cover
Cover design by Audrey Fox

The Devil's Mixtape Cover
Cover design by Audrey Fox

The Devil's Mixtape Cover
Cover design by Audrey Fox

Jaqui - by BigKat

The Devil's Mixtape FloatingHeads
Artwork by by Vilja Väisänen

The Devil's Mixtape Band Shot
Artwork by by Vilja Väisänen

ABOUT THE AUTHOR

Mary Borsellino is an Australian writer who works in the video game industry. She loves hearing from readers and her email address is mizmary@gmail.com. Her website is http://maryborsellino.com.

You might also enjoy:

Ruby Coral Carnelian

Little Ghosts

Thrive

Ice in Sunlight

The Wolf House Series
Origins and Overtures
Roads and Crosses
Fair Game
Fire Proof Heart
Last Girl

If you enjoyed this book please consider posting a review on Amazon and your favorite book site.

Printed in Great Britain
by Amazon